DEMON LOVED

THE WITCHES OF MINGUS MOUNTAIN - BOOK 5

CHRISTINE POPE

DARK VALENTINE
PRESS

DEMON LOVED

Copyright © 2025 by Christine Pope

ISBN: 978-1-946435-86-6

Published by Dark Valentine Press

Cover design by Indie Author Services

Ebook formatting by Indie Author Services

PROLOGUE

THE VOICE ECHOED ALL AROUND HIM, seeming to come from nowhere and everywhere at once.

"You have transgressed."

Belshegar frowned, then wondered if he should have allowed himself even that small reaction to those three damning words, which resonated on the air like a plucked bass string. The manner in which he'd been summoned here felt very different from those times when Elena Salazar had reached out from the mortal plane to ask for his company or his help, or when she needed a friendly voice during the times she thought she had no one else to turn to. Those summonings—if one could even call them that— had been much more like a casual invitation to tea, or perhaps like a familiar voice at the other end of a phone line…even though of course no phones existed on Belshegar's plane.

In fact, very little intelligent life could be found there at all. He knew others of his kind existed, but he'd only encountered a few of them in his long, long life, and they'd seemed content to acknowledge his presence and then move on so they could attend to their own business in the corner of the plane they inhabited. Odd as it felt to admit such a thing to himself, he found himself almost more at home in the world humans called theirs, even though Elena and her husband Alessandro…well, and the ghost Victoria, who'd inhabited their home before Belshegar helped her move on to the next world…were the only beings on the mortal plane who had ever seen his true form.

Whoever or whatever the voice belonged to, it had been no friendly invitation that had brought him here, to this gray, featureless place of eternal mist and not much more. However, the solid surface beneath his feet told him that it possessed some ground, even if he couldn't see it.

No, being called to this place had felt much more like being yanked out of bed on a cold winter night…or at least, how he imagined such a thing must feel, since he had no true frame of reference of his own.

"'Transgressed'?" he repeated, hoping he didn't

sound too timid…and that the owner of the voice wouldn't take offense at such a mild question.

Perhaps he would have felt comfortable being a bit more forceful if he hadn't known there existed a council of highly evolved beings whose sole purpose was to keep an eye on the doings of those on the lower planes, occasionally reining them in…or worse…when they overstepped. Belshegar had never had any interactions with them, but the knowledge of their existence still occupied some space in his mind. It was an understanding that lived at the core of his being, similar to the way he knew how to tend the gardens that surrounded his home without ever being taught… and how he knew that when such a summons came, even his great powers wouldn't be sufficient for him to ignore it.

As much as he racked his brains, though, he couldn't quite fathom why the voice believed he had committed a crime serious enough to require him to be brought here and then questioned about his wrongdoing. He'd been living quietly in his massive stone house, tending the lush plants in his gardens with their leaves of brilliant teal and blooms of fuchsia and cobalt blue, and he had no idea why he had been singled out by the Council.

"You put on a human guise and mingled among mortals, made them believe you were one of them," the voice said, its tone now bordering on contemptuous, as though it couldn't comprehend why an advanced being would wish to lower himself in such a way.

Belshegar's ebony skin was not the sort that would allow him to blush the way humans did. However, he couldn't quite hold back the wave of uneasiness that went over him at hearing the accusation, even as he thought,

That was so very long ago.

Time in his world didn't have the same meaning that it did for humans, of course, but because of his interactions with Elena Salazar, he thought he had a better grasp on it than most of his kind. That was how he knew it had been almost a year since the demon lord Loc—now married to a Castillo witch—had kindly bestowed a human guise upon Belshegar so he might attend Elena's marriage to Alessandro Escobar and dance with her at their reception, just as he'd promised. No one present had seemed to find anything out of the ordinary about him, and Belshegar thought he'd successfully carried off the impression of being a normal human being.

Apparently not.

"No one knew who I was," he ventured.

Even though he couldn't see the person addressing him, something about the atmosphere in the gray fog where he stood seemed to grow colder, almost tense, as if reflecting the mood of the being…or beings…who controlled it.

"That does not matter," the voice said. "It is enough that you allowed yourself to cavort with humans—wearing a disguise provided by a demon lord who himself has fallen from the true path. This sort of indiscretion must not be allowed to stand. Especially," it added, its tone growing even more sepulchral, "since this was not the first time you went to that plane and interacted with humans."

The thought flickered through Belshegar's mind that if he truly had made such a colossal mistake, it seemed odd that the powers-that-be had waited so long to take him to task regarding his so-called "transgression." The wedding had been a year ago, but Elena had first called him to the human plane more than a decade before that, and certainly no one from the Council had intervened during any of those occasions. However, he reminded himself once again that time was very different to him from the way it was perceived by humans and therefore must be an order of magnitude greater for those in the planes above. Because of this, he probably shouldn't allow himself to be too swayed by such a quibble.

And if they'd been tracking him this whole time, then the list of his transgressions was much longer than he'd first thought.

"How must I make amends?" he asked. He did not like posing such a question, but he also knew he should not dance around the issue and should instead accept his punishment, whatever it might be.

Hopefully not death. Even beings such as he could die, although their lifespans were much longer than those of humans. Belshegar had never feared the end of his existence, for he knew that relinquishing this body would only allow him to move on to the next plane, and yet he still didn't want to think of his life being cut short far before he had planned to exit this world.

Again, the atmosphere around Belshegar seemed to shift, and it now carried with it a note of something that felt almost like satisfaction. "Because you seem to enjoy being human," the voice intoned, "you will take on that guise once again. It has come to our attention that several artifacts which have no business being housed on the mortal plane are in the keeping of a certain witch and warlock, two mortals who have no idea what they have in their possession. As a human, you will travel to the place where those artifacts are located and retrieve them, then bring them back to us. Once you have completed that task, we will consider that you have successfully atoned for your…missteps."

Belshegar didn't like the sound of any of this,

not least because the mere mention of a witch and warlock made unease swirl in the pit of his stomach. True, the mortal plane had many witch clans, and there was no reason to believe that the two people the voice had just remarked upon were members of the same family that Elena claimed as her own.

But what if they were?

His oversized hands—ones that could have swallowed up Elena's delicate fingers many times over—clenched at his side. However, he made his voice mild and unassuming as he responded, "Where is it you wish me to go?"

"A place in Arizona," the voice said without hesitation.

"It is called Jerome."

1

Funny how the life of a witch could be so…mundane.

Brianna McAllister sat in the living room of one of her music students, Callie Mendoza, as Callie's small fingers struggled to find the proper positions for the minor seventh chord she'd just been taught. Although Brianna wanted to go over to Callie and gently press her fingers against the little girl's to show her the easiest method to duplicate the chord, she knew her student needed to find the way on her own if possible.

Sure enough, the discordant jangle gave way to a fairly respectable grouping of notes, and Brianna let herself relax slightly. Overall, Callie was quite talented, so Bree had guessed she would be able to master the fingering without too much outside assistance.

Every other Tuesday from three-thirty to four, she came to Callie's house to give these lessons, just as she visited her other students in Cottonwood and Clarkdale on the days when she wasn't performing at local wine tasting rooms and bars and resorts. Her current schedule wasn't anything Bree had exactly planned, was more a life she'd fallen into.

After all, what else was a witch without any singular talent supposed to do with herself?

Not for the first time, she did her best to dismiss the self-pitying thought. Everyone who knew her would have pointed out that, while her magical abilities weren't anything to write home about, she was very musically gifted. Those talents weren't necessarily magical, but in a way, she appreciated them even more because of that.

They were hers, and not something that had come to her simply because she was a member of the McAllister clan…or because she was Levi McAllister's daughter.

Levi McAllister, who'd been summoned to this plane to be the consort of Zoe Sandoval, the future *prima* of the de la Paz clan down in southern Arizona. She'd created him out of nothingness, and he'd been hideous when he first appeared. But he'd grown into his true form a few days later, and now—many years after he'd come to this world—looked like nothing more than a handsome blond man in his fifties.

Anyone who knew him, though, understood he was a lot more than that.

However, his otherworldly gifts hadn't been passed down to his two children. Bree's older brother Shane was an incredibly talented chef, thanks to a magical talent for cooking, and was already running the kitchen at The Asylum, the restaurant located in The Grand Hotel at the top of Jerome, but Bree…well, she had a little bit of everything, which was why her cousin Bellamy had referred to her more than once as the Swiss Army knife witch. She could do all sorts of things, as long as none of them were too powerful or too complicated.

And that was why she tended not to do much of anything at all.

"That's great, Callie," she said, knowing she'd let her mind wander far more than an attentive teacher should have. "Let's try the entire phrase now you've gotten that minor seventh in hand."

Callie nodded and bent her head over the guitar, delicate dark brows drawing together as she concentrated on the tricky notation. As always, she'd pulled her long, near-black hair into a scrunchie to keep it from falling into her face while she played, and she frowned in concentration as she began to work her way through the phrase they'd been studying.

Something about the combination of chords reminded Bree of the song she'd been working on for the past week, even though on the surface, they weren't much alike. Still, the way the A-minor chord melted into the seventh that had been giving Callie so much trouble prompted a moment of illumination, a way for Brianna to resolve the tricky bridge that she hadn't quite figured out yet.

Her fingers itched to pick up her own guitar and work on the phrase, but the instrument was sitting several miles away in her apartment in Jerome. Anyway, she was supposed to be focusing on her student, not writing a song no one would ever probably hear. Her audiences in the wine tasting rooms and bars wanted to hear covers of old favorites, not anything new, so she rarely trotted out her original work.

No, it just piled up in the trunk she used to keep all her notes. While she had songwriting software on her laptop, she rarely used it, preferring to do things the old-fashioned way.

Coming back to herself, she said, "That was great, Callie. Let's try it again."

Better to focus on the here and now, and not a song that would get trunked along with all the others.

Because it was a Tuesday, a typically slow time at the tasting rooms, Brianna didn't have any gigs scheduled for that night. She had a sort of standing invitation to go to her parents' house for dinner, but she wasn't sure if she wanted to do that today. It wasn't that she didn't enjoy spending time with them—she knew she'd been blessed with the best parents anyone could ask for—but more that she realized she was feeling restless, even though she couldn't say exactly why.

Maybe this unsettled sensation was due to the change of seasons and nothing more. The Verde Valley was plenty warm at the end of September, and the leaves wouldn't truly start to change for another month, but she still could feel the approach of fall in the shortening days and the way the quality of light had become more slanted, more golden.

Another year passing with not much to show for it.

She wanted to shake her head at herself for allowing such a self-pitying thought to pass through her mind, but it lingered despite her best efforts to dispel it. Stupid, really, since this was all her fault anyway. No one had held a gun to her head and told her to drop out of Northern Pines, the university she'd been attending in Flagstaff until this past summer.

Somehow, though, she hadn't been able to force herself to return, even though she only had one year to go. But what was she supposed to do with that bachelor's degree in music, anyway? Teach? Perform?

She was already doing both of those.

And although Flagstaff was beautiful and she'd had fun during her time in college, she'd also missed Jerome. Sure, it was only an hour and a half away, but it had still been a lot harder than she'd expected to carve out the time to make the trip home more than a couple times each year.

So…she was here, living her life, even though she wasn't sure what she really wanted to do with it.

Might as well go to dinner at her parents' house. Her mother always made plenty to go around, and there was even a chance—a very small one—that Shane might drop by as well. Technically, Tuesdays and Wednesdays were his days off, but he always seemed to be putting out one fire or another at work, sometimes literally, like the time when the new sous chef managed to catch one corner of the kitchen at The Asylum on fire. The blaze had been snuffed before it could do any real damage, and yet Brianna could see why her brother might want to at least stick his head in even when he wasn't supposed to be working.

Well, better to share a meal at her parents' house than sit alone in her apartment, brooding over all the things she'd done wrong with her life.

She picked up her phone and sent a brief text.

I'll be there for dinner.

Nothing about the house had changed much since she'd moved out, but, not for the first time, Bree was struck by how different it still felt to her as she walked in and gave her mom a quick hug.

It's not the house, she thought as she told her mother that everything was going fine.

It's you.

Well, she wasn't eighteen anymore. In less than a month, she'd be turning twenty-four, and that was around the time when you were supposed to be figuring out what to do with the rest of your life. Shane had always been committed to learning his craft, going so far as to attend culinary school in Phoenix even though his magical talent practically made him a Cordon Bleu chef without breaking a sweat. But he'd wanted the credentials to back up his gift, so he'd gone ahead and gotten his certification.

Next to him, Bree felt like a big lump of nothing.

Chicken cacciatore tonight, a nod toward the cooler weather that was coming despite temperatures that didn't want to drop out of the mid-eighties. Bree dutifully got out the bag of spaghetti after her mother asked her to fetch it and then dumped it into the big pot of boiling water that had been waiting on the stovetop.

"You're sure everything is all right?" her mom asked. Hayley McAllister was just as blonde and blue-eyed as her daughter, and still almost as slender as she'd been when she first met her children's father back when she was in her early twenties. More than once, the two of them had been mistaken for sisters rather than mother and daughter.

"I'm fine," Bree replied. Sure, that was a little white lie, but she didn't want to get into her current sense of near-angst, especially since she couldn't even say for sure why she'd been feeling that way in the first place. "Busy. I had a lesson with Cailie this afternoon, and then I've got a couple of gigs this week and the folk festival on Saturday."

Her mother nodded, although something close to concern flickered in her clear blue eyes. "Make sure you don't spread yourself too thin."

"Oh, I won't," Bree said. She only taught music two days out of seven, and most of her mornings were free. It wasn't as if she was putting in sixty hours every week like Shane. "But it always gets slower once we're past the holidays, so I figured I might as well get what bookings I could this fall and bank the money against the slow times."

The ebb and flow of the tourist trade in the Verde Valley was something all of them were used to, understanding it as intimately as the rhythms of their own bodies. Hayley nodded, lifted the lid of the crockpot so she could spoon out an experimental taste, then nodded. "Maybe not quite up to your brother's standards, but I think it'll do."

"I'm sure it'll do more than that," came Shane's voice, and both women turned to see him standing in the entrance to the kitchen, a grin pulling at the corners of his mouth.

At once, Hayley put down her spoon and went over to give her son a quick hug. "I didn't think you'd be coming tonight."

He shrugged. "Things are pretty quiet at work. Besides, it's nice to have something every once in a while that I didn't have to cook."

About all Bree could do was shake her head. That was such a Shane kind of thing to say.

Like everyone else in the family, her brother

had blond hair and blue eyes, although his hair was a few shades darker than hers and his eyes a cool, deep blue that looked almost dark if the lighting was dim enough. Right now, his shoulder-length locks were pulled back into a ponytail, although she'd seen him sport a man-bun from time to time…and had teased him mercilessly about it.

Not that the man-bun had proved to be much of a deterrent to any eligible cousins in the McAllister clan…or any unattached tourists who happened to catch sight of the man working in the kitchen at The Asylum. No, they would have followed him around like a bunch of sheep if he'd allowed it. Things were probably even worse now that he'd broken up with his girlfriend of several years, a civilian woman who managed one of the wine-tasting rooms in Cottonwood. Bree had been a little worried that the rift might have made Sara think twice about continuing to hire her ex's sister to perform at the tasting room, but so far, those fears hadn't materialized.

But Shane was now the focus of a lot of speculation among the clan as to when he might start dating again. It had been a couple of months since the breakup, and any cousins who were distant enough relations and in the right age bracket were starting to look at him like a dog might look at an especially juicy steak sitting on the counter...all the while praying that some mishap might send it flying to the floor so they could run off with it.

"It's nice to have the whole family here," their father put in, materializing somewhere behind his son. All right, he hadn't actually appeared out of nowhere...although he had the ability to do so... but had wandered in from the dining room, where Bree assumed he'd been busy getting the table set.

Yes, it was nice. She couldn't remember the last time they'd all been together like this, but she thought it had probably been for their parents' anniversary dinner back in July.

"Many hands will help get all this on the table that much faster," her mother said, sounding brisk. "Shane, could you get the salad? And Bree, can you check on the pasta?"

Everyone went to handle their various duties, and soon enough, they were all sitting at the big dining room table and passing around the food. She'd always loved the space, loved the big picture window that looked east toward Sedona and the Mogollon Plateau many miles away. There had been so many family dinners here where they ate and talked and paused from time to time to watch the moon rising.

No moon tonight, though; it would be nearly half full, she knew, but it wasn't due to rise until much later, long after they were finished with their meal.

That was all right, though. They chatted about the renovations her parents had planned for the empty bedrooms their children had once occupied —Bree's old room would become a kind of meditation space, while Shane's bedroom would be turned into the office their father had been wanting for years—and chatted about Jerome and the plans to finally update Spook Hall and make it a little more elegant than just a big, empty gathering place.

"They'll keep the floors, of course, and just refinish them," Hayley said as she passed the bowl of salad to her daughter. "But they're going to take out that awful drop ceiling and see if there's maybe some original tin underneath. If not, they'll probably put in real plaster so it's in keeping with the age of the building."

Bree thought that sounded like an excellent idea. Spook Hall—well, Lawrence Memorial Hall —had always been an important part of her life, since that was where the huge McAllister holiday potlucks were held and where the annual Halloween Ball had been taking place for decades. The spot was as familiar and comfortable as an old shoe, but she agreed that it could use a bit of a glow-up.

And while she'd experienced just the slightest

pang at hearing that her old room here at home would be transformed into something utterly different, she told herself it was for the best. Knowing that she couldn't just move back in whenever she wanted would force her to face this new adult life head-on…even if she wasn't all that comfortable with it yet.

After dinner, Levi and Shane handled the dishes, while Bree and her mother headed into the living room. Because the house was so old—it had been built in 1899—it was definitely more compartmentalized than more modern homes, and her parents had never wanted to knock down walls and open it up the way many other people had done with their vintage houses. No, they respected it for what it was.

Right now, that was probably just a good thing, because if the kitchen and dining and living rooms had been one big open space, then the two women wouldn't have had much privacy as they sat down near the fireplace. No fire tonight, of course, because the weather was far too warm for that, but Bree's mother put a candle rack in it during the hot months so it would always have some sort of flame dancing there.

The candles glowed cheerfully, and something about the flickering light they gave off made Brianna feel a little more at ease. No, she didn't live here anymore, but this place would still always be home to her.

Her mother crossed her hands over her knees and sent Bree a very direct look. "I was hoping you'd feel more settled in by now."

"I am," Brianna protested. After all, it had been more than three months since she'd moved into the apartment above the West by Southwest gallery on Main Street, plenty of time to adjust to her new reality. But even though the space was cute, with its age-worn wood floors and fun paint on the walls—a different color in each room—she'd never felt as comfortable there as she'd hoped.

Maybe she just needed a little more time to adjust to the place.

Hayley lifted one brow. "I'm sure we can find a different spot for you if it's not working out. I've been a little concerned that you don't have space for a piano there."

Well, that was true enough. The apartment was just a hair over five hundred square feet, big enough for one bedroom and one bathroom and a dinky kitchen she barely used except to make coffee in the morning. There was no way she could have squeezed even a spinet in there, not without sacrificing the sofa or the tiny bistro set that occupied the dining area. Maybe the dining set wasn't strictly necessary, but she hadn't liked the idea of not having anywhere to sit down and eat except on the living room couch.

So she practiced piano wherever she could— here at home, where the baby grand she'd learned to play on still had a place of honor in the library off the living room; at the various resorts where she had her gigs; at friends' houses whenever they offered. It seemed like enough, even though she knew the arrangement was a makeshift and nothing more.

"No, it's fine," she replied, glad that she sounded firm and sure of herself. "The view is almost as good as it is here, and I like being in the middle of things. New living spaces always take some kind of adjustment."

"I suppose so," her mother said, but she still looked worried.

However, Shane and Levi came into the living room then, and it seemed as if Hayley had decided it was better not to pursue the subject in front of them. Bree knew her father would always be sympathetic, but Shane...?

Maybe not so much. It wasn't that they didn't get along, but he'd always been so clear about what he wanted out of life that he didn't have a lot of patience for his sister's dithering.

And because he'd already bought a house for himself—a pretty little Victorian right here on Paradise Lane, walking distance to work—it wasn't as if he needed to worry about where he laid his head at night. No, Shane, as usual, seemed to have everything figured out.

Levi looked as if he could tell his wife and daughter had been discussing something important, but, being him, he didn't attempt to pry. Instead, he commented that he hoped they'd be able to do this again next week.

"One of the many things I like about being part of the McAllister clan," he said with a smile. "It's good to know that our children won't range too far afield."

Bree supposed that was true enough; people in witch clans always stuck to their territories except for brief periods to attend school, like she and Shane both had, or possibly if they'd met a witch or warlock from a different clan, fallen in love, and moved to their spouse's territory.

She didn't see that happening for either her or her brother any time soon. Shane had always relentlessly dated civilians, and she...well, she didn't have too many prospects at the moment.

Which was probably a good thing. She was enough of a mess without dragging some innocent guy into her neuroses.

Her mother smiled at Levi's comment, and Shane lifted an eyebrow, although he smiled slightly.

"Well," he said, "I've got my dream job now, so I don't plan on going anywhere."

No, he didn't.

Whereas Bree couldn't say for sure where she was headed.

She supposed she'd let fate figure that out for her.

2

YOU ARE BILL GARRETT, Belshegar reminded himself as he got out of the self-driving car that had brought him to Jerome. *Bill Garrett.*

He wasn't sure why the voice had decided that would be his alias, although he supposed it was possibly because it contained some of the same letters and syllables as his true name when it was rendered in the English language.

Now he could only hope he'd answer to it if anyone ever addressed him that way.

How all the arrangements had been made, he wasn't sure, but less than twenty-four human hours after he'd had that conversation with the voice, he was on the mortal plane, wearing the same face he'd put on to attend Elena's wedding and reception. It was a handsome enough face, he supposed, with a strong brow and chin and deep green eyes, topped by shaggy, shoulder-length, near-black hair, but it wasn't *his* face.

When Loc had conjured the human appearance for him that first time, Belshegar asked where the demon lord had gotten it from.

"A bit of this, a bit of that," Loc had replied almost carelessly. "Actors, mostly. People might comment that you remind them of someone, although the face I've given you isn't a copy of anyone in particular."

Would it be amusing to be mistaken for someone famous?

Probably not, he decided, especially since the voice had admonished him to do whatever he could to avoid attracting notice. He had been given a task to perform, and while the voice hadn't provided him with a precise timeline, Belshegar knew he should work his hardest to acquire the artifacts it wanted and then deliver them before anyone on the human plane began to think there might be something just a little strange about "Bill Garrett."

He would be staying at a place called The Grand Hotel, an imposing structure perched near the very top of Jerome, which appeared to be built into the side of a hill. The buildings he'd spied as the self-driving car brought him here had looked quite old, if not quite as old as many of the structures in Santa Fe, where he'd seen ancient adobe homes and shops that appeared almost as though they'd sprouted in place, like mushrooms, rather than been built with human hands.

Still, this was clearly no modern town, a small place with its own peculiar charm.

But the artifacts were here. He'd sensed them almost as soon as he got out of the car and went to the trunk to retrieve his luggage. Although he couldn't pinpoint exactly where they were located, he could still feel the pulse of their power somewhere in the distance.

Not too far, though. Definitely here within Jerome's town limits, just as the voice had said.

And Jerome, it seemed, wasn't very large.

He went inside the hotel and strode up to the front desk, hoping he looked as if he knew what he was doing. The voice had not only provided the face and form he now wore, but human cash and credit cards, a driver's license with his likeness on it, and a fictitious address somewhere in Los Angeles. Although that part hadn't been explained, he supposed the voice had decided to give him a place of origin outside Arizona so it would be easier to brush off any lack of knowledge about the place.

Belshegar had no idea whether any of his false background would hold up under close scrutiny, although he supposed he would find out soon enough.

However, the clerk at the desk—a woman who looked as if she might be in her early thirties, with light brown hair pulled up into a twist and heavy false eyelashes that reminded him of a couple of woolly caterpillars resting on her eyelids —took his I.D. and credit card, ran them through the machine in front of her, and then handed them back without so much as a blink.

"Thank you for staying at the Grand Hotel, Mr. Garrett," she said. "Do you need more than one room key?"

"One is fine," he replied. Of course he was traveling alone.

He'd always been alone.

"Very good," the clerk said briskly. "You're in room 316. The elevator is just around the corner, partway down the hall."

He thanked her and scooped up the key—which wasn't a true key at all, but a piece of plastic he assumed must be coded to the lock on the door to his hotel room—and then shouldered his overnight bag before going in search of the elevator. It was exactly where she'd said it would be, with an old-fashioned brass cage protecting the doors.

The cage opened easily enough, though, and he headed inside. As the door closed behind him, all his otherworldly senses went on the alert, telling him that other presences lingered here.

Perhaps not in the elevator itself at this exact moment, but they'd been nearby recently.

While he looked human, he wasn't human enough to experience a shiver or anything close to it. All the same, he found himself quite relieved as he exited the elevator and made his way to the room where he'd been staying.

Once inside, though, realized he was far from relieved. How could he be, when those same presences seemed to weigh on him even more heavily in here?

"Hello," he said politely, remembering his interactions with Victoria, the ghost who once had inhabited Elena's house in Santa Fe. "My name is Belshegar. Who am I addressing?"

Before he spoke, he'd wondered whether he should give the spirit his true name or the name of the man he was pretending to be. However, ghosts and spirits had a way of getting to the heart of a matter, so he didn't think it a very good idea to lie to whatever presence lingered in the space.

In the far corner of the room, a shadow grew more distinct, taking on the shape of a tall, thin man with hollow eyes. The ghost gestured toward its throat, then shook its head.

Was it trying to tell him that it couldn't speak? Victoria had certainly been vocal enough, but Belshegar supposed he couldn't expect all earth-bound spirits to behave the same, not when they'd been their own individuals in life.

And because he'd wanted to know something of where he was staying, he'd done a little research regarding the Grand Hotel on the device he'd been provided, a cellular phone that was much more like a pocket computer. That was why he knew this place had once been a sanatorium, where people with tuberculosis and syphilis and other dread diseases had gone to be cured. It didn't seem too strange that the spirit he saw now was someone who'd apparently suffered an affliction that had affected his ability to speak.

"Well, that's fine," he said, knowing he sounded a little too hearty. Although he'd certainly spent plenty of time talking to Elena Salazar over the years, he'd never had to worry too much about whether the tones he employed were precisely appropriate to human interactions. She'd already known exactly who and what he was.

This situation was very different, however. He needed to be as human as possible...even with a ghost.

"That is," he went on hastily, "I understand if you're unable to speak. Please rest assured that your presence here doesn't discomfit me in the slightest."

An expression flashed across the ghost's face, one of what looked like sheer annoyance.

Then he disappeared.

Did I say something wrong? Belshegar thought. He certainly hadn't intended to offend the spirit.

Perhaps the ghost was irritated because he'd hoped to frighten the person staying in this room. Being told he wasn't frightening in the least might have been the last thing he wanted to hear.

Unfortunately, there wasn't much he could do about it now. Perhaps there was a possibility that he could ask the ghost to return so he could explain he hadn't meant to cause any offense, but Belshegar decided that wasn't a very sensible course of action.

Best to let sleeping ghosts lie.

Instead, he took the clothes he'd been provided out of his bag and hung them in the antique wardrobe that faced the bed. There weren't many of them, four shirts and two pairs of pants, along with assorted socks and underthings, all of which he placed in the drawers of a nearby dresser, but he felt better knowing they wouldn't get any more wrinkled.

Now what?

Explore, he told himself. *You sensed the artifacts, but you don't know precisely where they are. Use the human form you've been given and wander through Jerome to see if you can get a better idea of where those things are being hidden.*

Not for the first time, he wondered why the voice hadn't provided him with their precise location. Surely if it had known that the artifacts were in the keeping of a witch and a warlock who lived in this town, then it must have also known their address.

But possibly it had been unable to pass that information along. While Belshegar had to admit that he didn't know very much about such things, he guessed the witch and warlock in question must have placed all sorts of wards on the artifacts to ensure they remained safely hidden. It was no great leap from there to believe those wards might also have prevented the voice from relaying the exact location of the items it wanted him to find.

Magic, after all, could be quite an unpredictable thing…and doubly so when employed by humans. Mortals could be oddly powerful, especially because they didn't have to abide by the same rules that Belshegar or other beings like him were forced to follow, and therefore they were always inventing new ways to wield their powers or bend magic to their wills.

All that aside, it looked like a fine evening, and what better way to enjoy it than to wander the streets of the former mining town and see what he could find? Although he couldn't come right out and ask where the witch and warlock who possessed the items he was seeking lived—

magical folks were naturally secretive about their talents, and therefore did not advertise the less conventional aspects of their natures—perhaps he could listen to people's conversations and possibly pick up a clue here and there.

Or not. While he knew from watching television with Elena that humans could have loose lips when they'd imbibed enough alcoholic beverages, he somehow doubted any self-respecting witch or warlock would let a secret like that slip, no matter how much they'd had to drink.

He allowed himself a shrug, getting a bit more used to this body and how it moved, and then headed out. The corridor just outside his room was empty of both humans and ghosts, but he still found his way to the stairwell and made his descent that way rather than use the elevator. This place also felt ever so slightly haunted, but nowhere near as badly as the elevator did.

Soon enough, though, he had emerged into the lobby, which wasn't precisely bustling at that hour but still had enough people occupying it to make the space seem a bit friendlier than the empty stairwell. And then he descended the steep steps to the street level, which in front of the hotel wasn't much more than a glorified parking lot.

However, he spied a set of stairs set into the hillside, beckoning him down to Jerome's main street, where he'd noticed shops and restaurants and bars as the self-driving taxi brought him up to the Grand Hotel. That certainly seemed like the best place to look for any clues that might lead him to the elusive artifacts.

Besides, he was hungry. In his true form, he did not need to eat, as he derived the sustenance he needed from the air he breathed and the energy of the universe itself, but this body was very different. Also, consuming food, while new and strange to him, wasn't a complete novelty anymore, not after he'd eaten various Salvadoran delicacies and had consumed an entire piece of Elena and Alessandro's lush chocolate wedding cake while at their reception.

Belshegar doubted he'd be able to locate any wedding cake here, but that didn't mean he couldn't find something interesting to break his fast.

As he walked along the main street, he noticed many cars were leaving their parking places and heading down the hill. True, evening was approaching, but he was still startled to see the way Jerome appeared to empty as the day wound down to a close.

A few signs of life remained, however. Several doors down from the spot where he stood, music spilled out through a door open to the warm, mild evening, the sound of the instrument known as a guitar accompanying a woman's voice, pure and sweet.

There was no music in his world, but he'd always been entranced to hear it during those times when he visited Elena in her attic bedroom and she would play something for him—quietly, of course, so as not to wake her father and grand-mother—on her computer.

This was even better, though, because he could somehow tell this was no recording, but someone singing and playing just a few yards away from him.

His feet moved forward as though pulled by an invisible force. When he drew closer, he saw that the establishment where the woman was playing appeared to be some kind of wine-tasting room. He'd drunk a little champagne at Elena's reception so he wouldn't look out of place and still didn't quite know what to think of it, but if he had to consume wine to fit in while he listened to the woman sing, then he would do what he must.

The place was larger than he'd thought, narrow but stretching at least sixty or seventy feet lengthwise, terminating in an enormous window that framed a truly spectacular view of the valley below and a series of red rock bluffs and purple mountains off in the distance. He noted that most of the tables were occupied, giving the lie to all the cars he'd seen driving away only a moment earlier.

Had these people decided to stay so they wouldn't miss out on the musical performance?

Even as that thought passed through his mind, he found his gaze drawn to the source of the sweet sounds that had drifted through the tasting room's open door.

The woman sat on a simple wooden stool and held a steel-string guitar in her lap. Her hair was pale gold, falling in soft waves past her shoulders, while her eyes were as blue as the sky must have been at noon, hours before he arrived in Jerome. Long, skillful fingers plucked at the metal strings.

She was the most beautiful thing he'd seen in this world…or any other.

"Can I get you something?" the man standing behind the bar asked.

Belshegar had been so focused on the woman's singing that he couldn't help startling a little at the sudden intrusion of a deeper voice. Hoping he hadn't made too much of a fool of himself, he said, "Yes…a glass of wine, please."

The man pushed a piece of paper toward him, one that seemed to include all the tasting room's offerings. "This is what we have available by the glass."

Although Belshegar had never been taught to formally read, his time with Elena had exposed him to the English language and the letters used to form its words, so he was able to grasp the contents of the wine menu well enough. Or rather, while he had no idea what a "chardonnay" or a "GSM blend" was, he could make out the words "white" and "red."

The champagne he'd drunk at Elena's wedding reception had been white. While he still couldn't say whether he'd cared for it, at least a white wine was something halfway familiar.

"The white blend, please," he said politely, and the man nodded, then went to fetch a bottle from one of the coolers behind the bar. As he was pouring the glass, Belshegar added, "Who is she?" and inclined his head toward the spot where the blonde woman sat on her stool and continued to sing and play.

"Brianna McAllister," the bartender supplied. "She plays here every other Wednesday."

Brianna. A beautiful name for a beautiful woman. Belshegar knew he probably shouldn't be thinking of her that way, not when he wasn't human and shouldn't have been able to feel even the slightest ounce of attraction toward a mortal.

Perhaps this wasn't an attraction, though. Perhaps this was only admiration, the same way he would admire one of Elena's skillful pencil sketches or one of the stunning sunrises he'd viewed from her attic bedroom after he'd spent the night comforting her and reassuring her that she would never be alone.

Yes, it was much better…and less unsettling…to think of this Brianna McAllister as a particularly beautiful work of art.

He thanked the bartender and found an empty seat somewhat farther away from the woman than he would have liked. However, he could still hear her and see her, if not from an optimal position.

To his surprise, the wine tasted good. Was he more accustomed to this human body now, or was it simply that the white blend he'd been served was more suitable to his palate than champagne?

He couldn't say for sure. The one thing he did know was that he was glad to be here, drinking this wine, listening to the woman sing…even if the reason for his presence in Jerome wasn't anything so benign as simple tourism.

Well, the voice hadn't given him a time limit for his mission, most likely because a being from a higher plane such as that didn't have as firm a grasp on the boundaries of time as a human might. Belshegar had no doubt that if he dawdled too much, he might be recalled and taken to task, but he doubted such a thing would happen after his first night here.

Besides, this was intelligence gathering…of a sort.

Because he realized, as he drank his wine and listened to the music, that this Brianna McAllister was a witch, just as Elena and Alessandro and the various members of their families had been. Probably not the witch he was looking for, the one who had the precious artifacts in her possession, but still, witches always belonged to clans, and that meant Brianna quite possibly would know where the items he sought were being kept.

Or perhaps not. Perhaps those treasures were so precious that the witch and warlock who possessed them hadn't spoken of them to anyone else.

Still, he couldn't dismiss the possibility that Brianna McAllister might be an important source of information…and that meant he needed to figure out a way to talk to her once she was done playing.

The mere thought of doing something so bold sent a frisson of worry through him. At Elena's reception, she'd introduced him to everyone as a cousin on her mother's side in order to explain his presence there. Because her mother had abandoned the family when Elena was barely a toddler and had been a "civilian"—nonmagical person—as well, none of the Castillos had asked too many questions. He had felt like an ordinary man to them, and they'd accepted him as such.

Well, except for the demon lord Loc and his wife, Catalina, who knew the real truth.

But in that situation, Elena and Alessandro had been the ones to make the introductions, and Belshegar hadn't needed to approach anyone on his own. Here, though, the only way he would be able to meet Brianna McAllister was if he went up to her of his own volition. She smiled sometimes as she played, but he noticed how she kept her gaze neutral, avoiding eye contact with anyone in particular, as if she'd discovered in the past that doing so would only invite attention she didn't desire.

That theory seemed logical enough. She was very beautiful, and he guessed some men would have pursued her even if they hadn't been given any real encouragement.

Which meant he needed to be neutrally friendly but not too bold. The last thing he wanted was to frighten her off.

He also noticed how magic seemed to thrum around her, although he could tell she wasn't consciously wielding it, wasn't doing anything that might bring attention to her witch nature. Indeed, he was fairly certain even another member of her clan or some other witch or warlock wouldn't have detected those energies, but because he wasn't human, he was able to sense the glow of the magic as it surrounded her, somehow resonating with the very beams overhead and the long sweep of the antique copper-topped bar.

Did she even realize what she was doing?

That was something he didn't know for sure. Although their magic was born within witch-kind, waiting to awaken when they reached the age of ten or eleven, each witch or warlock had to learn how to wield that magic—or not wield it, as the case may be, since they were so careful to make sure their true natures remained concealed from the outer world.

The song ended, and Belshegar swallowed some wine to brace himself. Brianna spoke then, saying she was going to take a brief break before she came back for her next set. Her speaking voice was as sweet as the one she employed while singing, friendly and clear.

She got down from the stool and leaned the guitar against it, then went over to the bar to get a glass of water. Belshegar watched her, knowing he needed to approach...even though he had no idea how to do such a thing without seeming painfully obvious.

But then she took her glass of water and headed outside, clearly wanting to get some fresh air before she began the next segment of her performance.

Now or never.

Belshegar set down his glass of wine and went in pursuit of his quarry.

3

Of course Brianna had noticed the man as soon as he entered the tasting room. While she tried to avoid eye contact with people when she was playing, that didn't mean she didn't take note of the comings and goings in her audience...or see right away when someone particularly noteworthy sat down to listen to her music.

And this guy was *super* noteworthy.

Tall, with dark hair that just brushed his shoulders, eyes whose color she couldn't quite make out because of the dim lighting in the space but were still way too sexy under those strong, level brows...the kind of cheekbones and jaw that seemed as if they might have been more suitable to the big screen than the Caduceus Cellars tasting room.

In fact, he kind of reminded her of someone,

maybe an actor she'd seen in a movie or TV show, although if pressed, she wasn't sure whether she could say exactly who.

And interestingly, he didn't carry himself like the sort of man who knew just how good-looking he really was. Something about him seemed almost diffident, as though he wasn't sure if he knew what he was doing but intended to try his best anyway.

That was why she couldn't be too irritated when she saw him emerge from the tasting room and glance down the street. From anyone else, she would have thought this was an obvious cover to make it seem as if he hadn't followed her outside, but in this situation, she couldn't be quite sure.

She found herself saying, "First time in Jerome?"

He turned back toward her and smiled. There was nothing practiced or flirtatious in his expression.

No, she saw what looked like relief.

Was he glad she'd been the one to open the conversation? In general, she didn't put herself out there like that—she was far more used to being pursued—but something about the stranger felt almost lost, and that quality about him seemed to have stirred her protective instincts.

"It is," he said. "I'd read about it, of course, but this was the first time I made the trip."

His voice was warm and deep, almost velvety, the kind of voice that made her think of hot cocoa and snuggling in a warm blanket on a cold winter night. Never mind that it had been pushing eighty-six degrees today, and even with the sun beginning to go down, the air was still plenty warm enough.

"So, what do you think?" she asked, doing her best to sound casual.

A lot of guys would have given her a significant look and then said something like, *Oh, I'm liking the view pretty well from here.*

But this man was obviously not the kind of person to play those sorts of games.

"It's very interesting," he said, his tone both thoughtful and serious, as if he was answering a question posed to him in class by the teacher and not by someone trying to have a casual conversation. "Older-feeling than I'd thought it would be."

"Well, we've done our best to preserve whatever we could," she said lightly. "Some buildings have already slid down the hill and couldn't be saved, but most of them have mostly stayed where they were supposed to be."

He absorbed her comment without even a blink. Then again, lots of people did at least some research on Jerome before they came up here, so she supposed it wasn't too strange that he would have already heard about how unstable parts of Jerome were, thanks to the extensive mining that had stripped away large chunks of the earth on Cleopatra Hill. You couldn't see the open mines from the center of town, but if you went up the hill a little way, it was fairly obvious that no one had worked too hard to remediate the mining pits, and they still gaped raw against the hillside.

"I'm glad so much was able to be saved," the man replied. "I find local history fascinating, so it's good to see the buildings in much the same shape as they were a hundred years ago."

If he really was a history buff, Bree was a little surprised that he hadn't visited Jerome before now. But then, she had no idea where the guy was even from. She couldn't detect a trace of any kind of regional or foreign accent in his voice, although she knew that didn't mean a whole lot. Plenty of people worked hard to erase all signs of their origins from their voices, whether out of embarrassment, a need to sound more professional, or any of a score of other reasons.

"Are you from Arizona?" she asked.

A pause. Then he smiled again and said, "No, I'm from Los Angeles."

Maybe he was an actor. They'd been standing a few paces away from each other, as though he hadn't wanted to intrude on her personal space, but now she moved a little closer to him and extended a hand. "Brianna McAllister," she said. "People mostly call me Bree."

Another of those hesitations, but then he reached over and shook her hand very gently, almost as if he thought it would break. Despite his caution, she could still feel the strength in his fingers…and in his well-muscled arm as well.

Dear Goddess, he was gorgeous.

"Bill Garrett," he told her. "I've been studying old ghost towns, and Jerome came up in my research."

He stopped there and looked around. Because it was nearly six, a lot of the people who'd come to town for the day had already decamped, but lights still glowed in the shop windows, and the traffic on Main Street never really ceased, thanks to all the people driving to Prescott from the Verde Valley or vice versa. Sure, there was a way to go around that didn't involve going up and over Mingus Mountain, and yet plenty of people would still rather brave the twisty highway to save themselves a little time.

"Although I suppose this isn't really a ghost town," he observed, expression now almost amused. "Not with so many people living and visiting here."

"It almost was," she replied, thinking of how Jerome had begun to dwindle after the mines closed in the early 1950s. Some brave members of the McAllister clan had hung on and joined forces with the free-spirited civilians who came to squat in the abandoned houses here back in the 1960s. Together, they'd kept the little mining town from turning into nothing more than a memory. "But it survived, unlike so many of those other towns."

"I'm glad it did," Bill said. "It's very charming."

Most of the time, the word "charming" wasn't something she would have expected to come out of the mouth of a guy who looked like he was in his late twenties, maybe thirty at the most. When Bill Garrett said it, though, there was something about the word that was, well…charming.

"We like to think so."

His head tilted to one side as he appeared to consider her comment. "Are you from here?"

"Born and bred," she replied. Her origins weren't a state secret or anything, so she didn't mind giving him that small piece of information. "Just like most of the McAllister family."

Again, not a secret. People found out pretty quickly that the McAllisters had been here for almost a hundred and fifty years. True, the clan had spread into Prescott and Payson and even down to Wickenburg, nearly to the edges of the de la Paz clan's territory in Phoenix and beyond, but Jerome would always remain its heart and soul.

Bill looked almost pleased by her response. "It must have been fun to grow up someplace so interesting."

Now she couldn't help chuckling. "Well, Jerome is charming, but there's also not a lot to do here. When I was little, Cottonwood didn't even have a movie theater yet, so we had to drive into Sedona or Prescott. And we still have to do a lot of driving to go shopping, or whatever."

His eyebrow lifted, and she could tell he was analyzing her reply. She had to believe that what she'd just described must have sounded utterly alien to someone from a big city like Los Angeles, a place where pretty much everything you wanted or needed was within arm's reach.

"I suppose I can see why it might have felt… limiting," he said. "But at the same time, it must also have been comforting to be in a place where you knew everyone and everyone knew you."

Bree supposed that was one way of putting it. While growing up, she'd chafed at how little to do there actually was in Jerome, even as she reminded herself that if she'd been born only a few years earlier, her life would have been much more circumscribed. At least she could go up to Flagstaff or down to Phoenix without too much trouble, whereas in the days before Angela and Connor got together, Flagstaff might as well have been on the moon thanks to the enmity that had

existed between the two clans. Sure, the McAllisters had been friendly enough with the de la Paz
clan down in the southern section of the state, but
you still couldn't visit there without clearing your
trip with the *prima* first.

"It's definitely small-town living," she said,
and decided to leave it there.

Anyway, it was probably time to head back
inside and play her final set. She was given free
rein to do pretty much what she liked, but the
tasting room closed at seven, and she wanted to
make sure they got their money's worth by playing
a decently sized final set.

"Time to pick up the guitar again," she told
Bill with a smile. "But it was nice meeting you."

Disappointment flitted across his handsome
features. However, he recovered himself, saying,
"Of course. You're very talented—I don't want to
keep you from your audience."

Polite *and* handsome?

Too bad he wasn't local.

"Well, it's not like I'm on the clock or
anything," she said. "But I don't want to cheat
everybody of a full set, either."

"I understand." Bill paused there, his gaze not
quite meeting hers. "Do you have any plans
afterward?"

Bree wasn't sure if she could really call them
plans, not when all she was going to do was head

back to her apartment, throw together a salad, and then watch some TV.

However, she also couldn't overlook the implications of the question he'd just asked.

Unless her instincts were all wrong on this one, she was pretty sure he was asking her to dinner.

Her first impulse was to say yes, she was busy, and manufacture some kind of excuse. But he was good-looking and seemed kind, and it had been way too long since her last date. Entirely her choice—she had guys hit on her all the time and could have gone out whenever she wanted—and yet something felt different about this situation. She was fairly certain that if she shot him down, he wouldn't keep pestering her to change her mind but instead would accept her wishes and go about his business.

She didn't want to shoot him down, though. No, she wanted to spend time with Bill Garrett and learn more about him. All right, it couldn't go anywhere, not when he lived hundreds of miles away, but what was wrong with a little distraction now and then?

"No plans," she said, even as she hoped she wasn't making a huge mistake. "What did you have in mind?"

"There seems to be a very nice restaurant in the hotel where I'm staying," he replied, and inclined his head toward the top of the hill where the Grand Hotel was located. "Would you like to have dinner there?"

In general, The Asylum wasn't the sort of place you'd go for a casual dinner, mainly because it was the most expensive restaurant in Jerome. However, it didn't seem as if Mr. Garrett was too worried about such things.

"You're sure we won't need reservations?" she asked dubiously. True, it was a Wednesday night and not the weekend, but still, the place was almost always busy, since it tended to be a destination for people celebrating birthdays and anniversaries and any other occasion that required something a little out of the ordinary.

And she absolutely wouldn't admit to herself that part of her reluctance stemmed from not wanting to be seen by her brother while out on a date. Logic suggested that, as the chef, Shane rarely emerged from the kitchen which was his realm, but Bree knew as well as anyone else that sometimes life could throw you some serious curveballs.

Even so, she was a grown woman and could do what she liked. If Shane happened to spy her and Bill together, what difference would it make? It wasn't as if she'd been seeing anyone else lately, and because there were a grand total of maybe ten restaurants in all of Jerome, sooner or later, you'd end up in the one fine dining spot the town offered.

"I can check on that," Bill said. "And if the restaurant doesn't have any tables available, we can go somewhere else."

It sounded as if he had all the bases covered. She could stand here and continue to come up with stupid excuses, or she could do what she knew she really wanted.

"Then dinner sounds great," she said.

4

SHE'D AGREED TO HAVE DINNER WITH HIM. Even now, after Belshegar had excused himself to call the restaurant and confirm there was a table available, he felt slightly dazed, as though he wasn't quite sure what to do about this astonishing turn of events.

Yes, Brianna McAllister had said she needed to perform her final set, and had suggested that she meet him at the restaurant because she had to go home and put her instruments and equipment away, but still, that shimmering, magical creature had said she would dine with him.

Belshegar couldn't be sure if the voice was watching his every movement. He didn't think so, mostly because he had to believe the voice had better things to do than monitor him continually, but even if he was subject to some kind of subtle surveillance, he could only hope the voice wouldn't object to this dinner. On the surface, this would simply look like him getting close to a member of the witch family that appeared to have inhabited this town for generations, just as the Castillos had in Santa Fe.

There was no need for the voice to think that Belshegar had any ulterior motives.

To be fair, he didn't think he did. This was all about fact-finding, and if said fact-finding involved talking to a very beautiful witch, what of it?

Those justifications sounded good enough to him. Whether they were entirely true was another matter.

He stayed through most of Brianna's final set of music, but slipped out about ten minutes before seven, figuring it was probably a good idea to go up to the hotel and confirm their dinner reservations, and perhaps change his shirt. From what he'd seen, Jerome appeared to be a very casual place, and yet he didn't know whether a simple, dark T-shirt was the proper attire for what appeared to be a rather fancy restaurant.

All of his clothes and other "personal" belongings had been supplied by the voice, which seemed to have had a better idea of what might be needed during this trip to Jerome than he ever could. Everything in the limited wardrobe he'd been provided appeared to be equally casual, just more T-shirts and jeans, but Belshegar told himself that was no real impediment.

It wasn't as if he didn't have powers of his own.

While he hadn't spent a great deal of time with any humans besides Elena, he'd still seen pictures in the magazines and books she'd kept in her attic bedroom, and had also seen what men had been wearing at her wedding reception. Quite possibly, a suit coat and tie wouldn't be needed here, but a dress shirt in a shade of dark green felt appropriate, along with a pair of lace-up shoes to replace the heavy boots he'd previously had on.

Now that he was properly outfitted, he went downstairs, confirmed his reservation, and then wandered around the ground floor of the hotel and did his best not to look too at loose ends. Although he could sense ghostly presences here and there, none of those spirits seemed inclined to approach him or interact in any way, which he had to admit was something of a relief. They were interesting, true, but he didn't want to do anything that might attract some attention.

At seven twenty-five, he went back up to the restaurant to wait. Not for very long, however, since Brianna McAllister appeared just a minute before their appointed waiting time.

It seemed she'd also decided her attire wasn't

entirely appropriate for The Asylum, since she'd changed out of the jeans and sleeveless blouse she'd worn for her appearance at the wine tasting room. Now she had on a simple dress in a shade of cornflower blue that echoed the color of her beautiful eyes, and her slender feet were adorned with a pair of low, silvery sandals.

He'd thought her stunning before, but now she looked like a goddess in that blue dress with her pink-painted toenails peeking from beneath the long, flowing hem.

"Hi," he said. Not the most eloquent of responses, he supposed, but it was still better than standing there and gawking as though a unicorn had just emerged from the elevator.

Which was foolish, he knew. Unicorns didn't exist on this plane.

"Hi," she replied. Was that just the slightest flicker of admiration in her eyes?

No, he must be imagining things. Although he knew the mortal form the voice had provided —and had originally been created by Loc—was considered quite attractive by human standards, he guessed it would take some kind of godlike being to impress someone as beautiful as Brianna McAllister.

To his relief, the woman standing at the desk up front—some kind of hostess?—seemed to realize their party was now complete, because she said, "This way, please."

Belshegar hung back for a second or two so Brianna could fall in behind the hostess. He took up the rear, noting that the restaurant was quite full on a day when normally it shouldn't have been very busy. Had it been simple luck that had allowed him to reserve a table, or was some force higher than he…or even the voice…stepping in to make sure his way was made as smooth as possible?

No, that was probably assigning himself—and his mission here—far more importance than it actually deserved.

However it had happened, it seemed his luck was meant to continue, for he and Brianna were given a table by a window, one that faced east and showed the twinkling lights of Jerome below and the near-dark landscape beyond. By this hour, everything was dusky purple, with no real features that could be discerned, but it was no less beautiful for that.

He and Brianna seated themselves and picked up their menus. While he was still mostly unfamiliar with human food, he knew he could eat any of it if necessary, for the body he wore was human enough, even if the spirit it contained was something entirely other. And because he didn't want to appear any more awkward than he already had, he'd perused the restaurant menu that had been waiting on the desk in his hotel room so he could familiarize himself as best he could with its contents.

That was why he knew he wanted to order the chicken tenderloins in poblano sauce rather than some of the heavier offerings. At Elena's reception, he'd consumed some beef and thought it too rich for his very new tastebuds, so he'd immediately gravitated toward the restaurant's lighter fare.

Brianna—Bree, he reminded himself, although he thought the longer form of her name suited her better—gave the menu only a cursory glance before setting it aside. Concerned, Belshegar asked, "Does nothing look good to you?"

At once, she smiled. "Oh, everything's good at The Asylum. It's just that I know the menu pretty much by heart because my brother is the chef here."

Startled, Belshegar stared back at her. Of course, he understood that most witches and warlocks had regular jobs—mainly because that was what Elena had told him, even though her grandmother hadn't worked, had stayed home all day so she could keep an eye on her troublesome, demon-summoning granddaughter—but still, he supposed he hadn't been expecting Brianna McAllister to have such a close connection to the restaurant he'd selected for their dinner.

"So I know all the food here is really good," she continued. "Tonight, though, I think I'll have the shrimp skewer. What about you?"

"The chicken tenderloins," he replied, and she looked pleased.

"Well, that'll make it easy to choose the wine," she said, then paused, a hint of concern touching her lovely features. "If you want to order a bottle, of course," she added hastily.

What would half a bottle of wine do to him?

Probably not all that much. The champagne he'd drunk at Elena's wedding reception didn't seem to have had much of an effect at all, so he thought it should be safe enough to share a bottle during his meal with Bree.

"A bottle sounds like an excellent idea," he said. "But you can choose. Perhaps something local?"

"They have a good selection," she replied. "And I've had pretty much all of them, thanks to performing all over the Verde Valley."

He hadn't thought about that aspect of her employment—probably because he hadn't noticed her drinking anything but water when she was performing earlier—but he supposed he could see how she would have been exposed to all the various vintages the local wineries offered.

After studying the wine list for a moment, she said something called Sandy Jones, a white blend from a vineyard called Chateau Tumbleweed, would be perfect for their meal. And her timing was excellent, since a moment later their server appeared and asked what they would like to drink. Belshegar thought he noted a subtle interaction between the two women, barely more than a very slight tilt of the waitress's head toward Brianna, and an even fainter lift at the corner of Brianna's mouth.

Clearly, they were acquainted with one another, not so strange a coincidence, considering she'd lived here all her life and her brother was the head chef at this restaurant. Still, the interaction put Belshegar that much more on edge, simply because it reinforced the impression that he truly was on his own here, surrounded by people he guessed would present a unified front against any outside intrusions.

As best he could, he brushed that unsettling thought away and then asked for the bottle Brianna had suggested. Since they already knew what they wanted to eat—and because he was doing his best to act as casual as possible—they also ordered their main courses. Once the waitress had departed, Brianna settled against the back of her chair and sent him a curious look.

"So, did you do much research about the Verde Valley before you came here?" she asked.

A neutral enough question, he supposed. He got the feeling she was doing her best to make conversation until the waitress returned with their bottle of wine, and he could only be grateful for that. Any topic that turned his thoughts away from his true reason for being here could only help.

And at least this time, he could answer her honestly.

Partly, at any rate.

"Not very much," he admitted. "I read about Jerome, of course, but I suppose I hadn't realized this area is so focused on wine."

"It's kind of hard to miss," she responded with a grin, although there wasn't anything overtly teasing about her tone or her expression. "Some days, it feels like almost everything here revolves around the wine industry. We've got our own AVA."

He raised an eyebrow. While he thought his grasp on the English language was quite good, he didn't think he'd ever heard that term before.

"American viticultural area," she explained, the corners of her mouth still curving in that beautiful smile. "You know, like Napa or Sonoma."

Belshegar wasn't sure he'd heard of either of

those places, either. But viticulture had something to do with wine, didn't it?

He thought so, and also took this opportunity to excuse himself for not being terribly familiar with some of the phrases Brianna had used. It wasn't as though he and Elena had discussed wine or winemaking during the times he'd come to keep her company and let her know she wasn't as alone as she believed.

"Ah," he responded, and was glad that their waitress had chosen to return at that moment, since her arrival saved him from having to say much of anything else.

Once their wine was poured, however, he realized he needed to make some kind of comment before they drank. Not a formal toast like the one that had been delivered at Elena's wedding by Alessandro's cousin Gabriel, but at least a few words to commemorate the moment.

"To unexpected meetings," he said, and Bree raised her glass and touched it to his.

"'To unexpected meetings,'" she echoed.

The sentiment behind the words was true enough, after all. It wasn't as if he'd come here for the express purpose of meeting Brianna McAllister. No, he'd arrived in Jerome to find the witch and warlock who held the artifacts the voice had requested, of course. But he'd had no idea he would meet someone so entrancing while here on his mission.

He couldn't allow her to distract him too much, though. After all, the entire reason why he'd approached her was that he'd hoped she might lead him to the people he was truly seeking.

Perhaps he was being a bit disingenuous, but he found he didn't want to analyze the entirety of his motivations too closely.

"I suppose it's a good thing that I decided to stay in Jerome rather than Clarkdale or Cottonwood," he said. "Otherwise, I wouldn't have been wandering along the main street, wondering what to do with myself."

"You did seem a little at loose ends when you came into the tasting room," Brianna remarked, and then sipped from her glass of wine.

Had it been that obvious? And here he'd thought he'd done everything he could to act as though he didn't have a care in the world.

Being human was more difficult than he'd thought.

"It was a little disconcerting to see all those cars leaving town at the end of the afternoon," he said. "I wondered if there would be anything for me to do here."

"Jerome does tend to roll up the sidewalks at night," Brianna replied. "A couple of the restaurants stay open, and the Spirit Room usually has live entertainment, but not on Wednesdays. And even then they don't start until around eight, so I can see why you might have thought you were doomed to eat room service or something."

Did the Grand Hotel even have room service? He only knew such a thing existed because Elena had mentioned taking advantage of it while she was staying at the La Fonda Hotel in Santa Fe, doing her best to lie low so her father and grandmother wouldn't realize she'd escaped the prison they'd created for her.

But he supposed the staff at the Grand Hotel wouldn't have put the restaurant's menu in his room if there wasn't some way of having the food delivered directly there.

"Then I guess it was very lucky that I heard you playing when I passed by the tasting room."

For a moment, her gaze met his. The lighting was dim enough in here that normal human vision probably wouldn't have been able to detect the pure blue hues of her eyes, but Belshegar's sight was anything but normal. He could detect the subtle shimmers of paler tones, almost crystalline gray, could see the dark ring around her irises, something that only served to make her eye color stand out that much more.

Even if the rest of her hadn't been equally as lovely, those eyes alone would have made her a beauty.

"I suppose it is," she said lightly. Her lips parted, as though she intended to ask him something else, but the waitress arrived with their food right then.

A moment was taken up by their plates being set down in front of them and the waitress asking if they needed anything else. Belshegar wasn't sure why she would pose such a question, not when they hadn't ordered anything other than their entrées, and those had already been delivered.

But Brianna smiled and thanked the other woman, and said she was fine and everything looked great. Picking up on her cue, he murmured much the same.

And then they were alone again.

He had to admit the food smelled delicious, and the first few bites only supported that impression. It seemed Brianna's brother must have used magic to create such dishes, for the flavors were blended so skillfully that he thought the food had become far more than the sum of its parts.

Of course he couldn't ask Bree if that was the truth, not when she knew she must never divulge anything about her magical nature to a stranger... and not when she thought he was no more of witch-kind than the woman who had just brought them their food.

To be fair, he wasn't witch-kind. No, he was

something far, far different, even though he possessed magical gifts of his own.

"How is your food?" he asked politely.

"Wonderful—but it always is when Shane's cooking." She paused there, fork resting against her plate. "How's yours?"

"It's excellent," Belshegar replied, knowing he could be truthful about that...if not a host of other subjects. "Your brother obviously has a gift for this sort of thing."

She blinked, clearly a little put off by the way he'd phrased the comment. But then something about her seemed to relax, as though she'd told herself it wasn't such a strange thing to say, and that people made remarks about "gifts" and "talents" all the time without those comments ever referring to the powers that a witch or warlock might possess.

"Yes," she said as she set down her fork and reached for her glass of wine. "He knew from the time he was really young that he wanted to be a chef, and he went to culinary school down in Phoenix. Still, landing the top spot in the kitchen here was kind of a coup for him, since he's only twenty-seven. Usually, you need to earn your lumps in a sous chef position for a few years before you're running the back of house."

Several of the phrases she'd used were unfamiliar to him, but Belshegar did his best to sort out her words. From what he was able to tell, she was saying that her brother was young for the position he currently held, and that was all due to his unique skills.

"I suppose it's always good to know what you want to do in life," he said.

Something about Brianna's mouth seemed to tighten, and he wondered if he'd said the wrong thing. But then her expression smoothed itself and became almost cheerful once again.

"And what do you do in life?" she inquired, her tone almost teasing now.

Damn. He hadn't taken the time to concoct much of a story about himself, mostly because he hadn't thought he would have to do anything more than pose as a tourist interested in local history.

He'd never thought he'd be sitting down to dinner with a member of the local witch clan.

But Brianna was gazing at him with those astonishing blue eyes, so he knew he had to think of something. For him to be here at a time that wasn't a holiday and with no real itinerary seemed to indicate that he had plenty of leisure time to do with as he pleased.

And he had the example of the Castillos to go on. True, many of them had some sort of career, if only to help obfuscate the true source of their wealth, but others seemed to do very little except paint or write or simply be.

"I live off my investments," he said, thinking that felt simpler than trying to explain a job he didn't even possess, and her eyes widened a little.

"Those must be some investments," she responded with a grin, and picked up her fork again.

Had he misstepped? Well, he'd said the words, so it wasn't as though he could retreat now.

"And an inheritance," he added, hoping that would help to explain the situation, and now she actually chuckled.

"Well, I'm glad you're being honest about it. So, you just travel where you like, when you like?"

"More or less," he said. That wasn't completely a lie. Except for those times when Elena had summoned him for companionship and comfort, his time had been entirely his own.

Until the voice sent him here to retrieve the artifacts, of course.

Perhaps some mortals would have said, "Must be nice," or something along those lines. However, Brianna only looked thoughtful.

"It's a great thing to be in control of your destiny like that," she said as she skillfully removed one of the shrimps from its skewer and speared it with her fork. "I like that you're using your time to learn new things. It's what keeps your mind active."

"Are you always learning new things?" he asked, genuinely curious.

Her expression sobered a bit. "Not as much as I would like, I suppose. But I'm teaching them, so that's something."

This response startled him. "You teach?"

Somehow, he couldn't imagine her in front of a classroom full of students, but possibly that was only because he had very little experience of such things.

Now she smiled again. "Music," she replied, then added, "Guitar and piano and voice. Just at my students' houses, and I don't have a lot of kids to teach. But it's a nice break from all the tasting room gigs."

Belshegar could see that. To share her love of music with a new generation—to guide them to appreciate it on their own?

That was no small thing.

"Have you always played?" he inquired next, and she nodded.

"As long as I can remember. My parents had a piano that belonged to my great-grandparents on my mom's side, so I played around with that. And then someone gave Shane a toy guitar for his birthday when he was eight or nine. He messed with it for a couple of days but wasn't all that interested, and I kind of took it over. I suppose you can say the rest is history."

Once again, Belshegar wished he could ask her if music was her magical gift, or whether she wasn't materially different from all the generations of mortals who had a natural aptitude for singing or composing or playing an instrument.

Unfortunately, he doubted they would ever get to a place where she would be willing to place such confidences in him.

"It's good when your talent is so strong that you can't think of anything else you would rather do in life," he ventured.

Her expression grew almost wistful. "I suppose it is," she replied. "And luckily, I never had parents who told me that pursuing music was silly and that I should get a business degree or become a doctor or a lawyer or something."

No, it seemed her parents had allowed her to find her own way. Was it like that in most witch families? He couldn't say for sure, not when his only real example had been Elena's father and grandmother…and they'd been anything but supportive.

However, he'd been able to tell at her wedding reception that most of the guests there seemed to be very happy with their lives. Certainly, it didn't seem as though they'd been forced into careers that were at odds with their talents and skills.

"So…." Bree went on, and again she seemed almost diffident, as if she wasn't sure how she should broach the topic even if it was something she wanted to discuss. "How long are you in town?"

Could it be that she wanted to see more of him?

That must be the case, or he doubted she would have even asked the question.

Hope fluttered with butterfly wings within his chest, but he tried to sound as casual as possible as he said, "My trip here is open-ended."

Of course it was. How could he know when he would be going back to his plane when he had no idea how long it would take for him to retrieve the artifacts the voice had requested?

Thank all the various forces in the universe that he'd already provided Brianna McAllister with a perfectly plausible reason as to why he could stay in Jerome for as long as he liked.

Her mouth pursed, partway to a smile. "Well," she said, also in tones that he knew were deliberately nonchalant, "there's a folk festival coming up this weekend, and I'm playing Saturday afternoon. Maybe you'd like to stick around for that?"

Belshegar could think of nothing he'd like better. Of course he had no real interest in folk music, but he would take every possible opportunity to spend time in her company.

"That sounds like it would be fun," he replied.

She seemed to relax against the back of her chair, although he could tell she was doing what she could to hide her relief by spearing another shrimp and popping it in her mouth. Once she was done chewing, she said, "There's lots of other stuff besides music, too. There'll be food trucks and a craft fair. We started having the festival about ten years ago, and it keeps getting bigger every year."

"Then I suppose it's a good thing I already have a hotel room," he told her.

Now her eyes met his, and he could see the anticipation shining in them.

"Yes," she said. "I suppose it is."

5

Had she really just invited Bill Garrett to the folk festival?

It sure looked like it.

Well, she couldn't take back the words now. And honestly, she wanted him there to see her perform. True, he'd already heard her playing at the tasting room, but this would be different. She wouldn't be covering the same old songs that everyone wanted to hear.

No, at the folk festival, she'd have one of the few opportunities that came her way to play her own music, to see how people reacted to the songs of her heart.

Which meant she needed to get the one she'd been working on for the past few weeks completely out of her head and down on some paper.

Luckily, Bill didn't seem awkward about the situation, and instead asked a few questions about the festival and the sorts of things he could expect. Nothing about his tone or expression made her think he thought it a little strange that a woman he barely knew had asked him to hang around and attend a local event.

They chatted about the sorts of things he might do to occupy himself over the next couple of days—she told him he needed to visit Sedona and maybe drive up to Flagstaff to see the aspens, since, charming as Jerome was, there wasn't so much to do there that you still didn't need to find alternatives during a multi-day stay—and when Tori came back with the check, he reached for it so smoothly that Bree didn't even have a chance to protest.

Not that she should have, she supposed. After all, he was the one who'd asked her out to dinner.

And she also knew she shouldn't worry about the chunk he'd dropped on their meal, not when he was independently wealthy or something. From a lot of other guys, she would have thought that was only a line designed to get her into bed, but she didn't think so. Something about Bill seemed too inherently trustworthy to allow him to lie to her like that.

In fact, he even offered to walk her home, despite him staying right here in the Grand Hotel and not needing to do much more than go over to the elevator to get to home base. She thanked him but said she was fine.

"Jerome is the safest place in the world," she said, knowing that was pretty much true. Sure, there was the occasional tourist-caused fender-bender from time to time, but residential and personal crime was practically nonexistent.

It was kind of hard to pull off that kind of stuff when you were surrounded by witches and warlocks, some of whom had the ability to sniff out those sorts of illegal activities…or anyone who'd be inclined to lie about them.

Bill looked dubious, but after she told him again that she would be fine, he let it go, although he still walked her over to the steps that would lead her down to the street level below them. From there, she'd have to descend once more, but once she got to Main Street, it was pretty much a straight line downhill to her apartment over the gallery.

No attempt at a kiss, either, and she wasn't sure what to make of that.

It's because he's a perfect gentleman, she thought as she waved goodbye and then began to make her way down the stairs. They were steep but had been renovated recently, so at least they weren't uneven anymore.

Or maybe, despite all evidence to the contrary,

Bill Garrett hadn't leaned in for a kiss because he wasn't that into her.

She didn't want to believe that, though. If he wasn't interested, she doubted he would have asked her out to a dinner that had lightened his wallet by a few hundred bucks.

Maybe he was holding back because he was here on vacation and would eventually return to L.A., even if he'd agreed to stay longer than maybe he'd originally planned.

That theory made more sense, although she knew there were plenty of men in the world who wouldn't have any problem with indulging in a holiday fling before they headed back to their ordinary lives.

Bill Garrett didn't seem to be most men, however. It wasn't just his extraordinary good looks—no, something about him seemed more thoughtful, more kind, than anyone else she'd ever met.

Not the sort of quality you'd expect from a trust fund baby.

If that was even the source of his wealth. There were plenty of ways to live off an inheritance without it coming from a trust, she supposed, but that did seem to be the most likely reason why Bill could live his life exactly as he pleased.

She emerged on Clark Street, cut past the

Haunted Hamburger, and then descended the rest of the way to Main Street. The Spirit Room was open, so she could hear the murmur of voices and the background hum of canned music, but it still felt pretty subdued compared to the way the place could get jumping when a popular band was playing.

Even though she knew it was silly to be annoyed by something so minor, she still kind of hated knowing she'd probably never get booked there. It wasn't a lack of talent that kept her from playing the venue, but instead a focus on the kind of music that generally didn't get people's toes tapping.

Well, that was on her. If she'd concentrated her talents in a different area, maybe she could have been her generation's answer to Lady Gaga, or whatever. As things stood, though, she knew she was a folksy singer, and it felt too late to shift gears now.

A few lights shone through the gallery's windows, just enough to guide Bree to the stairs that led up to her apartment. Belatedly, she remembered that she had to watch the place tomorrow afternoon, since Chelle, the owner, had an appointment in Scottsdale and wouldn't be back until well after closing.

Usually, Brianna would have been okay with the interruption to her schedule, if only because minding the store offered her a small change of pace. Now, though, she didn't much like the idea of being trapped in the gallery for half the day, not with Bill Garrett wandering around town.

And he didn't say one word to you about getting together tomorrow, she scolded herself as she touched a finger to the door to unlock it and let herself in. Most of the time, she went through the show of using her key just so no one could see what she was doing, but this part of Main Street was utterly deserted tonight. It wasn't as if there was anyone around to see how Brianna McAllister had managed to unlock her front door with a mere touch.

Because she often came home after dark, she always left one light on, the pretty little mercury glass lamp that sat on top of her bookcase. It didn't do a whole lot to illuminate the space, but it was just enough to prevent her from tripping over something.

She dropped her purse on the dining room table and went into the kitchen to pour herself a glass of water. Yes, Tori had brought them water during dinner, but her throat still felt dry.

All that talking, probably. She and Bill had talked a lot.

The conversation had never felt forced, though, and had flowed naturally from one topic to another. Throughout dinner, Bree had been just the slightest bit tense, wondering if Shane was going to emerge from the kitchen and pull some kind of big-brother act on her, but either Tori had kept her mouth shut about how his sister was dining at The Asylum with a hot stranger, or Shane had decided he should keep his distance.

Either way, any scenes had been happily avoided, and she could only be grateful for that. She didn't want any awkwardness between Bill and her…even while she knew there was no way the two of them could have any kind of a real connection. Getting together with a civilian wasn't impossible, true, and neither was a long-distance relationship.

Both of those things at the same time?

Not so much.

It was far too early to get ready for bed. Instead, she went into the hall closet, which was surprisingly large for an apartment of this size. Inside was her beloved old acoustic guitar.

She took it from its case and then pulled out one of her two dining room chairs. Sometimes she played on the sofa, but she knew she had much better posture when she sat on a hard seat.

No song at first, just her fingers finding their way through a progression of minor chords, their melancholy a fitting accompaniment to her current mood. Maybe it was foolish to feel this way when she'd just had a wonderful dinner with

Bill and the promise of him accompanying her to the folk festival in a few days.

And yet....

Figures that the first decent guy I meet in a long time is a civilian from L.A., she thought, strumming away quietly. There wasn't any real need to keep the noise down, not when the buildings on either side were fully commercial and didn't have anyone living there, but the habits she'd acquired during her childhood when she was trying her best not to blast everyone in the house were hard to shake.

Besides, banging on the guitar like a kid enthusiastically playing in her first recital didn't fit her current mood. She couldn't be sad, not when she'd had such an enjoyable evening, but at the same time, she also didn't think she had as much to celebrate as someone looking in from the outside might have thought.

Well, all she could do for now was focus on the positive. She would spend time with Bill or not, and things would progress...or they wouldn't. Sitting here and feeling sorry for herself wouldn't change a damn thing.

Maybe she should see if Bellamy was available for coffee or something tomorrow morning. Her best friend was currently house shopping with Marc Trujillo, the de la Paz hottie who'd basically fallen in her lap just a month earlier, but thanks to

Bellamy's recent windfall lottery win, it wasn't as if she had a job she needed to go to or something.

And Bree didn't have to be on duty at the gallery until one.

She set the guitar aside and reached for her purse, which luckily was within arm's reach. A quick text to her friend—and a faster response than she'd expected.

> Breakfast tomorrow sounds great. Meet at the Mine Shaft at 10?

Brianna would probably be way up before then...she'd always been an early riser...but that was fine. She could have some coffee, putter around the apartment for a bit, and then go see Bellamy at the restaurant, which was only a block uphill from her place. Whether her best friend would really have some useful advice to offer was up in the air, but on the other hand, it was always good to talk things over with someone who would lend a sympathetic ear.

> Sounds great. See you then.

Bellamy responded with a smiley emoji, and that seemed to be that.

At least Bree now had part of her day occupied.

She set down her phone and reached for her guitar again. Smiling, she began to work on the passage in her current work-in-progress that had been giving her so much trouble.

Sooner or later, she'd get it figured out.

Bellamy looked all glowing and happy the next morning when she slid into the booth Bree had secured for them. And why shouldn't she be? Everything had gone amazingly right for her so far.

You will not be jealous, Brianna scolded herself. *Just…no.*

The green-eyed monster subsided a bit, but she knew it was still lurking there in the background, waiting to pounce if she let her guard down too much.

"So, what's up?" Bellamy asked as she pushed a strand of copper-red hair back over her shoulder. That red hair and her sparkling gray eyes often made people turn to look, but she'd always treated her prettiness in an off-hand sort of way, as though she wasn't sure exactly what to do with it. Like Bree, she didn't bother to glance at the menu, not when she already knew every single item the café offered. "Something about your text message made this feel urgent."

"No, it's not urgent," Brianna replied at once. "A couple of friends can't get together for breakfast?"

Bellamy lifted one russet eyebrow. "Sure they can. But this is the first time you've asked since Marc and I got together."

"I didn't want to bug you when I knew you guys were busy."

This response earned her another raised eyebrow. Luckily, though, the waiter—a guy named Andre who Bree knew was getting his enology degree at the community college in Cottonwood—came by to take their orders. Bellamy ordered coffee and a breakfast burrito, while Brianna asked for tea and waffles.

Once that was handled, though, Bellamy leaned against the back of the booth and sent her friend a very direct look. "You want to tell me what's really going on?"

The words escaped Bree's lips without her even stopping to think about what she wanted to say. "What would you have done if Marc was a civilian?"

"A-ha," Bellamy said, now smiling a little. "So…you've met someone?"

"Kind of," Bree replied. She was now wondering whether this had been such a good idea after all, but since she'd broached the subject, there wasn't much she could do except plow forward. "We had dinner last night. He's good-looking and charming and seems like a really great guy."

"But he's a civilian," her friend supplied for her.

Bree nodded. "And he's from L.A. It's hopeless, right?"

"Nothing is hopeless," Bellamy said, her tone firm. "I mean, since he's a civilian, he can go where he wants, right?"

Well, that much was true. Especially when you factored in that he wasn't tied down to a job and appeared to be similarly unencumbered by a serious relationship. Sure, he could have left a girlfriend or wife behind in Los Angeles, and Bree wouldn't have known the difference, but....

Or maybe not. The one or two times she'd tried to make her ever-shifting gifts allow her to see into someone's mind, she hadn't been at all successful, but sometimes magic had helped her discover whether a person was telling the truth. It wasn't a surefire thing, and yet she thought maybe if she asked an innocent question about any significant others, she might be able to determine if Bill was lying when he responded to an off-hand question about any relationships he might have in L.A.

Andre came by with their coffee and tea and let them know their food would be out in another moment. However, the interruption wasn't quite enough to prevent Bree from providing the answer her friend clearly expected.

"I guess he has that kind of freedom," she said. "From what he said at dinner, it sounds as if he doesn't have to work, so I think he isn't all that tied down." She paused there to pick up a bag of English Breakfast and dunk it in the hot water their waiter had provided. "It's kind of stupid for me to even be thinking about this sort of stuff when Bill and I have only just met."

"Bill and Bree," Bellamy said, then grinned. "You sound like a musical act or something." Then her expression sobered a little, and she added, "I think it's different for wi...for people like us," she amended quickly, since a couple of older women, probably tourists, occupied the booth across the way from them, close enough to overhear what she and Brianna were saying. "We tend to know up front whether there's any sort of spark or possibility for something more than a casual date. You've already gone out with this Bill guy once, so I don't see anything wrong with letting your thoughts wander in that direction. You had a nice time, obviously, or none of this would even be an issue."

Yes, she'd had a nice time...a *very* nice time. Sure, it had felt a little anticlimactic to leave and head down the hill without a goodnight kiss to end the evening, but at the same time, she thought she liked that Bill had held back. It was sweet, and a lot more old-fashioned than she'd been expecting.

Still, that didn't mean she didn't want to know what it would feel like when he pressed his lips against hers.

If that ever even happened.

"I suppose you're right," she said. Her tea was probably still too hot to drink, but she picked it up and blew on it anyway.

"I know I'm right," Bellamy replied firmly.

Andre came over with their food, so they paused while he set their plates in front of them and asked if they needed anything else. Once they'd reassured him that everything was great, he headed back toward the kitchen.

"Anyway," Bellamy went on, apparently content to let her food cool a bit as she continued their conversation, "have you made any other plans with him?"

At least Bree had something positive to present on that front. "We're going to the folk festival on Saturday."

Triumph flickered on Bellamy's features. "Well, then. I doubt he would have agreed to go to an all-day event like that if he wasn't into you. That kind of thing requires commitment."

The same thought had passed through Brianna's mind as she was taking a shower that morning. At the time, though, she'd wondered if she was reading too much into the whole situation. For all she knew, Bill had been glad of the chance to find something to do to pass the time, and spending the day with her might have been incidental to that particular goal.

She hadn't gotten that vibe from him, however…unless she was completely misreading the guy.

And she also had a feeling that if she tried to present that particular argument, Bellamy would shoot it down with all the laser accuracy of a surface-to-air missile.

Maybe she should just check her insecurities at the door and wait to see what happened.

Worst case? They'd have some fun together, and then he'd head back to L.A., and that would be the end of it.

Best case?

For some reason, Bree was almost more worried about that outcome….

6

Belshegar had no real plans to explore Sedona and Prescott and Flagstaff, of course. Doing so would only take him away from the place where the artifacts had been hidden. During dinner the night before, he'd learned from Brianna that she would be working at a gallery down on Main Street for most of the afternoon, so he thought it shouldn't be too hard to avoid her. All he had to do was stay in his room until he knew she was safely ensconced at the gallery, and then he would be free to move about the town without too much interference.

That was why he spent most of the morning engaged in meditation, allowing his mind and spirit to drift and, he hoped, gain some inner calm.

He knew he needed it after the dinner they had shared.

Ever since, he hadn't been able to stop thinking about her—about the gleam of her beautiful blue eyes, the smoothness of her skin, those glorious golden waves of hair that fell about her shoulders. Never in his very long life would he have ever thought he might be attracted to a human. In all those hours he'd spent with Elena, he'd never once experienced even the slightest flicker of desire.

True, he'd met her when she was a very young girl, and if he'd had to explain their relationship in human terms, he might have said he was a protective older brother. But Elena had certainly grown up to be beautiful enough, and he still barely noticed, except perhaps to be glad that she'd found someone in Alessandro who admired both her inner and outer attractions.

Brianna, on the other hand….

It took some effort, but eventually he managed to banish her from his mind and to simply be. His consciousness ranged to the place he called home, and he saw that the gardens he'd tended so carefully still looked just as they always had, lush and full of colors that had never existed on Earth. Deep down, he knew those gardens would flourish without him, and he'd mainly taken care of them because tending the plants and flowers gave him something to do.

And when he came back to this plane and glanced over at the digital clock on the bedside table, he saw it was nearly two o'clock in the afternoon. Brianna would be at the gallery, and that meant he should be free to wander the streets of Jerome…as long as he avoided the block where her place of work was located.

The sky was once again bright and blue, the air warm. He donned human attire of jeans and a dark green T-shirt, got out a pair of sunglasses— even though he didn't really need them—and prepared to sally forth to see what he could find.

The town seemed a little busier today. Was that because of the approaching weekend, or because people were coming to Jerome early for the folk festival that would begin the day after tomorrow?

Not knowing the usual rhythms of the place, he couldn't hazard a guess. However, he believed the additional foot traffic could only be helpful, as he thought it might assist in concealing his movements.

The night before, he hadn't seen any sign of the ghost that had appeared in his hotel room, but he'd sensed it moving around the building, along with others whose presences weren't quite as easy to detect. He felt something of that now as he left the Grand Hotel and walked past a place called the Haunted Hamburger—apt, he thought, for that place had at least two or three resident spirits, possibly more—and continued on his way.

Jerome's history had been a violent one, he'd learned from a brochure he picked up in the hotel lobby, one of gunfights and drunken brawls and crimes of passion. As the years wore on, it became a little more sedate, but blood had already been spilled here many times, and some of those victims—and perpetrators—had never found a way to move on to the next plane.

But the ghosts, while interesting, were not his main concern.

No, he needed to pick up the thread of the energy he'd felt the day before, a low thrum of magic that was entirely different from the powers he sensed whenever a witch or warlock passed him on the street. There were quite a few of them here, but he didn't find that too strange, not when he was in the heart of McAllister territory. Their energy was bright and sparkling, not so different from champagne in its own way.

The other magic, though, felt more like a background hum, similar to the sound an old-fashioned car's engine might make. Unfortunately, those pulses, while discernible to him, didn't seem to emanate from any single place that he was able to detect.

By design, he was sure. Although Belshegar didn't completely understand how humans used magic, he guessed whatever wards had been placed on the artifacts would have been designed to ensure that anyone looking for them wouldn't be able to determine their exact location.

No, the only way he could trace them to their hiding place would be to discover whose home or other property concealed them. He guessed the witch the voice had described must be the *prima* of this clan—and the warlock her consort—since tradition held that the strongest witch of a particular generation was always the one to lead them.

Fine and good, but although he could sense witch powers, he wasn't able to determine who among them was stronger and who was weaker.

And that meant the *prima* could have passed him on the street, and he would have been none the wiser. He might have been an extradimensional being, but that didn't mean his powers were limitless.

Well, he would have to do this by means of simple deduction. If a *prima* was the head of her clan, then that meant she probably held some sort of first-among-equals status. Therefore, she would probably live in one of the nicer homes in town.

Even though Jerome was quite small, there was still a good bit of it that most people would never even know existed, since it seemed clear to him that the tourists generally stayed on its main streets, the ones that were basically a part of the highway before it continued up and over the heavily wooded mountain that towered above the town.

The question was, how could he poke around in the residential areas without someone wondering what he was doing there? Saying he was lost might work once or twice, but he had a feeling word would soon get out that a stranger was snooping around their homes, and his activities would be shut down by whatever means necessary.

Well, he'd told Brianna just the day before that his hobby was researching old ghost towns, so he didn't think it would seem too strange for him to be inspecting the architecture of the various houses that had been built during Jerome's boom times more than a hundred years ago. In fact, he would bring a sketchpad and some pencils with him to bolster his story. Although he would certainly never call himself an artist, he'd spent many years watching Elana draw and thought he could fake it well enough, to use an utterly human phrase.

He could have conjured the sketchpad and pencil, but it turned out there was a shop near the top of Main Street called McAllister Mercantile that sold the items in question. The credit cards he'd been given were loaded with so much money that he knew he could never spend it all, so he wasn't too worried about purchasing such trifles. He noted at once that the pretty brown-haired woman working there that morning was a witch as well, and she gave him a cheerful smile and said she hoped he would have fun sketching the sights. Their exchange also played well into his plans, because if anyone made a comment about seeing him with the sketchpad, she could comment that she'd sold it to him.

All very normal, completely ordinary.

Once he was armed with his drawing supplies, he wandered down the street, passing the tasting room where he'd first met Brianna McAllister. The door was open, and he could see people inside, but there was no music, of course, not this early in the afternoon.

Still, he couldn't help experiencing a pang when he saw the place, and wished he did not have to continue deceiving her as to who he was and why he was here in Jerome. But the voice could take away his pleasant home if it wished… could even end his very long life if it was sufficiently displeased with the work he was doing. Lying to Brianna, while uncomfortable, was certainly better than dying.

Wasn't it?

His jaw tightened then—such a human reaction—and he forced himself to continue toward a neighborhood he'd noticed when he was wandering around the town the day before. Perhaps the *prima* and her consort wouldn't turn out to dwell there after all, but he thought he had to start somewhere. Later on, if his search in this location didn't bear any fruit, he would find a map of Jerome and see if there were other more likely streets he could search.

As soon as he turned onto Rich Street, however, he realized that most of the homes here were quite modest, small bungalows of only one story, with the occasional clapboard farmhouse similar to the home where Elena had grown up to give some variety to the neighborhood's architecture.

This street was much quieter than the main thoroughfare, of course, and he knew he must look terribly suspicious. No foot traffic to shield him, and several of the people who passed in their cars sent him wary glances, as though they could tell he had no business there.

Well, that was what the sketchbook was for.

He opened it up and commenced composing a quick drawing of the house before him, an attractive bungalow with a large front porch and cheerful roses blooming in various shades along the front walk. Since he hadn't spied any cars in the driveway or any other signs of life, he guessed the people who lived there must be away for the day, most likely at work or school or engaging in whatever activities might occupy them during the daylight hours.

And then he heard Brianna's incredulous voice. "Bill?"

Startled, he looked up from his sketch to see her approaching with a bulky brown paper–wrapped parcel under one arm. Based on its size and shape, he guessed it must be a painting of some sort, perhaps one of the pieces from the gallery where she was supposed to be working this afternoon.

However, the presence of a painting didn't explain why she was here rather than safely tucked away at the gallery.

"Hello, Bree," he said calmly, hoping he didn't sound as rattled as he felt. "What brings you here?"

Although she was wearing sunglasses to shield her eyes from the bright, sunny afternoon, he could still see the way her brows drew together. "I might ask you the same thing."

Immediately, he held up the sketchbook, gladder than ever that he'd come up with the simple subterfuge to explain why he was so off the beaten path. "I enjoy sketching some of the houses and buildings I see during my travels. It didn't appear as if anyone was home, so I didn't see the harm in making a drawing of this one."

She moved a little closer—not too close, because the bulky canvas she carried prevented her from doing so—but enough so she could see the drawing he'd begun a few minutes earlier. "That's really good," she said, sounding almost surprised.

Perhaps some men would have taken umbrage at the intimation that she didn't believe he could create a worthwhile drawing. Belshegar, on the other hand, was only pleased that she thought it wasn't dreadful.

"It is?"

She shifted her burden to the other arm. "You've really captured the charm of the house."

"Let me help you with that—" he began, reaching with his free hand to take the canvas, but she only shook her head.

"No, it's fine. I need to drop it off at Helen Doyle's house anyway."

"It's a painting from the gallery?"

Brianna nodded. "Yes. She bought it a week ago but wanted it reframed, and it just came in today. I guess she's having the members of the historical preservation society over for tea later this afternoon, so when she heard it was ready, she insisted that I bring it over right away so she could hang it above her fireplace."

Quite a demanding customer. Belshegar

wondered if this Ms. Doyle was also a member of the McAllister clan, or simply a civilian who'd lived here for decades.

Not that he could ask, of course.

"Well, then, I won't keep you," he said, and couldn't help adding, "although I'd be happy to carry the painting the rest of the way."

Even though Brianna had declined his offer of help only a moment earlier, now she looked almost hopeful. "Are you sure?"

"Absolutely," he replied at once. "You can take my sketchbook, if that makes you feel better."

She chuckled. "It's a deal."

He closed the book and handed it over to her, and she gave him the painting. It was quite heavy, and he wondered at Ms. Doyle for demanding that Brianna drop everything to bring it to her home.

For him, of course, the burden was nothing at all, and he followed Bree to a house at the end of the street, definitely the largest on the block. It was also farmhouse in style, but with an extensive wraparound porch and leaded glass windows flanking the sturdy oak front door.

Could it be that Ms. Doyle might be the clan's *prima?*

Brianna knocked, and a moment later, a short, rounded woman with close-cut ginger hair opened the door. Belshegar couldn't sense anything magical about her at all, which told him she was no *prima,* but merely a civilian accustomed to getting her own way.

In fact, not only did she take his presence in stride—perhaps she thought he also worked at the gallery—but she bustled him into the living room, and before he knew exactly what was happening, he had a nail in one hand and a hammer in the other, and was pounding in the nail so the picture could be hung.

He had to admit it was quite an impressive piece, a rendering of a lazy summer river with cottonwoods flanking it on either side and a cloud-dotted sky above. The frame was wide and made of what he thought was oak, the same shade as the mantel that topped the stone fireplace and the furniture that accented the room.

No wonder she'd wanted to have the frame changed out to match her exact specifications.

And although Ms. Doyle thanked them, she also ushered him and Brianna out quickly, saying she needed to get ready for her guests before she closed the front door behind them.

"Thank you," Brianna told Belshegar once they were heading down the rose-bordered path to the street. She looked as if she was about to burst out laughing at any moment, and he supposed he could see why there had been something somewhat amusing about the situation. "I'm sorry you got roped into that."

He wasn't entirely certain as to the meaning of "roped" in that context, but he assumed it had something to do with being coerced. "It's fine," he said. "I'm glad I could help."

"Helen Doyle's kind of a force of nature," Brianna went on as they began to walk down the street toward the main thoroughfare. "I don't think I've ever heard anyone say no to her. I suppose that's why she's so effective as president of the historical preservation society—people fall in line and make the necessary upgrades or repairs rather than get on her bad side."

"She is somewhat terrifying," he agreed, and now Brianna did chuckle. The sound was as musical as her singing voice, and he knew he wanted to hear her laugh as often as he could.

"Well, here's hoping she doesn't plan on buying anything else from the gallery anytime soon," she said. "But she fell in love with that painting of Connor's, and I have to admit it does look really good in her living room."

"'Connor'?" Belshegar repeated. Something seemed significant about the name, although he couldn't say why. "He's the artist?"

Now Brianna's expression looked almost guarded. However, she sounded neutral enough as she said, "Yes. Connor Wilcox. He's kind of famous around here—does lots of *plein air* landscapes of the Verde Valley and Sedona and Flagstaff."

Belshegar wasn't sure what "*plein air*" meant. But at least he knew what a landscape painting was, so he nodded and hoped he looked as if he understood what she was talking about.

Aside from the painting, though, he was beginning to see how truly difficult it was to be in Brianna McAllister's presence and not betray anything of how she affected him. Out here in the sunlight, her hair glinted like pure spun gold, and although the brighter illumination should have revealed any flaws in her complexion or her features, he certainly couldn't find them.

If he were at all intelligent, he would find a way to end their conversation quickly so he could go back to exploring Jerome and doing his best to discover where the *prima's* house was located. However, when he opened his mouth, he found himself saying, "I know we're meeting Saturday to go to the folk festival, but would you be interested in having dinner again tonight?"

Her mouth quirked. Her lips were too perfectly formed to become precisely lopsided, but there was something endearing about her expression for all that.

"I would," she said, her tone serious. "Only I'm buying this time."

"I'm the one who asked—" he began, but she just shook her head.

"You asked first," she told him, that hint of a smile still playing around her mouth. "But the thought had entered my mind, too, so it only seems fair that this one is my treat. How about we meet down at Bocce in Cottonwood?"

He assumed "Bocce" was a restaurant of some sort. That would have been fine, except....

"I don't have a car," he said. "A taxi brought me here."

Which was only the truth. Yes, that taxi had materialized out of nowhere rather than bringing him to Jerome from the airport in Phoenix, but Brianna didn't have to know that.

She didn't seem too put off by his revelation that he didn't have a car of his own at his disposal. "Then I'll pick you up at the hotel. Seven o'clock?"

"That would be fine," he replied.

And would give him the rest of the afternoon to continue with his exploring. At least now Brianna would only think he was out sketching again, rather than doing his best to discover where those magical artifacts had been hidden.

"I need to get back to the gallery," she said. "But I'll see you at seven."

She lifted her hand in a wave and began walking toward Main Street and her place of business. Belshegar stood on the sidewalk and watched her go.

And although he wanted to shake his head at himself, he wouldn't bother wasting energy on such a human gesture when there was no one around to see it. Instead, he shifted his sketchbook to the other hand and turned onto a small cross street they'd passed on their way to Helen Doyle's house.

Perhaps there would be nothing to find here, but he thought he should at least appear as if he was making an effort.

Just in case.

7

Although Bree kept telling herself she had no real reason to be nervous about this second date with Bill Garrett, she still couldn't ignore the flutters in her stomach as she pointed her ancient Chevy Suburban up the hill toward the Grand Hotel. A single date with a person could be discarded easily enough, tossed aside like an old movie ticket or a receipt for groceries that had been consumed weeks ago.

But a second date? In a lot of ways, that was much more fraught. Seeing a person a second time meant there might be a possibility of a future between two people.

Well, technically, this would be the third time she'd seen Bill, thanks to the way they'd bumped into each other down on Rich Street earlier today. At first, she'd been startled, but she'd accepted his explanation about sketching the town's architecture without too many questions. She'd heard her artist cousins say that they felt much more connection to a place or an object when they drew it rather than merely taking a picture with their phones, so she could see why Bill would want to do the same thing.

And he'd been such a sport about helping Helen Doyle, hanging that picture without a single raised eyebrow. Brianna didn't think she knew too many guys who would have been quite so mellow about being roped into providing free labor like that.

Which meant Bill seemed a lot more promising as a romantic partner than anyone else she'd met in a very long time.

Except for the part where he was a civilian… where he wasn't even from Arizona.

She allowed a breath to escape her lips, mostly because she was alone in the car and didn't have to worry about anyone giving her grief for being overly dramatic. Best to get it out of her system now.

Especially with the Grand Hotel coming up on her right. She pulled into the gravel-paved parking lot and was pleased to see Bill waiting at the base of the wide steps that led up to the hotel's entrance. He wore a dark camp shirt and jeans and appeared completely casual, but he still looked like a movie star who was trying to maintain a low profile while out mingling with the common folks.

She brought the Suburban to a stop near the steps, then waited while he came over, opened the passenger-side door, and climbed in. As he fastened his seatbelt, he sent her a glance that could only be classified as amused.

"This is…quite a vehicle."

"It is," she said equably, and began to turn the hulking SUV around—no mean feat in the tight quarters of the Grand Hotel's somewhat skimpy parking lot.

"I haven't seen many gas-powered vehicles around here."

"That's because there aren't very many." They were heading back down the hill now, the Suburban chugging along and playing its usual symphony of grumbles and creaks. Every six months, she had a mechanic in Cottonwood who still had the know-how to service an internal-combustion engine look over Sally—Bree's nickname for the SUV—so she knew the vehicle was running just fine, but she also realized it could sound alarming to people who weren't used to her ride.

Bill shifted in his seat so he could look at her a little more directly. "But you prefer this type of vehicle?"

Bree didn't know if "prefer" was precisely the right word to describe her feelings on the subject. "Not exactly," she replied. "It's not that I have something against electric cars. But none of them seemed to have the space I needed to haul my equipment around, and a cousin of mine was practically giving this one away, so...." She shrugged, even as she guided Sally around the long, banking curve that would send them down to Cottonwood. "Everyone thought I was crazy for taking on an antique like this, but she works."

Even as she spoke, she wondered if she was being a little disingenuous. Sure, Sally could carry pretty much anything Bree could throw at her, but still, there were plenty of modern EVs that had some decent hauling capacity. However, what they couldn't give her was the opportunity to be in the driver's seat at all times, and she liked the feeling of control.

Well, that and the way pretty much everyone who lived in the Verde Valley and wasn't a tourist recognized the vehicle and would wave when she went by. It made her feel…included, she supposed, which was something she appreciated. Obviously, she was a member of the McAllister clan, but her relatives also knew that she and Shane were something just a little bit other, thanks to their father not being from this particular plane of existence.

Shane had never seemed to be bothered by that otherness, though. Bree supposed it could have been because he was so secure in his magic, whereas she....

Your magic is just fine, she told herself. *It's just a little wimpy.*

Okay, a *lot* wimpy, especially when you considered that both her parents were power-houses on that front. And although her mother's gift was enhancing the magical powers of anyone nearby, even that rare and useful talent didn't seem to have any effect on her daughter. No one could say exactly why, although her father had theorized it was most likely because Brianna shared his blood and therefore wasn't an ordinary witch.

Even though she thought she was far less than ordinary when it came to using magic.

Bill appeared to be interested in watching the landscape pass by the Suburban's windows and didn't seem to have too much of a problem with the way they'd both fallen into silence after he'd nodded at her reply. Well, the world outside was all new to him, or at least mostly new; she supposed he'd seen this landscape while the taxi was bringing him to Jerome, but things often looked a little different on the way down than they did on the way up.

For a Thursday night, Cottonwood was busy, and Bocce looked packed. Bree wasn't too worried about that, though, just because the restaurant's current hostess was a McAllister, and she knew that Tally would get them in without it looking too much like they'd been bumped to the head of the line.

And they lucked out on parking, since someone was pulling out of the public lot across the street from the restaurant just as she guided the Suburban in.

Maybe she should take that as a good omen.

"I suppose I should have asked if you like pizza," she said as they waited for a break in traffic so they could cross the street.

Bill only smiled at her. "Is there anyone who doesn't like pizza?"

"People who are lactose-intolerant?" she responded, and his smile broadened.

"Luckily, that isn't something I need to worry about."

Thank goodness. A gap in the passing cars presented itself, and the two of them hurried over to the restaurant, where Bree caught Tally's eye through the window. Her cousin nodded, and that was enough reassurance for her to know that they wouldn't have to worry about waiting very long.

Sure enough, Tally seated two groups ahead of them, but soon afterward, she guided Bree and Bill to a table near the window and handed over a couple of menus. "Your server will be with you shortly," she said, sounding professional enough, but Bree could still see how her cousin's big hazel eyes were dancing.

No doubt the story would be making the rounds that Brianna McAllister had been spotted having dinner at Bocce with a handsome stranger. Or maybe it was already circulating amongst the clan; The Asylum tended to be a place for tourists or those in the family who were celebrating a milestone of some sort, and that was why she hadn't seen anyone she recognized at the restaurant the night before, but that didn't mean someone might not have spied her as she said goodnight to Bill before heading home.

Either way, she knew she wouldn't have been able to keep this secret for very long…if she even needed to.

After all, this wasn't the bad old days. She could date anyone she liked.

Theoretically.

But their waiter wasn't a McAllister, so she relaxed a little as they ordered wine and pizza and one of Bocce's famous wood-fired veggie salads. Once that was taken care of, she asked, "So…did you sketch the rest of the afternoon?"

"I did," Bill replied. "There are a lot of very interesting structures in Jerome. I even saw a building that looked as if it had collapsed and slid down the side of the hill."

"The Cuban Queen," Bree said, naming the former brothel that had once occupied a spot behind Hull Street. Some efforts had been made over the years to try to prevent the whole thing from going south—or east, she supposed, since that was the side of the hill that it now occupied —but the expense had proved to be too much for anyone to want to take on the project. "The hill is unstable in some parts, thanks to all the pit mining they did in Jerome back in the day. There wasn't any way to save it, and after a windstorm knocked it down and its ruins began to slide down the hill, trying to remove them might have created more instability, so the town decided to leave the debris where it was."

Bill shook his head. "This is why Jerome is so fascinating to me. You see things here that you couldn't possibly find anywhere else."

His gaze lingered on her as he spoke, and she could feel her cheeks beginning to heat up.

The waiter came by with their glasses of wine, though, so she was saved from having to make a reply that acknowledged his remark without actually commenting on its content. And once their server was gone, it just seemed easier to clink their glasses together and then have a sip.

"Jerome is kind of a trip," she admitted. Bill's

brows drew together for just a fraction of a second, as if he was trying to puzzle out the meaning of the word when she used it in that context, but then he smiled.

"It's definitely a fascinating place. I hadn't expected it to be quite so haunted."

She tilted her head, amused. After all, Jerome prided itself on its spirit population, so she couldn't be too startled by his comment. "You've seen a ghost?"

"Oh, yes," he replied, then sipped some of his chianti. "And felt them all over the hotel—and in other places around town."

"So…you're psychic?" She didn't feel too strange asking the question, just because she knew for a fact the ghosts were real, even if she hadn't directly communicated with any of them herself. On the other hand, she was a little surprised that Bill would make such an admission when a lot of guys didn't want to venture into such woo-woo territory.

His shoulders lifted. "I wouldn't go so far as to say that. Many people who aren't psychic have had encounters with ghosts. And, for whatever reason, their presence seems to be very strong here in Jerome."

That was true. She still didn't like to take the elevator at the Grand Hotel because it positively gave her the creeps. Angela had said once that it had been used to transport a lot of very ill people from their rooms to the operating center on the lower level, and some of them had died en route, so that was a lot of negative energy concentrated in a very small space.

She supposed that same concept could be applied to the town as a whole. Sure, there had been plenty of law-abiding people in Jerome back then…but there had also been a whole lot who weren't.

"You should be glad you didn't stay at the Connor Hotel," she remarked, and he sent her a questioning look. "The hotel above the Spirit Room," she explained, then went on, "There are lots of stories of people having the covers yanked off their beds, or hearing a baby crying in the hallway when there isn't anyone there. And there's also a ghost kitty that comes and sleeps on your bed, although most people don't have as much problem with that. While there are also plenty of ghosts at the Grand Hotel, they generally aren't quite as in your face."

"Then I suppose I made the right choice," Bill said.

For a moment, his gaze met hers, and once again she got the feeling he wasn't referring to the actual topic of their conversation.

"If you want to get some actual sleep, yes," she responded, taking care to keep her tone light. "If you're trying to do some ghost hunting, then I suppose it might be a toss-up."

"Ghosts weren't the main reason I came to Jerome," he said. "Maybe they're the cherry on top?"

She couldn't help smiling at that comment, and then the waiter came by with their appetizer, effectively ending their discussion of that particular topic. They dished some portions onto the small plates their waiter had also brought along, and when the conversation resumed, Bill had apparently decided to move on to something a little less supernatural.

"How many people will be performing at the folk festival?" he asked.

That question was easy enough to answer. "Twenty," she replied. "There'll be eleven of us on Saturday and nine on Sunday, since the festival ends earlier that day. We each get a half-hour set."

Which, under normal circumstances, wouldn't make her bat an eye, since she routinely played forty-minute sets or even longer when she was working the tasting rooms. During those sorts of performances, though, she was only providing background music. She wasn't there to be the center of attention.

Whereas on Saturday, all eyes would be on her.

Deep down, she knew that wasn't precisely

true. People would still be wandering up and down Main Street and visiting the shops and not paying any particular attention to what was happening on the main stage of the festival.

But there would still be plenty who'd come there to listen and nothing more.

She wouldn't speak about those insecurities to Bill, though, not when she had a hard time admitting them to herself.

"It sounds like quite an honor," he said, and she shrugged, then realized it probably had looked a little rude to be so dismissive of his comment.

"I suppose so," she replied. "We do all have to be invited—it's not the sort of thing you can just audition for. And there are some very good musicians here in the Verde Valley…and Flagstaff and Prescott and Payson. People come from all over."

"But not Phoenix?" Bill asked, and she couldn't help smiling.

"We figure Phoenix is big enough that it can take care of itself."

His mouth quirked in response. "I suppose I can see that."

They settled down to eat their vegetables—which had been roasted with balsamic vinegar and were positively divine—and soon enough afterward, the waiter came by with their pizza, which was pesto and chicken and was also heavenly.

Bill took a bite before giving an appreciative nod. "I can see why you would want to eat here."

"I've never had a bad meal at Bocce," Bree replied, which was only the truth. Also, while the food and the setting at The Asylum had been wonderful, it was a lot more relaxed here, and much more her style.

His lips twitched. "Neither have I."

She shook her head at his joke but couldn't help smiling a little in response. Yes, they both seemed more at ease today, although she couldn't be sure whether that was due to their surroundings or the simple fact that this was their second date, and therefore they'd had a chance already to get a little acquainted with one another.

"I'm sure you must have had lots of good pizza in L.A., though," she said. "It's a foodie kind of place, isn't it?"

For just a second, Bill looked almost panicked. But then he reached for his glass of wine and said in too-casual tones, "There's lots of great food in Los Angeles. I think this pizza is on par, though."

A normal enough response. And yet there had been that flash of fear in his deep green eyes, as if she'd asked him a question he wasn't sure how to answer.

Could it be that he wasn't from Los Angeles after all?

But why would he lie about such a thing?

Bree had no idea. Okay, if he was from some hillbilly place in the Deep South or something, then maybe he wouldn't want to talk about it, and yet she didn't think that was what was going on here. For one thing, Jerome wasn't a place with a lot of pretense. It wasn't as if Bill was trying to impress someone from Beverly Hills or Palm Beach or whatever.

If he was even trying to impress her at all. She still wasn't entirely sure about that.

Better to let it go. She supposed she could have completely misinterpreted his expression. It wasn't as though they'd known each other long enough for her to be confident in reading his moods.

She'd kind of like to be, though.

"I'm sure the chef would be glad to hear that," she said, and now there was no mistaking the relief that passed over his handsome features.

"Another brother?" he asked, almost teasing, and she just had to smile.

"No," she replied. "The chef here at Bocce is a woman. She's been here forever."

"Which would explain why the food is so excellent."

After that, they went on to talk about some of the other restaurants in Cottonwood—not, Bree, thought, because she was angling for another date, but just because she thought it seemed like a neutral enough topic. Bill seemed interested in absorbing as much local area knowledge as possible, so the rest of their meal passed comfortably enough, with neither of them touching on any subjects that were even remotely problematic.

Once they were done with their meal, he suggested that they walk up and down Main Street so he could get a better look at Cottonwood's historic downtown.

"There's not a lot open right now," she warned him.

Well, except the Copper Jackalope, a bar located right next to Bocce, or Kaktus Kate's, another bar farther down the street.

Not that Bree could really imagine Bill at Kate's. That was where the bikers tended to hang out, and although she'd gone slumming there with friends a few times and could attest that they made a mean Long Island iced tea, it didn't seem like his kind of place.

"It's fine if we can't go into any of the shops," he said. "I drove through here on the way up to Jerome, but I wasn't able to get a good look at anything, so it would be nice to see the stores up close at least."

"Then we'll wander," she replied. "And maybe you can get another taxi to bring you down here tomorrow so you can really explore."

She supposed she could have offered to be his

chauffeur since she didn't have much going on tomorrow except a voice lesson at three-thirty, but something made her hold back. Why, she wasn't sure, except they'd gone out two nights in a row and would be seeing each other pretty much all day on Saturday until she had to go on stage, and that seemed like an awful lot of togetherness with a guy she hadn't even known two days ago.

Even though some part of her wanted to spend every single minute with him that she could…right up until the time the taxi arrived to take him back to the airport.

Whenever that would be. He'd made it sound as if he planned to stay through at least the weekend, but what would happen after that?

You'll find out when it happens, she told herself. *In the meantime, stop being such a worrywart.*

Easier said than done. Maybe they hadn't discussed anything earth-shattering over dinner, and yet she thought the most significant thing about their meal was how easy it had been, how the conversation had mostly flowed from one topic to another without much awkwardness.

Except when she'd asked him about the food in L.A. No matter how you looked at it, that flash of fear in his expression had been downright mystifying.

Then again, maybe he didn't go out much but

didn't want to confess that fact to her and sound like a stick-in-the-mud.

There was so much about him she didn't know…and she had no idea whether she'd learn any of it before it was time for him to leave.

They were about halfway down the block before he said, "Do you play at all these wine-tasting rooms?"

"I do," she replied, glad of the question, since it was one she could answer honestly. "Not every week, obviously, but I manage to cover all of them within the space of a month, give or take."

"And in Sedona, and other places around here," he said, clearly remembering her off-hand comment about that when they'd had dinner at The Asylum the other night.

"All over the Verde Valley." A thought struck her, and she wondered if it would be too awful if she made the invitation, especially since they'd be spending all day at the folk festival together.

Well, if he didn't want to go or had other plans, he could just tell her. They might not have known each other very well, but they were still both adults and could act like reasonable people.

"In fact," she went on, "I'm playing at Alcantara on Sunday afternoon. It's a gorgeous winery a little south and east of Cottonwood, right on the Verde River. You'll feel like you're in Tuscany or something."

For a second or two, he didn't reply, and she wondered if she really had put her foot right in it.

But then he smiled and said, "That sounds like fun. It seems as if there are always new and interesting places to explore around here."

She thought so. Maybe once upon a time, the Verde Valley didn't have much going on, but there was plenty to see and do now.

Well, as long as you were into wine.

"Great," she replied, hoping her relief hadn't seeped into her voice too much. "How about I pick you up around two? I need to get there a little early to set up."

"That sounds good." He paused there before saying, his tone almost diffident, "I can help you with your equipment, if you'd like me to."

Oh, she'd definitely like it. Not just because he'd make the world's best-looking roadie, but also because hauling her guitars and her amp and her mic and all the assorted other paraphernalia required for her performances could be a little exhausting. Having someone to lend a hand would make the gig a lot more fun.

"Then it's a date."

He was silent for a moment. But then his eyes met hers, and she found her mouth going a little dry at the need she saw in his gaze.

"Yes," he said softly. "It definitely is."

8

THERE HAD BEEN A MOMENT RIGHT AFTER Brianna asked him to come to her performance on Sunday when he'd looked into her eyes and understood that if he'd bent down and pressed his lips to hers, she wouldn't have stopped him. He'd seen the need in her gaze and felt the thrum of attraction between them, so different from the low-level hum of the hidden artifacts he'd sensed while exploring Jerome.

The moment had passed, though, as Belshegar had known it must. Whatever his heart and his body were telling him, he knew he couldn't act on that impulse.

He looked human to her, but he wasn't.

And he had no doubt she would recoil in horror if she were ever to see his true form.

Then again....

Perhaps he was underestimating Brianna's strength. He had to admit to himself that she did not seem like the sort of person to be afraid of something just because it was alien to her.

However, he also knew they were of two different species, utterly unlike one another, and therefore he could not allow himself to indulge these new and strange feelings…even if he very much wanted to.

So he had turned away, pretending to be interested in an unusual mineral specimen displayed in the shop window behind them.

But he hadn't turned quickly enough to miss the confusion and disappointment in her eyes.

Brianna hadn't said anything, of course. No, she'd only told him about the store and its collection of rocks and minerals, and how he should take a look when he came back tomorrow after it was open.

He was good at guarding his emotions—he had to be, considering his reasons for being here in this world—but he thought she might be even more skilled than he.

Afterward, they'd walked back to the parking lot where she'd left her oversized vehicle, and then she'd driven him back to the Grand Hotel. They'd promised to meet a little before noon so they could get lunch from one of the food trucks that would be servicing the festival, and that appeared to be that.

Was there something else he could have said or done?

Probably not...unless he wanted to lead both of them down a path he knew they should never travel.

Now he sat in his hotel room and stared at the picture of Sedona's red rocks that hung on the wall opposite the bed. It was a painting, not a photograph, and Belshegar could only think that the artist Connor Wilcox, who'd painted the landscape they'd hung over Helen Doyle's fireplace, would have done a much better job.

What was it about Connor Wilcox? That name still seemed to hold some deeper significance than merely belonging to an artist who specialized in northern Arizona landscapes, even if Belshegar didn't know what it might be.

Well, the voice had supplied him with a phone, since it was unheard-of that any citizen of the world in the twenty-first century would try to exist without one.

And Elena had shown him how to search the internet to discover those pieces of information that one wasn't able to unearth on one's own.

Unfortunately, an internet search didn't reveal anything of much use. Connor Wilcox appeared to be an ordinary man in his fifties, someone who was inspired by the natural beauties of northern Arizona to create some truly outstanding landscapes. There was absolutely nothing in his online biography to show he was anyone except who he seemed to be.

Clearly, intuition didn't seem to be of much use at the moment.

Annoyed, Belshegar set his borrowed phone down on the bedside table and leaned against the pile of pillows on the oversized bed. It seemed that so far, he had very little to show for his efforts.

Except for several enjoyable evenings in Brianna's company, with the promise of more to come. They hadn't made any plans for Friday night, and he guessed that was probably because she had to perform at some tasting room or another, perhaps one as far away as Sedona. This begged the question as to why she hadn't invited him to that performance, just as she'd asked him to come see her play at the winery called Alcantara, but perhaps that was because her Friday night venue wasn't nearly as picturesque.

Or perhaps she'd decided that being with him every single night was a bit too much, even leaving aside the very real attraction that had begun to grow between them.

Difficult to say since, despite the time they'd spent together, he still knew very little about her thought processes, or why she would proceed one way in a certain matter and an entirely different direction when it came to the next one.

What he did know was that he was spending entirely too much time thinking about her and not nearly enough pondering how to track down the artifacts he was supposed to find.

He picked up the phone again, this time to study the online map of Jerome and do his best to determine where the *prima's* house might be located. It certainly wasn't in the neighborhood he'd explored earlier today, so he focused his efforts on other areas that seemed promising.

The problem was, even though this "Google Maps" promised street-view images of any given area, there seemed to be some streets in Jerome that hadn't been mapped in such a way. Was that because the residents had made sure none of those cameras would infiltrate their quiet neighborhoods, or was it simply that those included other areas where structures had slid down the hill like the Cuban Queen and were now off-limits to street traffic?

Weighing all the facts he had in hand, he thought either scenario was equally plausible.

But just because Google hadn't provided the information he wanted, that didn't mean Belshegar couldn't set out on foot to see what he could find.

Now that he'd analyzed the map of Jerome, he

had the town's layout firmly fixed in his mind and could access it any time he liked. And, even though he had no concrete evidence that the voice or those who might work for it were watching what he did, he still thought it best to make it seem as if he was doing whatever he could to locate the artifacts rather than spending far too much time wining and dining Brianna McAllister.

Deep down, he didn't believe he could ever spend too much time following those pursuits, but he doubted the voice would have the same opinion of the situation.

It was too late to set out to investigate those other sections of Jerome—not because he couldn't see what he was doing just as easily at night as he did during the daytime, but because he guessed that the people who lived in those neighborhoods wouldn't be too pleased to see a strange man wandering around and sketching their homes after the sun had gone down.

And although he could make himself invisible and undetectable if he put away this borrowed human appearance, he didn't know for sure whether he would be able to assume it again without the voice's help.

Better not to risk it.

He'd wait until morning…and then he would see what he could find.

The homes in this part of town were much grander, that was for certain. High above the busy tourist traffic on Jerome's main street was a quiet little eddy of a road called Paradise Lane. All the houses were carefully restored and built in the style he knew was Victorian, since the home in Santa Fe that Elena shared with her husband Alessandro possessed similar architecture. Some of them had more scrollwork and stained glass than others, but they'd all been built with large front porches and multiple stories, as well as paint schemes that included sometimes as many as five different complementary hues.

He'd walked here from the Grand Hotel, where he'd had green tea and toast and fruit for breakfast. Quite possibly, he didn't need to eat at all, but he'd found himself feeling better after the light repast and wondered if somehow this human form he currently wore was affecting him on a level he didn't quite understand.

On this Friday morning, Paradise Lane was very quiet. He'd waited until the people who lived there most likely would have already departed for their various schools or places of work, although if the street was inhabited mainly by McAllister witches and warlocks, he supposed some of them might still have lingered there. Based on what he'd seen of the Castillo clan, it seemed that many members of the magical community either worked from home or had their own businesses, so their schedules were somewhat different from those of most of the mortal population.

But no one seemed to be out and about today, except a woman at the far end of the street—a cul-de-sac, really, since the narrow road terminated in a steep hillside partially obscured by a small grove of tall trees, oak and sycamore and a few graceful willows—who appeared to be intent on tending the luxuriant rose bushes that grew in a bed in front of her home's front porch. Even at this distance, Belshegar could tell she wasn't a witch, and although she looked up and sent him what he thought was a curious look, she didn't seem so discommoded by his presence that she felt it necessary to ask what he was doing there.

Well, the neighborhood offered many splendid examples of late Victorian architecture, so he assumed he wasn't the only traveler who'd wandered up here to take a look at the houses and their colorful paint, their stained glass windows and fanciful turrets and weathervanes and gingerbread trim. He had his sketchbook tucked under his arm, and he pulled it out and began drawing the house closest to him, one that was painted pale blue with white and darker blue and deep red as its accent colors.

Was it the *prima's* house?

He didn't think so, just because there were several on the street that were a good bit larger. Once he was done with his sketch, he began moving toward one of the bigger homes, this one pale yellow with trim in various shades of sage-hued green. When he got closer, though, he stopped, small shockwaves going through him as he sensed the energy that seemed to flow out from the place in all directions.

This was Brianna's house.

But…that couldn't be right, could it? She'd already told him that she lived in an apartment above the gallery where she sometimes worked.

And yet, the yellow house practically shimmered with echoes of her presence.

Her childhood home, he guessed. She might not live here any longer, but the place where she'd grown to adulthood was still full of her essence, her energy.

He tilted his head to gaze up at the second story, wondering which of those windows was the one that opened into her former bedroom. Had she looked out onto the street, or was her room one of the chambers that gave a view of the backyard?

Impossible to know for sure, of course, although he thought most likely she and her brother had occupied the rooms at the rear of the house, where their sleep wouldn't be disturbed by any traffic on the street.

Of course, considering how quiet Paradise Lane appeared to be, he didn't think the rooms that overlooked the street would have been very noisy, either.

As he stood there on the sidewalk, trying to decide whether he should attempt to sketch the house or move a little farther down, perhaps to the big white house with the green shutters that seemed to be the largest on the block, the front door to Brianna's house opened and a tall man emerged. His hair was even lighter than hers, with what looked like glints of silver at the temples, and he appeared to be in his middle or late fifties as humans reckoned time.

That wasn't what took Belshegar aback, however. No, it was the subtle aura of power which surrounded the man, one that was very strong and at the same time alien. It didn't feel like the magic he'd sensed around regular witches and warlocks, not at all.

In fact, what it reminded him of most was the power he'd sensed shimmering around Loc, the demon lord who'd married a Castillo witch and who'd given Belshegar a human appearance so he might attend Elena's wedding.

Was this man also a demon lord?

An impulse to flee came over him, even

though Belshegar knew running away was probably the worst thing he could do. No, he had to pretend he hadn't sensed anything out of the ordinary about the man and that he was nothing more than the tourist he was pretending to be.

The stranger's eyes met his, clear blue.

Nearly the same shade as Brianna's, although hers weren't nearly so piercing.

Was this being her father?

Before Belshegar could attempt to analyze the implications of such a possibility, the man spoke.

"Good morning," he said. If he'd detected anything out of the ordinary about the stranger who stood on the sidewalk outside his house, sketchbook tucked under one arm, he didn't give any sign of it. "Are you looking for someone?"

"No—no," Belshegar replied quickly, and then pulled out the sketchbook, brandishing it like a shield.

In a way, he supposed it was, since it provided him with an excuse to move around Jerome without anyone questioning his motives too closely.

And he also had to hope that the same enchantment which had given him a mortal face and form and also masked his inhuman nature would be enough to hide his true identity from the man—well, more than a man—who faced him now.

"I'm interested in architecture," he explained. "This is a wonderful collection of Victorian homes."

The man nodded. "That it is. And you're certainly welcome to draw whatever you like, although I'll have to ask you to leave off any street names or house numbers from your sketches, just to protect the privacy of the people who live here."

"Oh, of course," Belshegar said immediately. As far as he could tell, he wasn't able to detect any suspicion in the other man's face and expression, although he wouldn't allow himself to relax. "These sketches are just for me," he added, hoping that extra bit of information would help to reassure Brianna's father…if that was even who the man was. "I certainly have no plans to share them with anyone else."

The stranger lifted an eyebrow and then directed his attention toward the sketchbook. "May I?"

When presented with such a direct question, Belshegar knew there was no way to demur without possibly raising some questions. Irrationally, his heartbeat sped up a little as he handed over the notepad. Foolish, he knew, but he couldn't always control this human form's physical reactions.

"Of course."

The man took the book and flipped through

it. There weren't so many sketches, maybe ten in all, but Belshegar hoped he could explain that away by saying he'd only begun working on them after he arrived in Jerome.

A nod, and then the stranger handed the sketchbook back to him.

"They're really quite good," he said. "You might want to reconsider not sharing those with anyone else."

"Thank you," Belshegar replied, since there didn't seem to be any other way to respond. He couldn't explain that he didn't have any real talent, that he was only mimicking what he'd seen Elena do as she learned more about her art and had gotten more sure of her talent. Her prodigious gifts hadn't truly begun to blossom until she'd escaped from the house that had been her prison for so many years and she'd had the freedom to work in the oils that were her true medium, but her pencil sketches had been lovely as well, somehow strong and delicate at the same time.

"Enjoy yourself," the man said, and headed back into the yellow house.

Belshegar wouldn't allow himself to sag with relief—not when he couldn't be sure if someone else might be in the house watching him through a window—but he drew in a breath anyway, thanking the universe in general for the spells that were doing such an excellent job of hiding the truth of his nature from everyone around him.

But because he couldn't be sure he wasn't being observed, he knew what he needed to do. He shifted his position on the sidewalk to allow himself a better perspective of the big yellow house.

And then he flipped to a new page in his sketchbook and began to draw.

9

HER FRIDAY NIGHT GIG AT 1912 WINERY HAD helped to distract Brianna from her upcoming performance at the folk festival and her day date with Bill Garrett, but now that the morning had come and she was pushing her way through the clothes in her closet, trying to decide which outfit would be best for both activities, she couldn't ignore the nervous ache in the pit of her stomach.

Just breathe, she told herself, deciding one top would be too warm and another too casual.

Maybe a dress?

She released a huff of annoyance and went back into the dining room, where her half-drunk cup of coffee sat waiting for her on the table. A few sips didn't seem to help very much, but she swallowed some more anyway.

Green tea might have made her less jangly, but there wasn't much she could do about that now.

All right, maybe she should double-check the weather reports.

A glance at her phone told her it was going to be eighty-five degrees and sunny today. Certainly warm enough for a tank top and sandals and one of the pretty sequined peasant skirts she'd bought at a boutique in Sedona when they were having an end-of-summer sale last year.

But would the sequins catch the sunlight too much and possibly annoy some of the members of her audience with their dancing reflections?

Okay, now you're really overthinking things, she scolded herself. *Stop screwing around.*

Bellamy had said once that Bree tended to go back and forth whenever making a decision because she was a Libra, someone who needed to weigh all the possible angles when faced with a choice. While Brianna still wasn't sure how much stock she should place in astrology, she'd been forced to admit that her friend had a point there.

One last swallow of coffee, and then she marched back into the bedroom, resolutely pulled out the skirt she'd been thinking of, one that swirled with tie dye in shades of turquoise and soft green and deeper blue, along with a green tank top she'd bought a while back because it was the perfect pale mint color to go with the skirt. Some silvery flip-flops and turquoise jewelry, and she figured she had herself a pretty decent performance outfit.

And date ensemble. She honestly had no idea how the day was even going to go—would she and Bill realize they were good together in small doses, but an entire afternoon was a bridge too far?—and yet she also realized it was way too late to do anything except proceed as planned. It wasn't as if she could pull out of the folk festival at this late date, and it also wasn't as if she could cancel things with Bill, either.

Okay, she probably could do that if she really wanted to, although any excuse she tried to manufacture sounded impossibly weak in her mind.

Also, she really did want to see him. She'd thought that maybe a day away from him would have given her some perspective, would have allowed her to concede that, sure, he was a nice guy, but nothing terribly special.

Except that assessment would have been dead wrong. The more she was out and around other people, the more she realized how truly unique he was. A man who looked like a male model but didn't seem to notice how handsome he was? A guy who would drop everything to help her install a painting at a total stranger's house?

Men like that didn't come along very often.

Actually, they hadn't come along at all…well,

not until Bill Garrett arrived in Jerome. Even if they didn't have any kind of a future together, Brianna knew she'd be stupid not to spend every moment with him that she possibly could until it was time for him to go back to L.A.

Now that she'd firmed up that particular reality in her mind, she felt better about getting in the shower and performing the rest of her preparations that morning. Most of the time, she didn't wear a lot of makeup, just some mascara and a bit of lip stain or gloss, but because she would be performing, she knew she needed to put in more effort than that. Foundation with sunscreen, since she'd be outside most of the day, and blush and eyeshadow and a hint of liner to go with her usual mascara. Lip stain rather than gloss, though, because whatever she put on needed to last as long as possible.

At least she'd finally found her way through the bridge of the song that had been giving her so much trouble. She could have replaced the piece with something else, she supposed, but she'd wanted to perform it today, and an hour of practicing and polishing after she'd gotten home from her gig the night before had told her the song was as ready as it would ever be.

Well, she hoped it was, anyway.

Eleven o'clock. Her hair was still a little damp —she tended to let it air-dry when the weather was warm enough and allow its natural wave to take hold—but that was all right. It would be completely dry by the time she met Bill.

The folk festival was being held at the lower park, located down on Hull Street. If they wanted to, musicians could check in early and leave their instruments and other equipment to be looked after by some of the festival's volunteers, and that was exactly what Bree planned to do. That way, she'd have minimal setup when it finally came time for her to perform at four o'clock.

Although the park was only a block away from her apartment, she still loaded everything in Sally and drove it over, since trying to lug two guitars, her mic and mic stand, and an amp over there all by herself would have been a little too difficult. When she got to the park, she saw that Angela and Connor were helping with the check-in. From what Brianna had heard, a lot of *primas* and their consorts weren't nearly so hands-on, but the couple had always let their instincts guide them rather than be ruled by so-called expectations for clan heads.

"Hey," Connor said as she approached, a guitar slung over each shoulder. "What else do you need help with?"

"My amp and my mic equipment," Bree replied, not surprised that she hadn't even needed to ask for assistance but that Connor had immediately volunteered. It was just the way both of them were.

"On it," he said cheerfully.

Angela had been standing at a table, checking in one of the musicians, but it seemed she must have been almost finished because she stepped away almost immediately. "Hi, Bree," she said, also sounding utterly upbeat.

Well, why shouldn't she? Maybe she'd been through some pretty rough stuff in the past, but it had been smooth sailing for her and Connor for the past twenty-five years.

The two of them weren't dissimilar in coloring, both with dark hair and green-hued eyes, although Angela's were a brilliant emerald that looked almost like contact lenses, while Connor's were a lot darker, more like nephrite jade. They both also seemed much younger than the fifty-plus they actually were, but Bree guessed that decades of happiness could do that for a person.

Even though she knew she shouldn't have allowed the thought to enter her mind, it crept in there anyway.

What would it be like to share that many years with Bill Garrett?

She shooed the notion away as best she could. Even if everything else about him had been perfect—namely, that he'd turned out to be a warlock from Arizona rather than a civilian whose home base was in L.A.—she knew it was way too early to be thinking about him like that.

Except that witches and warlocks sometimes did know this early in a relationship when someone was the exact right fit in every possible way.

"Do you want me to take those?" Angela continued, tilting her head toward the guitars Bree had slung over each shoulder.

"Oh, right," she replied. Hopefully, the *prima* hadn't noticed the way she'd been lost in the clouds.

Probably she had, though. Angela might act casual and laid-back, but she didn't miss a trick.

Since Brianna knew that trying to comment on her absentmindedness would only make things worse, she slipped off first her six-string and then the steel twelve-string and handed them over. The *prima* picked up a couple of tags that had been sitting on the table behind her, then tied one on each guitar so it would be obvious which ones were hers.

Connor came over right then with the mic and the amp—the festival was supplying the mic stands—and Angela also tied tags on those.

"How many people are you expecting to attend?" Bree asked, figuring she should try to make some conversation. Besides, she hadn't gotten a final tally from the festival organizers, a couple of civilians who ran the Main Stage club down in Cottonwood, and it would be nice to know what kind of crowd was going to show up.

"The latest number we got was around two hundred," Angela said. "But there are always people who show up at the last minute and want to buy tickets at the gate, so we'll probably get about fifty more."

"And then we'll be at capacity," Connor chimed in. "The park won't hold any more than that."

No, it definitely wouldn't. Lower Park—maybe it had had a real name once upon a time, but Bree had never heard it referred to as anything except that—ran alongside Hull Avenue for fifty yards or so and was often used for art shows and other musical events, but there was a limit to how many people could gather there.

Then again, Jerome was so small that you'd probably be able to hear the music no matter where you were. She wasn't sure how she felt about that; true, she was no stranger to performing, but having maybe twenty or thirty people listening to you at a wine tasting room was a far cry from having the entire population of Jerome become your audience.

Well, the time to worry about that was long past. Right now, she just needed to focus on giving the best performance possible.

"That's great," she said brightly. "I'm glad the event is doing so well."

"Yes, it's grown a little each year," Angela replied. "We can't get any bigger than this, though."

No, they couldn't. There were bigger venues down in Cottonwood—or even in tiny Clarkdale, which at least had a nice big park near downtown, a park with its own gazebo, but that would sort of defeat the point of having a Jerome folk festival.

She thanked Angela and Connor, and reassured them she'd be back at three forty-five to await her turn on stage, then headed over to the spot where she'd parked Sally so she could drive back to the gallery. It was a good thing the apartment came with a designated parking spot, because Jerome was going to be packed this afternoon. The parking spaces nearest the festival were going to be taken over by the food trucks, so a lot of people were probably going to have to leave their cars in the satellite lot out by the old Gold King mine and then either hike down to the park or take the shuttle the town offered during the weekend.

Those logistics weren't her problem, though. Now that she'd dropped off her equipment, she could get around on foot just fine.

No, the biggest problem would be trying to

navigate her time with Bill…and not give away how much she knew she already cared for him.

He definitely looked cheerful when they met up by the food trucks a little before noon. Unlike a lot of the crowds who'd already gathered to listen to the music—the first act started right at twelve—he wore another of his short-sleeved camp shirts rather than a T-shirt, this one in deep burgundy that looked great with his lightly tanned skin and dark hair.

And possibly she'd been imagining it, but she thought she saw his hazel eyes light up in admiration when he caught sight of her walking through the crowds, her sequined skirt sending off little happy sparkles as she moved.

"This is much more than I imagined," he said after they'd exchanged greetings.

Yes, she had to admit that a couple of hundred people gathered in a not-very-big space felt like quite the crowd. Also, the food trucks were accessible to everyone, not only those who'd bought tickets to the festival, so the lines there were also pretty impressive.

"I think we'd better queue up now," she replied. "Otherwise, we're going to be waiting forever to get our food."

"A good idea," he agreed as he surveyed the crowd. "Which one looks best to you?"

"Anything," she said simply. "You can pick."

He studied the various food trucks—there was one from the Mustang Grille in Cottonwood, and one offering Mexican food, and two more beyond that, a truck that specialized in good old American food like hamburgers and hot dogs and one that had Mediterranean fare like shish kebab and falafel and shawarma.

"Let's try the barbecue one," he said. "It sounds interesting."

Bree would probably rather have had the Mediterranean food, since the Verde Valley was pretty short on restaurants like that. But maybe because Bill liked to travel so much, he had a habit of sampling the barbecue wherever he was. She'd heard it could vary regionally quite a bit, although she'd never been able to venture out of Arizona to find out for herself.

They got in line. The queue wasn't quite as long as some of the others, and she guessed that was because anyone attending the festival who lived in the Verde Valley knew all about the Mustang Grille, since they had restaurants in Cottonwood and Sedona and Prescott.

Thanks to that, they were able to get their food fairly quickly, and managed to snag a spot at one of the picnic tables just as several of the early birds were getting up to leave.

Bree could only hope that kind of luck would continue to follow her for the rest of the afternoon.

"Did you get over to Sedona yesterday?" she asked, thinking that was a neutral enough question.

Bill hadn't started eating yet, so it wasn't as though she'd interrupted him. Still, she noticed how he paused before saying, "Oh, I decided to stay here in Jerome and explore a bit more. Also, I knew today would be busy, so I thought it might be better not to go running all over the place."

She wasn't sure whether taking a trip of less than a half hour to see Sedona's red rocks could exactly be classified as "running all over the place," but she decided not to comment on that. If he'd wanted to stay put and do more sketching or whatever, that was his prerogative.

"I hope you found some interesting stuff," she replied before taking a bite of her pulled pork sandwich.

He nodded. "Paradise Lane. There are some beautiful Victorian houses up there."

Bree wasn't sure why such an admission startled her. Maybe it was because not many tourists made it to the street where she'd grown up, thanks to the way it was so cut off from the normal flow of traffic through Jerome—by design, she was sure. Several civilians lived there, too, but the majority of the residents on Paradise Lane were also McAllisters.

And since he'd already been there, she didn't see the point in trying to hide that it was her former home base.

"I grew up there," she said, reaching for a French fry.

Now it seemed to be his turn to be surprised. "You did? Which house?"

"The yellow one with the green trim," she replied. "My parents still live there. My brother lives on Paradise Lane, too. He bought a house near the end of the cul-de-sac—the pink one. He hates the color, but it was such a steal that he snapped it up anyway. I think he'll repaint it in the next year or two, though."

As she said all this, she couldn't help wondering if Bill would look at her as kind of a loser for living over a gallery when her brother had just bought his first house. All right, Shane was a couple of years older and farther along in his career, but….

"What's wrong with pink?" Bill asked, sounding genuinely curious.

"I guess he thinks it's too girly or something." She couldn't help smiling a little as she made that remark, mostly because it probably was a bit foolish to say one color was more feminine than another.

Expression considering, Bill scooped up a forkful of brisket. "I think pink is a nice color."

"So do I," she said, then added, "but I'm not sure I'd want a pink house, either."

He nodded and ate the brisket, washing it down with a swallow of iced tea. "What's your favorite color?"

Maybe that was the sort of thing you asked on a first date, but Bree was just glad he'd posed such a simple question to her. "Blue," she said, "but more like a teal or turquoise kind of blue. What's yours?"

"I suppose I hadn't thought about it," he responded, and she found herself lifting an eyebrow.

Were there really people in the world who didn't have a color preference?

"Oh, come on," she urged him. "There must be something you gravitate toward more than others."

His expression turned thoughtful. "Then green, I suppose. There isn't much of it where I—"

The words broke off then, as if he'd been about to say something he hadn't intended. Once again, Bree allowed herself an inner frown.

Had he been about to say there wasn't a lot of green where he came from?

Considering his home base was Los Angeles, she didn't find that too strange. Lots of people had lawns there, and she had a vague impression that there were golf courses everywhere, too, but the native landscape was almost as dry as it was here in Arizona.

Probably better not to press him on the subject.

"Well, I like green a lot, too," she said cheerfully. "It's my second favorite color."

They were sitting across from one another, so there was no mistaking the way his eyes—also green, although not the bright green of fresh grass but the dark, smoky color of a pine forest, with flecks of amber and gold—held hers for a moment.

"I'm glad we have that in common."

Color touched her cheeks, but she told herself it wasn't a big deal, not when it would probably be hidden by the blush she'd applied earlier, or maybe just the regular flush she got from sitting out in the sun for any length of time.

However, she tried not to let awkwardness overwhelm her. After all, this was the reason why you went out with a person multiple times—to get to know one another, to find out if you really were compatible.

"Since we're on the subject of favorites," she

said, and hoped it didn't sound as if she was forcing the issue, "what about music?"

Bill set down his fork and reached for his cup of iced tea again. "I like what you play."

Well, that was nice of him, but that wasn't what she'd asked. "Before you heard me play."

Now he smiled, as if he'd guessed that his first answer hadn't been the right one. "Guitar," he said. "Solo classical guitar, I suppose. It's…soothing. But I very much like what I've heard from you as well."

Once again, their eyes met. She wasn't sure what she'd been expecting to see—maybe another flash of the amusement she'd spied just a few seconds earlier—but this was nothing like that.

No, it was naked need.

Warm blood rushed through her, but then he blinked and the moment was gone.

And they were sitting here in public, surrounded by couples and families enjoying their food truck lunches, and she knew there was no way in the world she could possibly ask him what he'd been thinking.

If she hadn't just imagined what she saw, of course.

Then she heard the voice of Brad Otis, one of the organizers of the festival, coming through the speakers, and she realized with infinite relief that the music was about to start.

She wouldn't have to say anything at all, could pretend as if that moment had never happened.

"Welcome, everyone, to the tenth annual Jerome folk festival!"

Everyone applauded, and Brianna set down her sandwich so she could join in. Bill clapped as well, although she noticed he did so only after everyone else had started to put their hands together, almost as if he wasn't sure what he was supposed to do until he'd seen other people doing it.

"We're kicking off five hours of music today, and four hours tomorrow," Todd Otis continued. "Our first performers are Skinny Lizard, down here today from Payson. Let's give them a warm welcome!"

Everyone started clapping again, and Todd stepped away from the microphone so the band could come on stage. Although Bree didn't know them well, she'd heard Skinny Lizard before and knew they tended to be a little more bluegrass than most of the other acts that would be performing today.

That was fine, though. A little variety never hurt anyone.

Hearing the banjo player start picking away only made her realize, though, that she'd be going onstage in four short hours. All these people who were tapping their feet along to the music or nodding their heads would be listening to her.

The food she'd just eaten seemed to congeal into a ball in her stomach. Looking back at Bill, she saw he now gazed at her with concern.

"Everything all right?" he asked softly.

The music was loud enough that she was a little surprised she'd been able to hear him clearly.

Or maybe she'd just read his lips…those strong, kissable lips.

"I'm fine," she managed. "Just a little attack of stage fright, I suppose."

He reached across the table to touch her hand. It was their first real physical contact, and she couldn't ignore the warmth that flowed through her at even that small pressure of his fingers on hers.

"You'll be wonderful," he said. "I've heard you play and sing. You have nothing to worry about."

Easy for you to say, she thought.

He was only trying to help, though. And his words did encourage her, if only a little. She wasn't an amateur, after all. No, she'd been performing locally for years now, ever since she'd gotten paid to sing at the Arizona Stronghold tasting room when she was only eighteen, years before she could even drink their wine.

This was going to be fine.

Wasn't it?

10

Belshegar could tell Brianna was suffering something of an attack of the nerves, so after lunch—which had been excellent, very different from the other red meat he'd eaten and something he thought his system could manage a bit better—he thought perhaps it would be a good idea to walk around Jerome and have the music as a backdrop to their afternoon, rather than standing right at the stage to listen. If they'd done that, he guessed she might have started imagining herself on that stage and begun to worry again that her performance wouldn't measure up.

No chance of that happening, of course. He'd been taken aback when she asked him what kind of music he liked, but then he'd remembered how Elena had often played classical guitar in the background when she painted or drew. Although he knew very little about it, he also realized how soothing that sort of music could be, so that was the answer he'd given Brianna.

She seemed to have been content with his reply, and to his relief, hadn't asked him about his favorite musicians or pieces. Those were questions that would have been much more difficult to answer, mostly because Elena had never talked much about the music she listened to, and instead had simply been happy to have it going in the background so she wouldn't have to work in dead silence.

And although he knew that Bree must be just as familiar with the shops in Jerome as she was with the offerings on its various restaurant menus, she hadn't seemed at all bored by the way he wanted to look at a kaleidoscope composed entirely of semiprecious stones, or how he surveyed the various minerals in another shop, deciding in the end on a chunk of something the label said was black tourmaline. He wasn't quite sure why he'd been drawn to the stone, only that it had felt comforting in his hand.

As they left the shop, she asked with a grin, "Trying to ward off evil spirits?"

His fingers touched the chunk of stone, which now resided in his jeans pocket. "Is that what it's meant for?"

She slipped her sunglasses on her nose.

Although he hated to have her beautiful eyes obscured, the sun was quite fierce today, so Belshegar could see why she would want to protect them.

"That's the story," she said. "Actually, I guess it's more than a story, because there's more evidence out there than you might think that some crystals really do have the qualities they're rumored to possess. Black tourmaline is all about warding off or maybe even absorbing negative energy." A pause, and then she looked up at him, her eyes a flash of blue behind the dark glasses. "Put that under your pillow, and you probably won't have to worry about ghosts."

He hadn't been precisely worrying about them, but he could see why it might be good to know that the first fellow who'd appeared in his room—the gaunt man who'd been visibly annoyed when the person he was trying to haunt hadn't been frightened at all—would be chased away by the energies emanating from the black crystal.

Or perhaps it would also prevent the voice from getting too close or spying on his activities here.

No, that was the wrong way to look at the situation, wasn't it? The voice wasn't a negative form of energy, was only a member of a council that made sure the beings on the upper planes didn't abuse their powers.

And yet....

Something about the entire situation was beginning to feel wrong in a way he couldn't quite quantify. If the voice knew where the artifacts were being held, why hadn't he or the other members of the Council swooped in to collect them? Surely their powers must be much greater than those of the McAllister *prima,* even though Belshegar supposed she must be a very strong witch in her own right.

Perhaps he'd been too naïve, too trusting. Some people might have thought it odd to apply those adjectives to a being who'd existed for millennia, but Belshegar had had very few dealings with other sentient creatures.

Not until Elena had summoned him that one night, and he'd realized he could offer her some comfort in his own odd way.

All he knew was that everyone he'd met in Santa Fe had appeared to be kind—even Alessandro, who'd wrestled with his own demons at first but had eventually opened his heart to Elena.

And everyone here in Jerome had been friendly as well. Yes, including the fair-haired man who Belshegar now knew for certain had been Brianna's father, a man who wasn't exactly a man at all.

Why her powers weren't nearly as strong as her father's, he couldn't begin to guess. Just the idea that a being from another plane could have a life here, could presumably have a wife…could have children…had made all sorts of ideas begin to spring up in Belshegar's mind like wildflowers after a summer rain.

What if he also could do that very thing?

Because Brianna was now looking at him, clearly expecting an answer to her question, he knew he had to attend to her and not the dazzling possibilities that had begun to present themselves.

"Oh, the ghosts have been quiet the past few days," he said, forcing a smile. "I have a feeling they wanted to meet the newcomer, but since they didn't get a rise out of me, I suppose they moved on to people who are easier to frighten."

He was proud of himself for using the colloquialism; he'd overheard a man saying that very thing in the bar at the Grand Hotel just the night before, and had gone to his phone to look up the phrase to see what it meant. To be sure, he also learned a great many other things from the website he visited, a place called The Urban Dictionary, some of which he thought he could have done without.

But Brianna returned his smile, which meant what he'd said had sounded completely normal to her.

"Ghosts can be tricky," she said. "I suppose they like being whimsical. I mean, if you're not bound to an earthly existence anymore, you might as well have your fun where you can, right?"

That was one way of looking at it. Of course, by their very natures, spirits were bound to this plane, but they could leave whenever they wanted, just as soon as they acknowledged that it was time to move on. Otherwise, they would be trapped here forever.

A chime sounded from the phone he knew she carried in her purse, and some of the humor vanished from her expression. "That's my alarm," she explained after she'd reached inside the bag to turn off the alert and prevent it from continuing to sound. "I need to head down to the festival and get ready for my set."

She sounded very calm as she spoke, and yet Belshegar could still see the tension in her neck and the set of her slender shoulders.

"Then let's go," he responded at once. The day had gone by so quickly that he was surprised to see it was already past three-thirty. "Do you need me to help you with anything?"

A quick smile, and she said, "Thanks, Bill, but I brought my equipment down to the site earlier today. All I need to do is show up and wait my turn."

He supposed he should have thought of that.

Whoever was running the festival, they seemed to be quite organized.

"But I still appreciate you being there for moral support," she added, almost as if she'd feared he might continue to wander around the town rather than being there to watch her perform from nearer the stage.

"Of course I'll be there."

After giving her that encouragement, he headed toward the street, with her only a pace behind. They had to wait a moment for an opening in traffic so it would be safe to cross, but soon enough, they were on the other side and moving toward the sounds of music drifting up from below.

If possible, the park seemed even more crowded than it had been when they got lunch from the food truck, and Belshegar guessed that quite a few people had arrived late to miss the first rush. However, Brianna threaded her way through the crowd with some ease.

Or possibly people recognized her and stepped out of the way to allow her passage.

Whatever the case, she made it to the roped-off area for the performers quickly enough, where she paused to reach out and give his hand a quick squeeze.

"This is it," she said. "I'll come find you in the crowd when I'm done."

He wished he could pull her close and give her a reassuring hug—perhaps even more than that, although he knew he would rather not share their first kiss in such a public place—but because they hadn't even gotten to the hugging stage yet, he had to settle for what he hoped was an encouraging smile.

"I'll be sure to be in the front row," he promised.

A flash of a returning smile, and then she was hurrying into the roped-off area, speaking to the woman who appeared to be guarding the musicians' instruments and other equipment.

No point in lingering, not when Brianna would be looking for him in the audience. Instead, Belshegar shouldered his way through the crowd as best he could, trying to get as close to the front as possible without actively pushing anyone out of the way.

The person currently performing was a man with reddish-blond hair pulled back into a ponytail. His voice was good, but Belshegar only wanted him to be done so he could hear Brianna sing.

That wish was granted, because the man finished his song, said there would be a brief break while the next performer set up, and then left the stage.

The people in the crowd around Belshegar

murmured and shifted, but he could tell no one wanted to move too far from their current positions lest they lose their places. All the same, he was still able to move a bit closer...and then froze as he sensed a sudden rush of powerful energy, rather like hitting a warm current when swimming in a cold lake.

Standing next to him was the fair-haired man from Paradise Lane.

Brianna's father.

It seemed the man recognized him at once, because he said, "Checking out some more of the local sights?"

"Yes," Belshegar managed. From what he'd been able to tell, Bree hadn't said anything about him to her family—and why would she, when they were only casually seeing one another during these few days he was here in Jerome?—so there was no reason in the world why her father would think of him as anything other than the man who'd been sketching the Victorian houses in the neighborhood as his own way of sightseeing. Thinking he needed to elaborate, he went on, "I heard about the folk festival from someone at the Grand Hotel, so I thought I'd come down and check it out."

"You're in for a treat," the man said. Then he held out a hand, surprising Belshegar a little. "I suppose I should have introduced myself earlier.

I'm Levi McAllister. And this"—he inclined his head toward the blonde woman who stood next to him, someone whose golden hair and clear blue eyes echoed her daughter's—"is my wife Hayley. Our daughter is performing next."

"Very nice to meet you," Belshegar murmured, shaking the woman's hand next. "And you must be very proud of your daughter."

"Oh, we are," Hayley McAllister said. She was tall and slender, like her daughter, and didn't seem quite old enough to have a child in her mid-twenties. "Brianna doesn't get the chance to play her original music very often, so we definitely didn't want to miss this."

And neither did Belshegar. Brianna's voice was as beautiful as her face, and she was clearly a skilled guitar player, but he hoped when he heard her play her own songs, he might get to learn a bit more about her, to see past the public face she'd presented during this time while they were still getting acquainted.

A little rustle went through the crowd, and he looked away from the McAllisters to see Bree walking on stage, a twelve-string in her right hand and the other guitar in her left. She leaned that one against a stand that had been placed there for that purpose, then lifted the twelve-string and slung it over one shoulder.

"Hello," she said into the microphone, her

voice carrying clearly across the crowd and out toward the rest of Jerome. "I'm Brianna McAllister. I'd like to play you a few of my songs."

Everyone clapped, and Belshegar could sense how many of the men in the crowd seemed particularly attentive. Well, she was very beautiful, with her pale hair falling in mermaid ripples past her shoulders and the full skirt and tank top she wore hinting at her form without obviously flaunting it.

The first song was livelier than he'd expected, with a sort of rhythm that made him think of water rushing through a creek full after a summer storm. Around him, the crowd seemed to fall into the spell of the music, clapping along and tapping toes, all while her voice carried clear and strong above it all, speaking of dusty roads that needed to be traveled and a longing for a life that might exist far beyond the small town where she'd grown up.

Was that truly how she felt? Was she constrained by her life as a witch, made restless by a need to see something more than this one small corner of Arizona?

Perhaps. He hadn't encountered such sentiments in Elena, but then, she'd been so happy to be set free from the house that had been her prison, she had thought Santa Fe on its own was more than enough to keep her happy, let alone the entirety of New Mexico.

But you are free, Brianna, he thought then. *Free in the love of the people who surround you.*

It was an odd thought to emerge from the mind of a being who could go anywhere and do almost anything. And yet, even though he'd been given that freedom, he knew he hadn't done much with it. No, he had been content to stay at home and tend his gardens. Somehow he'd known that seeing more of the universe wouldn't change the emptiness he carried inside.

He hadn't felt empty the past couple of days, however. Even when he hadn't been around Brianna McAllister, it had still seemed as though he carried something of her within him.

The song ended, replaced by another, slower, one that talked about the simple beauties found in the everyday, whether it was watching the sun rise or lying in the tall grass and breathing in as clouds passed by overhead. Once again, Belshegar was struck by the way she could capture the essence of those moments in just a few words and a few carefully chosen chords.

Around him, the crowd had fallen mostly silent, listening carefully rather than chatting or texting or one of a hundred different things humans did to distract themselves when their minds or their hearts weren't fully engaged. This, he thought, was true magic, even though he could tell it had nothing to do with whatever gifts Brianna might have inherited from her parents.

No, this was all her.

The set went on, with songs sometimes faster and sometimes slower. From time to time, she would put down the twelve-string and pick up the six-string and stay with it for a song or two. As the set wound down, though, she reached for the twelve-string again and settled it in her lap, causing some of the silver sequins on her skirt to sparkle like little stars. Her expression grew almost melancholy, and she bent her head toward the strings, a few locks of golden hair falling forward to obscure her lovely features.

And then she sang again.

> Midnight roads stretch endlessly
> The horizon keeps its secrets
>   from me
> I'm walking through valleys deep
>   and wide
> With mountains of questions I
>   keep inside

The ache in her voice was so pure, so true, that a similar ache awoke in Belshegar's breast, one he wasn't sure he could ever explain. Once again, he wanted to take her in his arms...only this time, he thought it was more to soothe himself than to comfort her.

> I've painted dreams in crimson
>   and gold
> Of worlds beyond what these eyes
>   can hold
> Standing at the edge of what
>   I know
> Feeling the pull of where I
>   might go

Yes, now he could feel it, that desire to go beyond the constraints of the world she lived in. Some might have said she was a lucky woman, blessed with brains and beauty and the voice of an angel, but still, she couldn't do whatever she liked.

She would always have to keep the truth of her soul, her spirit, hidden from most of the people she met.

Except for times like now, when she allowed just a little of it to slip out.

And then she slowed, shifting into another minor key as she echoed the chorus one last time.

> There's a distance in my soul
> That no map could ever show
> Like shadows between stars

So close, yet so far
So close, yet so far....

The song ended there, the final chord drifting off into utter silence. All around him, the people in the crowd stood quietly, as if they weren't sure what to do next.

But then someone started clapping, and another, and the applause turned thunderous, echoing off the buildings across the way and the tall retaining wall that kept the street above from sliding down into the park. Belshegar clapped as well, clapped until his palms began to hurt.

Pain. It was such a human thing.

In that moment, he would have given anything to be human, to be one with the people in the crowd all around him.

A few feet away, Brianna's mother was wiping tears from her eyes. "How does she know?" she asked. Her voice was only a little more than a whisper, the words intended for her husband and no one else, and yet Belshegar was still able to hear them well enough. "How does she know what it feels like for us?"

"Because she's a poet," Levi McAllister replied in equally low tones. "Along with so many other things."

Then Levi looked over at Belshegar, and his

expression shifted, becoming one that seemed far more public, friendly and open. "What did you think?"

"I think she was amazing," he said honestly, and Levi smiled.

"We think that, too."

Up on the stage, Brianna was making awkward little half-bows, as if she knew she needed to acknowledge the adulation from the crowd even while being horribly embarrassed by it. After a minute or so, however, she made her escape, fleeing with her twelve-string in hand. A few seconds later, the woman who had been watching the musicians' equipment came up to retrieve the six-string Bree had left behind, shot a brilliant smile at the audience, and then hurried off again.

Belshegar had no idea who had been scheduled to follow her, and he rather pitied them in that moment. He might not have been human or understood all the subtle nuances of their interactions, but even he realized that appearing after such a scintillating performance must be trying, to say the least.

He and Brianna had exchanged phone numbers at the end of their second date, so he thought he would leave the park and go to the Vino Zona tasting room not too far from her apartment and see if she would like to meet him there. That was just far enough away from the park where the festival was being held that it would allow her a bit of separation.

So he murmured a goodbye to her parents and made his way through the crowd to the sidewalk, then walked to the end of the street and continued his way down the hill. This part of town wasn't nearly as flush with visitors, probably because so many of them were in the park, listening to the music.

In fact, he was the only one in the tasting room, and after he told the woman who was tending the place that he was going to check and see if his friend wanted to meet him there, she nodded and headed toward the back of the space, allowing him some privacy.

He got out his phone.

> I'm at Vino Zona. Would you like me to buy you a drink?

The seconds ticked by with no response. Perhaps Brianna's parents had scooped her up and taken her out for a congratulatory treat, or perhaps she was so thronged by admirers that she hadn't even had a chance to look at her phone.

But then his cell phone chimed, and he let out a breath of relief.

You have no idea how much. I'll
be there in a few.

He smiled and turned toward the woman who
worked at the tasting room.

"My friend will be here shortly."

11

Maybe Bill Garrett was a mind reader. That seemed to be the most likely explanation for why he knew she needed a drink.

It wasn't that the performance had gone badly —just the opposite, if the crazy applause that had greeted the end of her final song was any indication—but doing a set composed solely of her own music had felt a bit like stripping naked in front of all those people.

She could only hope that a glass of wine would settle her nerves.

It had taken longer to get away from the festival site than she'd thought, since she had to say goodbye to her parents and all the other McAllisters who had gathered there to see her perform, accepting their congratulations and their hugs with the best grace she could muster. Luckily, she wouldn't need to be back to pick up her equipment until after six, well past the time most of the crowd would have left, since the festival ended at five today.

After about fifteen minutes, though, she managed to tear herself away and head down the hill toward Vino Zona. It crossed her mind that her apartment was only a few shops down from the wine tasting room, and that meant it might not be too difficult to coax Bill over there once they were done with their drinks.

Or maybe it would. Although he'd touched her a few times today, it had only been to give a reassuring pat here and there, the sort of thing her brother Shane might have done in a similar situation. She still wasn't getting too many vibes that Bill was interested in anything more than some companionship while he was visiting Jerome.

Best not to project too much about what might or might not happen. The important thing was that he'd invited her to meet him for a drink —and in the tasting room located farthest away from the festival site, which meant he probably understood that she wanted to put some distance between herself and the crowds that had watched her play just a little while earlier.

He was sitting in one of the chairs near the front entrance when she came in, but he immediately stood up once he spotted her. Vino Zona was decorated with an eclectic and fun collection of modern and antique furniture arranged into several groupings that could accommodate either a couple or a larger gathering, like the pair of two married couples who occupied the big pink sofa and the chairs that faced it farther back in the space.

They sent her a mildly curious glance when she came in but immediately returned to their conversation, which seemed to be a signal that they hadn't seen her performance and had no idea who she was.

Good. Safe anonymity sounded just about perfect right then.

"I had the place to myself up until a few minutes ago," Bill said in a murmur after they'd greeted one another and both sat down. "But then that group showed up."

His tone was mildly disapproving, and Bree wanted to chuckle. However, she only replied, "It's fine. Honestly, sometimes it's better if there are more people, because that way, Nina doesn't feel the need to hover."

He nodded, which told Brianna that the tasting room's owner had already introduced herself while he was waiting for her to arrive. "I suppose that makes sense. What would you like to drink?"

"The Birds and Barrels petit sirah," she said immediately, and he cocked an eyebrow.

"Very specific."

She smiled. "The winery makes it just for Vino Zona, so this is the only place where you can get it. And I want something with a little more oomph than a white."

That was for sure. All her nerve endings still felt jangly and raw, twanging like a bunch of broken guitar strings, and she knew she needed something that would help smooth away the rough edges.

To be honest, maybe they should have skipped the wine and headed down the hill for some Long Island iced teas at Kaktus Kate's.

But they were at Vino Zona now, and Bree was pretty sure she'd feel much better after she had a few sips of petit sirah inside her. Bill excused himself and went over to let Nina know what they wanted to drink. As he came back to join her near the front window, she couldn't help noticing the way one of the women in the other group watched him with appreciative eyes. She was probably at least ten years older than he and obviously married, but that didn't seem to have prevented her from getting an eyeful.

He appeared oblivious, however, and told Bree as he seated himself again, "Nina said she'll bring our wine right over."

"Thank you."

A pause as he seemed to study her, and then he said, "How are you doing?"

Good question. Brianna wasn't quite sure yet. Now that she was away from the stage and someplace relatively quiet—well, sort of quiet, since the foursome seated a few feet away sounded as though they must have hit at least one other tasting room on their way down here—she found herself a little steadier, but she knew it would still take a while to analyze her performance and its response.

"I'm okay," she said. "I suppose I wasn't expecting that kind of reception."

"You were incredible," he replied.

Blood rushed to her cheeks, but she managed to reply steadily enough, "Well, I don't know about that. I suppose I'm just glad that I didn't forget any of the words to the songs or bust a string or something."

Some men might have smiled. Bill, on the other hand, only looked thoughtful. "Do you really think you would have forgotten your own lyrics?"

Most likely not. Still….

"Well, I only finished that final song last night," she said. "So it's not as if it's had months to get engraved on my brain."

His brows lifted, but he had to hold back his

response, since Nina arrived then with their glasses of petit sirah. She must have been able to tell that there was no need to go into her usual spiel about the winery and how this particular wine was made specifically for the tasting room—probably since Bree had heard it multiple times before—because she only handed over their wine and said briefly, "Just let me know if you need anything else."

They both promised her they would, and she headed over to the foursome, who called out that they wanted another round.

Once they were all safely occupied, Bill held up his glass. "To your performance."

Brianna thought maybe it was a little much to be toasting her own singing and playing, but since he was the one who'd brought it up, she figured she might as well go along with his wishes for now. However, she couldn't help remarking, "If you say so."

His deep green eyes crinkled with amusement around the corners. "I do say so. And I think it's even more impressive that you only finished that final song last night. It was amazing."

She wanted to squirm in her seat like an unprepared child asked a question by her teacher. Since that wouldn't have looked very adult—and she knew she needed to learn to accept praise, no matter how difficult it might be—she only said, "Thank you."

"I'm surprised you haven't been approached to record your music," he commented next.

Her mouth twisted a little, and she drank some of her petite sirah before saying, "Acoustic folk isn't exactly hitting the top of the charts these days."

He sipped from his glass as well. "It isn't? I don't pay too much attention."

Kind of hard for her to believe that when he was from Los Angeles, the heart of the music industry, but then again, just because you were surrounded by something didn't mean you had to participate in it.

And he had told her just yesterday that he preferred to listen to classical guitar. That genre wasn't exactly burning up the Top 40, either.

"It's fine," she said. "I like playing live, even though it can be nerve-wracking sometimes. I feel like something might get lost when it's reduced to a bunch of ones and zeroes."

For just a moment, his forehead puckered, as if he wasn't quite sure of what she was talking about. But then his brow smoothed and he said, "I suppose I can see your point."

She wouldn't mention that a year or so earlier, an agent from Phoenix had heard her playing at Page Springs Winery and had talked about wanting to sign her and record an album. But as enticing as the prospect had sounded at first, she'd known she couldn't go down that path, not when being a witch was all about lying low. Some might have argued that any kind of public performance wasn't exactly flying under the radar, either, although in her mind, she thought there was something very different about playing live to a limited number of people versus having recorded music that could be out there on Spotify or Pandora or some other streaming service.

So she'd turned down the offer, even though it had hurt a little, and stuck with what she was already doing.

It wasn't as if she had a huge amount of alternatives, not when one of the most important directives she had to follow was to make sure she didn't attract too much attention.

"Well," Bill said after he took another sip of wine, "I don't think you're going to need to worry too much about playing your original work from now on. People seemed to respond to it very positively."

That they had. Then again, the audience at a folk festival was a little different from the crowd you'd get at a tasting room, people who were there to drink first and listen to music a very distant second. Bree doubted they would want to be presented with something that made them think too hard.

She would worry about all that later, though. For now, it was enough to enjoy some of the lingering endorphins from her performance, and to know she'd gotten through the thing without embarrassing herself.

Far from it, actually.

Bill seemed to sense that she didn't want to talk about her contribution to the folk festival anymore, and he shifted the conversation to the logistics of her performance tomorrow at Alcantara Winery and how he was just fine with meeting her at her apartment so she wouldn't have to drive up to the Grand Hotel to fetch him.

That seemed like the perfect opening to invite him over there after they were done with their drinks here, but something seemed to hold Brianna's tongue. She couldn't say for sure if that was because she knew deep down there was no reason to have things get that serious, or whether it was a simple case of cold feet.

Either way, she told him that sounded great, and they left it there.

See what happens tomorrow, she told herself, and yet she still didn't know if that would be the right time for them.

Maybe it would never be.

~

He hadn't asked her to dinner, and she'd let it go, telling herself that they'd spent most of the day together and she shouldn't monopolize his time. All the same, she couldn't stop herself from wondering exactly what he'd done that night after they parted ways at Vino Zona.

When he appeared at her apartment exactly at 2:30 the next afternoon as she'd requested, though, he looked rested and full of energy at the same time, so whatever he'd been up to, it couldn't have been too taxing.

He helped her load her guitars and amp and cords and the rest of it in the back of her Suburban, and then they rattled their way down the hill. Bree took the upper route through Cottonwood since that wasn't her destination, then turned onto Highway 260, which would take them down to Alcantara.

As they drove, he sat up a little straighter in the worn leather seat, his gaze seeming to take in everything about the landscape around them. Bree couldn't say that it looked too different from the country up near Clarkdale, was only more rolling hills covered in yellow grass that had faded since its green heyday during monsoon season, but she supposed the contours of the land were just different enough to hold his interest.

They turned off the highway onto a rough road that eventually switched over to gravel, taking them past a trailer park full of travelers enjoying the last bits of summer before autumn truly arrived, then down a steep incline that led onto the winery property. Acres of grapevines stretched on either side, and the building that housed the tasting room looked like a Tuscan villa set down in the center of the Arizona countryside.

"It's beautiful," Bill said, and Bree nodded.

"Definitely. I think it's one of the prettiest tasting rooms in the area, and we've got plenty to choose from. Let me show you where we need to set up."

Suddenly looking brisk, he tilted his head in acknowledgment and opened the door to let himself out of the Suburban. Brianna did the same, then lifted the back hatch so they could pull out all her equipment. Since she'd done this dozens of times before, she knew exactly where to guide him—around to the back, where the lawn was perpetually green except in the depths of winter, and anyone enjoying their wine on the back patio could enjoy a stunning view of more vineyards sloping down to the Verde River.

Although she could tell he wasn't familiar with setting up audio equipment, he was good at following directions, and she had everything placed where she wanted it and properly connected much faster than she would have if she'd had to do all this by herself. When Dave Miller, one of the winery owners, came out to check on her progress, he seemed a little surprised that she'd gotten her setup together so quickly.

"Guess it helps to have a roadie," he said, his blue eyes twinkling good-naturedly as she introduced him to Bill. Dave looked as if he would have liked to ask a few more questions—he'd known her since she was barely able to drive—but had decided it wouldn't be good manners to probe too much when the man he was curious about was standing right there and listening to everything they said.

"I like to help," Bill said.

That he did. Not a single word of complaint, no "helpful" advice on how to perform a task she could probably have done in her sleep. No, he just did as she asked without question—and with a smile on his face.

Too bad she couldn't bottle whatever made Bill, Bill. She'd be a multimillionaire overnight.

Dave offered them both a glass of wine and some water, and she went ahead and said that sounded great. She didn't always indulge when she performed—and if she did, she limited it to one glass—but sharing a drink with Bill made this seem a little more like a date of sorts, even if she was going to be working most of the time.

The winery had been open for several hours, so a few groups of people wandered out from the tasting room to see what was happening on the patio and then seated themselves when they seemed to realize there was going to be live entertainment. Sure, Dave posted information about the various performances on the chalkboard in the tasting room and on the sandwich board near the entrance to the winery, but it still kind of amazed her the way people didn't pay attention to those sorts of things.

"I'm going to start in a few minutes," she told Bill after Dave had brought them their glasses of Albariño, a crisp white perfect for the warm autumn afternoon. "So you should find a place to sit."

For just a moment, he hesitated—had he thought he was going to hover her near her during the performance, waiting in the wings in case she needed him to hand her a spare string, like a nurse at a doctor's elbow during an operation?—but then he seemed to relax and said, "Of course. I thought I saw an empty seat near the edge of the patio."

"Then go ahead and take it," Bree replied, guessing it probably wouldn't be occupied any time soon. Her experience had taught her that a lot of listeners didn't want to seat themselves too near the performer, reminding her of her old classmates who'd never wanted to sit too near the front in case they got called on by the teacher.

Not that Bill needed to worry about that. Probably his biggest concern should be how many women might try to hit on him while he was sitting there alone.

Everyone out on the patio appeared to be paired off, but because they hadn't gone in the tasting room proper, she had no idea how many sharks might be swimming around, looking for chum.

And now she just wanted to laugh at herself.

Jealous much? she thought.

Bill Garrett wasn't her property. There was nothing formal between them. True, it would be a little tacky for him to chat up another woman while the person he was currently seeing stood only a few yards away, but still, he was a free agent.

Bree couldn't really imagine him doing anything like that, though. If nothing else, he was far too polite.

He gave her a little wave and, wine glass in hand, went up the steps to the patio and sat down at the table he'd mentioned a few minutes earlier. The low murmur of conversation reached her ears, letting her know that no one was paying any particular attention to her.

Which was just how she wanted it. She'd had

enough eyes on her yesterday to last her a very long time.

And she'd already decided to perform all covers this afternoon. Although Dave had never told her what she could or couldn't play, it just seemed better, on this mild, mellow Sunday afternoon, to stick with the tried and true.

So she opened with "Desperado" and segued into "Black Velvet" after that, sticking with the old standards everyone seemed to love. Although Bill's seat was partially obscured by the railing that protected the raised patio, she could still see him well enough as he sat there and listened and took the occasional sip from his wine glass. No one had approached him, and she allowed herself a sigh too small to even be picked up by her microphone.

Maybe someday she'd learn to stop borrowing trouble.

Her first set passed without incident, and she picked up her glass of wine so she could go sit with him and relax for the ten minutes she allowed herself for breaks between sets. His face lit up as she approached, and once again she found herself marveling at how good-looking he was.

Bill Garrett was about much more than looks, though. Bree was pretty sure she'd be just as attracted to him if he were the Hunchback of Notre Dame.

Okay, maybe that was taking it a bit far. Still, he didn't need to be movie-star handsome, not when he was so uniquely…himself.

"You haven't played any of your own songs," he said as she seated herself.

His tone wasn't quite accusing, but she could tell he was disappointed. "I thought I'd take a break," she said lightly. "You know, just in case any of the people here heard me yesterday at the festival."

That was probably a long shot but not entirely out of the bounds of possibility.

Bill seemed to accept that explanation, however, because he nodded and didn't seem inclined to press the issue. "I suppose I can see that. How many sets do you usually play?"

"Three," she replied at once, since that was an easy enough question to answer. "I'll finish up around five-thirty."

And she stopped there, not sure if she should say anything else.

Bill, on the other hand, didn't seem nearly so reticent. "Then possibly we could get something to eat afterward?"

The very question she'd been hoping he'd ask. "Sure," she said, doing her best to seem as if this was all off the cuff and not something she'd been thinking about for most of the afternoon. "But since it's going to be kind of early, how about we go into Sedona instead of heading back to Cottonwood? That way, you'll still be able to see something of it."

And such an outing should be safe enough. Yes, Bellamy and Marc had pretty much established that sleeping overnight in Sedona near one of the energy vortexes there enhanced their inborn witchy powers, but just being there for a few hours didn't appear to affect anything. She and Bill could have dinner someplace with a view—maybe the Mesa Grille, up by the airport—and at least that way he would get a chance to see the red rocks. It just didn't feel right to her that he'd traveled all this way and didn't seem to have made any effort to spend a few hours exploring Sedona's beauties.

"I think I'd like that very much," Bill replied. "Will we need a reservation?"

"On Sunday night? Probably not," she said, answering her own question. "At least, not where I'm planning for us to go."

"Then I'm looking forward to it."

She smiled and took another sip of her wine. In a moment, she'd need to head down to the lawn and pick up her guitar again, but for now, she was content to simply be here with him.

However long it might last.

12

He realized he had made a huge mistake in not traveling to Sedona before this, even though he doubted he could have justified such an expedition to himself...let alone to the voice or whoever else might be watching his movements.

Sunset was still half an hour off or so, but the rocks that rose on either side of the town's main thoroughfare blazed with their own reddish light nonetheless. There was power here, the power of the earth itself, concentrated in certain spots that seemed to glow like beacons on the landscape.

Could Brianna sense any of that? She certainly seemed matter-of-fact enough as she guided them through surprisingly heavy traffic and then turned off onto a winding road that led up to a spot called Airport Mesa, according to one of the signs they passed. However, he guessed that just because she was a witch didn't mean she was able to sense the energies that seemed to swirl all around them.

Those energies only grew in strength as the oversized vehicle climbed what felt like at least five hundred feet or maybe more. In fact, the pressure from those energy sinks was so overpowering, he had to force himself to take a breath.

"Are you all right?" she asked as she sent him a worried sideways glance.

He hadn't said anything, but it seemed she'd been able to detect something of the way the landscape around them was acting upon him.

"I'm fine," he managed. "This place is…breathtaking."

In every possible sense of the word.

"It is," she agreed. "Every time I come into Sedona, I ask myself why I don't visit more. Then I get stuck in traffic and remember why it's sometimes a good idea to stay away."

He was able to chuckle. The pressure on his body was beginning to lessen, although he had a feeling that was more because he was becoming acclimated to those energy sinks than because the power they were emitting had diminished in any fashion.

"I think it's worth the traffic."

She smiled. "Maybe you're right. Anyway, I took a gamble and figured it shouldn't be so bad on a Sunday evening, especially since this isn't a holiday weekend or anything." A tilt of her head toward the parking lot they were approaching, and she added, "There aren't a ton of cars, so it looks like I was right."

An assertion that was proved correct in the next moment, since the hostess took them to a table right away rather than making them wait to be seated. It was placed up against the windows that created a wall of glass on one side of the restaurant, windows overlooking a small runway.

"Sedona Airport," Brianna said in response to his questioning glance. "We might see a few planes coming in for a landing, but I doubt anyone will be taking off because we're so close to sunset."

"The airport isn't open at night?"

Not that he had any great knowledge of such things, but some of the movies he'd watched with Elena had shown the characters coming and going from airports at what appeared to be all hours.

"No," Brianna replied. "Too dangerous. The runway isn't very long, and with the airport perched up here on the top of the mesa, there's too much risk of something going wrong. If you need to land at night, you'd need to go up to Flagstaff, or maybe over to Prescott. I have to admit I don't know too much about it—I've never flown."

This was possibly not that strange a comment

coming from someone who didn't seem to have ever left Arizona. Something about her words had sounded almost challenging, though, as if she wanted to underline that her experience of the world wasn't very large.

Well, neither was his. He'd learned new things every day he was here, and yet he understood that this world held so many treasures, it would require lifetimes to explore them.

"You're not missing much," he said, remembering all the complaining the people in Elena's movies and TV shows had done about the inconveniences of airports and the cramped conditions on the planes themselves.

Now Brianna smiled. "I suppose you might be right about that. Anyway, we should probably take a look at the menu so we'll know what to order when our server comes over."

True enough. Belshegar dutifully picked up his menu and studied its contents, deciding that he would like to try an enchilada. He knew they were something of a specialty of Elena's husband, who was an excellent cook, but he hadn't ordered one since coming to Arizona in human disguise. Might as well try something of the local cuisine while he was here.

The waiter must have noticed the way they set down their menus, because he approached their table and asked what they would like to order. A bottle of wine, of course, another white, since both he and Brianna were ordering lighter fare.

With that settled, Belshegar shifted so his back touched his chair and he could get a nearly unobstructed view of the red rocks to the east of town and the mesa beyond. The light had shifted enough that they were redder than ever, looking almost as if they were illuminated from within.

In a way, they are, he thought. *But with their own energies and nothing else.*

If everything had been open between them, he might have asked Bree about the power he'd sensed in this place. Doing so, unfortunately, would signal to her that there was far more to him than met the eye, so instead he pretended that he was admiring the beauty of the scenery.

Which of course he was. It was only that he also knew those red rocks hid their own secrets.

After the waiter had brought their wine and poured each of them a glass, Brianna fiddled with the stem, her eyes studiously directed down at the tabletop. Belshegar could see the way she pulled in a breath, almost as if she was steeling herself for something.

Then she said, "So…is it back to L.A. after this?"

Ah, there was the source of her discomfort. He supposed he could see why it might have been difficult for her to push past her reticence and broach the subject.

"Not right away," he said, and her slender form almost visibly relaxed. Today she was much more casual, in a turquoise-hued sleeveless top and jeans rather than a sparkly skirt and silver sandals, but she was still the most beautiful thing he had ever seen. "Now I'm fairly certain I'll be here through the end of the week, possibly more."

As long as it took to find the artifacts. All right, he hadn't been looking very hard the past couple of days, although he excused this to himself by thinking there had always been the chance that Brianna might let something slip about her *prima* and where she lived.

Well, that was the excuse he'd planned to use if he was questioned about why it was taking so long to find the artifacts. He'd been in Jerome for five days now, and he thought that even a being without much concept of time might start to become frustrated at his utter lack of progress.

At once, her eyes lit up, although Belshegar had the impression that she was trying her best not to seem too encouraged by this development.

"You've really found that much to do in Jerome?" she asked, her tone almost teasing.

"I have," he said steadily, meeting her gaze.

This time, she didn't look away. "I'm glad to

hear that," she said. "I've had a lot of fun these past few days."

So had he. That might not have been his original intention when he came here, but he couldn't remember the last time he'd enjoyed himself so much, or had the hours pass so quickly. Perhaps at Elena's wedding, and yet when he'd attended that event, his happiness had arisen mostly from seeing her so utterly content and so free at the same time, like a butterfly that had finally escaped its cocoon and was now beginning to experience all the joys and experiences it had missed. For himself, he knew he'd been self-conscious, doing his utter best to make sure nothing he said or anything in how he acted might give away the truth of his being, that he was certainly not human.

Perhaps he had felt that way when he first arrived in Jerome, but as the days had passed and no one seemed to notice anything exceptional about him, he'd allowed himself to relax somewhat.

Or possibly more than merely "somewhat." Otherwise, he wouldn't have allowed himself to even entertain the idea of something romantic happening between him and Brianna.

He'd held himself back, of course. He'd told himself such a thing was impossible.

And yet…and yet he couldn't prevent himself

from wondering what it would be like to feel the silky strands of her hair running across his fingers…to imagine how sweet her lips must taste.

So many things that he knew must be utterly forbidden to him.

"Me, too," he replied. "So I changed my plane ticket to a week from tomorrow."

Perhaps he shouldn't have said anything, because he noticed at once how her expression darkened slightly. It seemed she wasn't too happy to hear that he'd put an end cap on his stay in Jerome, even if it was still a week off.

But she forced her lips into a smile and said, "Well, if you're going to be here that long, then maybe we can figure out some other things for you to do. If you have the time, of course," she added hastily, as if she'd realized that inserting herself in his plans in such a way might have been a little too presumptuous.

"I do," he said at once. Although he knew he needed to be more dedicated in his search for the artifacts, he also realized such a pursuit couldn't take up every hour of every day. "Which days do you have free?"

"Tomorrow," she said promptly. "No winery gigs—a lot of them are closed on Mondays—and no music lessons, either."

That sounded good to him…until he reminded himself that he really should dedicate a portion of his day to his search, even if that resulted in him doing nothing more than sitting in his hotel room and racking his brain in a vain attempt to discover the artifacts' hiding place.

"In the afternoon?" he returned. "I have something I need to do in the morning."

She didn't seem put off by that modification to her plan, because she nodded and said, "That's fine. If you want to go sightseeing, we can drive up Oak Creek Canyon and maybe do a little hiking. It's really beautiful, and on a Monday, the trails shouldn't be too crowded."

Belshegar had no idea what Oak Creek Canyon even was, but if it involved more breathtaking scenery, then he was definitely on board with the idea. He didn't have any real hiking shoes, although he knew that wasn't an impediment, not when he could conjure anything he might require for such an outing.

"What time?"

"Does two o'clock work?" she said. "Normally, I wouldn't go for a hike that late in the day, but because the elevation is a little higher in the part of the canyon I want to visit and there are a lot of trees for shade, the heat shouldn't be a problem."

He hadn't thought of that aspect of the situation—fluctuations in temperature didn't affect him very much, even in his assumed human guise

—but he certainly didn't want Brianna to get overheated.

"Two o'clock sounds fine," he replied. Surely that would give him enough time to do whatever he needed to do, and then he could go on this hike in the canyon without worrying whether he'd given his mission its due diligence that day.

"Then you can meet me at my apartment... unless you want me to pick you up?" she added, her voice now uncertain, as if she'd realized that making him walk down to her place right before they were going to head out on an extended hike might not have been the most considerate thing in the world.

Belshegar didn't mind, though. Such a short walk certainly wouldn't be taxing in the least, and it did seem rather foolish for her to drive up to the hotel, just to turn around so they could head back down the hill.

"No, there's no reason for you to do that," he said. "I don't mind meeting you at your apartment. It'll save us some time, if nothing else."

"And gas," she said, although she was smiling, and he guessed she wasn't too worried about that.

Still, he hadn't stopped to think about how much these excursions must be costing her. True, she would have gone to Alcantara for her performance even if he hadn't tagged along, but she certainly wouldn't have gone to the Mesa Grille for dinner…and he doubted she would have decided to head off to Oak Creek Canyon tomorrow if she hadn't had someone she wanted to show it to for the first time.

And although he had very little knowledge of such things, he also had to assume that the gasoline was fairly expensive, just because it was a rarity these days and he doubted there were many places where she could even get it.

"I can chip in for gas," he said, but she just smiled.

"It's fine. I'm used to going all over, since my gigs can get pretty spread out. But thanks for the offer."

Her tone was firm enough that he doubted there would be much point in attempting to press the issue. Instead, he told himself he could pay for dinner afterward, or perhaps only an afternoon snack if it turned out Bree didn't want to extend their excursion into the evening.

"Then it sounds like we have a plan," he said, and she nodded.

"I think we do."

They hadn't lingered too long at the Mesa Grille, and afterward, she drove him back to Jerome and dropped him off in the Grand Hotel's parking lot.

"See you tomorrow at two," she said, then drove off.

No real opportunity for a goodnight kiss—even if he'd been inclined to press the issue. Oh, he'd wanted to kiss her...this human body he wore had been telling him how very much he wanted such a thing...but if that moment ever came, he certainly didn't intend to give in to those instincts while sitting in the front seat of an ancient Chevy Suburban.

So he'd gone to bed and done his best to sleep, and when he woke up the next morning, it was with a renewed resolve to achieve some progress on his search for the artifacts, if only to make him feel a little less guilty about sharing another afternoon with Brianna.

The problem was, he had no clear idea as to where he should look. It wasn't that he couldn't sense the artifacts anymore—the low-frequency hum of their presence had continued the entire time he'd been in Jerome—but because he seemed unable to pinpoint where it was coming from, he had no clear idea what exactly he was supposed to do about it.

Well, as blocked as he might currently feel, he knew he wasn't going to learn anything new by sitting in his hotel room and brooding about the situation.

Once again, he ordered room service—toast

and fruit and tea, just like the day before—and showered and got dressed so he could venture out into Jerome to see what he could find.

It was cooler today, with a few large white clouds floating above the landscape and somehow making the sky seem even bluer. Now it almost felt as if fall was on the way, even though only a few leaves on the trees around him had begun to turn, and he guessed it would still be some weeks before autumn was truly upon this part of the world.

Something in the cool, fresh breeze seemed to hearten him, however, and he wanted to believe that was a hopeful sign.

For some reason, he couldn't stop thinking about the painting he and Brianna had hung in Helen Doyle's house. There hadn't seemed to be anything exceptional about it—certainly, it hadn't contained any magical qualities except the inherent skill with which it had been painted—but Belshegar still felt there was something significant about the artist who'd created it, even if a cursory online search hadn't revealed anything particularly special about the man.

Well, often the best research was what could be performed in person.

The gallery where Brianna sometimes worked wasn't the only one in Jerome. Belshegar had noted that an artist's co-op was located just up the street from West by Southwest, and he thought perhaps someone would be employed there who might be able to tell him a bit more about the mysterious Mr. Wilcox.

It was now well after ten o'clock, so there was no reason to believe the co-op wouldn't be open. Or perhaps not; Belshegar had been in the small former mining town for less than a week, but he'd already noticed that many of the shopkeepers here appeared to be rather lax about their schedules and showed up to work when they felt like it rather than adhering to the hours posted on their shop doors or in their windows.

But the door to the artist's co-op stood open when he approached, probably to let in that fresh morning breeze. He allowed himself a moment of relief, then stepped inside.

The space was larger than it had looked from the outside, with high ceilings and white-painted walls to set off the art hung there. Like so many of the other spaces he'd encountered in Jerome, it had many interesting angles and small rooms that didn't seem to have much connection to one another. In a way, Belshegar thought that was a good thing, since it allowed a visitor to be alone to immerse themselves in the art in front of them rather than being distracted by what was going on in other sections of the gallery.

An older woman with shocking bright blue

hair had been setting out a collection of hammered brass and copper jewelry in the display case by the cash register when he came in. She looked up at once and smiled, her fuchsia lipstick a friendly contrast to her blue hair.

"Good morning," she said pleasantly. "Are you looking for something in particular, or did you just want to wander?"

Belshegar had already noted that there seemed to be a plethora of interesting things to look at inside, whether it was the brightly painted pottery displayed on a cunning multi-level shelving unit or the colorful abstracts on the wall behind the pottery. However, he was here on a mission, so he couldn't allow himself to be distracted.

"I was wondering if you had any paintings by Connor Wilcox?"

At once, the woman's face brightened. "Yes, a few. They're over in the next room. Let me show you."

She came out from behind the counter and led him to the space next to where they'd been standing, a larger room that appeared to be dedicated to oversized canvases.

"We only have three right now," the woman continued. "He tends to have his paintings in quite a few different spaces, so it's difficult to find a lot of them in any one place."

"That's all right," Belshegar replied. "I'd heard

about him and saw a couple of his pieces online, so I thought it would be good to view them in person."

"There are a few more in West by Southwest just down the street," said the clerk—or perhaps she was an artist as well, since this was a co-op and he'd read on the website for the shop that many of the artists took turns minding the store. "And if you're up for a drive, I know they just added some to Van Gogh's Ear in Prescott."

"This should do for now," Belshegar told her, which was only the truth. The Connor Wilcox collection here might have been limited to just three of his works, but still, they were all impressive in their own right. One was nearly six feet tall and showed towering red rocks peeking out from behind pine and oak and cottonwood trees, with a wide, rocky creek cutting through the foreground. Another portrayed a dense pine forest, deep and dark, while yet another was similar to the one he'd helped Brianna hang at Helen Doyle's house, a landscape that had a slow-moving river as its main subject, although in this one, the sky above was brooding and dark, perhaps hinting at a monsoon storm to come.

He'd experienced some of the monsoons during his visits with Elena in her childhood home in Las Vegas. Those summer storms had fascinated him with the way they sometimes arose from the heat of the day and at other times descended in the middle of the night, bringing with them thunder and lightning and torrential downpours. Although he was enjoying the warm, bright weather of the region at the tail end of September, he thought it would also have been interesting to be here earlier in the summer and see if the monsoons in northern Arizona were substantially different from the ones he'd experienced in New Mexico.

"What can you tell me about the artist?" he asked next. Perhaps that was too bold a gambit, but the woman with the blue hair was clearly a civilian, and she obviously thought he was no more than an ordinary tourist. It didn't seem too improbable that she might share the sort of information that Brianna would never divulge.

A smile that showed white teeth against the woman's fuchsia lipstick. "He's originally from Flagstaff—his family has been there for generations. Now he divides his time between Flagstaff and Jerome because his wife, Angela McAllister, is from here."

Angela McAllister. Again, Belshegar wasn't sure why a certain name would resonate so much within him, but somehow he knew she was just as significant as Connor.

Perhaps more.

Trying to make sure he sounded nothing more than idly curious, he said, "Is she an artist, too?"

"A silver artist." The woman paused there and pointed toward a display case in the other room that held a collection of silver jewelry. "She's an excellent silversmith—got it from her father, I suppose, since he's part Navajo and is also a jeweler. We have some of her pieces here, but there are a lot more at McAllister Mercantile down the street, since her family has owned the store for generations."

Of course they had, because the McAllister clan had been in this place for decades…more than a hundred years, from what he'd been able to determine.

"I'll have to take a look," he said, adding, "My girlfriend loves silver jewelry."

An utter lie. Or rather, while he'd noticed that Brianna McAllister only wore silver, it wasn't as if she was his girlfriend or anything close to it.

Probably better not to attempt to quantify their relationship.

"I'm sure you'll find something you like," the woman said. Another pause, and she went on, "Are you interested in any of the paintings?"

They were all beautiful, and if Belshegar had possessed an earthly home, he probably would have bought one on the spot. The rendering of the canyon with the red rocks spoke to him particularly.

However, he didn't see how he could transport it to the dwelling on his plane, and it wasn't as if he would do the painting the disservice of propping it against a wall in his hotel room for a few days and then leaving it behind.

It deserved more respect than that.

"My living situation is a little fluid at the moment," he replied. "But I'll keep these in mind in case things change."

A smile. "Let me get you a card, and I'll write down the name of the painting just in case. Most of Connor's pieces sell pretty quickly, though."

Belshegar could see that. They were somehow masterful and casual at the same time, conveying an almost effortless combination of light and shadow, of brushstrokes that were strong without overwhelming a piece.

The woman went to fetch a card and wrote something down on it, then brought it back to him. "Here you go," she said. "We're open seven days a week, so drop by any time you like."

He took the card and thanked her, then headed outside. A glance at the back of the card told him the name of the painting was "Oak Creek Reflections."

The same Oak Creek he'd be visiting in a few hours?

It must be. He had a hard time believing there would be two of them in the same general location.

A coincidence, most likely. Still….

He slipped the card into his jeans pocket and made his way down the sidewalk. Perhaps it would be too much to ask that someone might simply provide him with Angela and Connor's address here in Jerome—he could tell the woman at the co-op had known and had withheld that vital piece of information—but he still knew much more than he had even ten minutes ago.

Sooner or later, he'd be able to track them down…and the artifacts as well.

13

BILL WAS RIGHT ON TIME. NOT THAT BRIANNA had expected anything less of him, but still, it was nice to know he could be relied on not to show up half an hour late with a mouthful of excuses.

She didn't have a lot of patience for that kind of behavior, not after one of her college boyfriends had been the type of person to have only a nodding acquaintance with anything remotely resembling a schedule.

And she also noted that today Bill was much more casual, in faded jeans and hiking boots and a light blue T-shirt. A pair of sunglasses hung from the neckline of that shirt, although she'd never seen him wear any before and had figured he must be one of those people who didn't have a problem with lots of light.

Apparently not. Or maybe he'd come to

realize after spending some time in Jerome that the hard, bright sunlight of northern Arizona was a lot different from what he was used to in L.A.

"Ready?" she asked, and he nodded. He'd given a brief glance around the room after she let him in, probably to get an idea of what her furniture and decor were like, but it wasn't as if he'd been openly staring or anything. Since she did pretty much the same thing whenever she was in a new place, she couldn't exactly give him grief for that.

"I'm looking forward to seeing Oak Creek," he said.

So was she. Every once in a great while, she had a gig in Flagstaff, but most of the time, she had no real reason to go that way, which meant she only went into the canyon for the sole purpose of wanting to soak up its beauties.

"I think you'll be pleasantly surprised," she said lightly. "I've already got some bottled water and snacks in Sally, so we're ready to go."

"'Sally'?" he echoed, now looking confused. "Who's that?"

"My Suburban," Brianna replied. "Don't ask me why I gave her that nickname. She just felt like a Sally to me."

His shoulders lifted, but it appeared he was ready to go with the flow, since he only said, "Then let's get in Sally and get going."

Smiling, Bree picked up the backpack-style purse she used for these sorts of outings and slung it over one shoulder, then waited while he stepped onto the landing so she could lock the door behind them. With a key, of course; she wasn't stupid enough to lock up her apartment by merely touching her finger to a door handle with him standing there.

The apartment had one parking space carved out between the rear of the building and the side of the hill directly behind it, and she led him back there so they could both get in the SUV. A moment to back out and another to reorient the vehicle so they were pointing in the right direction to pull onto Main Street, and then they were on their way.

Should she ask him what he'd been up to earlier today? That kind of query felt like regular small talk to her, but she didn't want him to think she was prying or anything.

Probably better to start with the weather. That was innocuous enough.

"I'm glad it's cooler today," she remarked as they made their descent toward Clarkdale. "We'll probably be able to last a little longer."

"Yes, I noticed that," Bill replied. "It feels more like fall."

It did. Not that they probably wouldn't peak in the upper seventies, but that was still better than the mid-eighties it had been for the past week. Brianna tended to keep an eye on the weather reports just because some of her gigs were outdoors and it was always good to know if there might be a last-minute switch to an indoor location if it got too windy or started to rain, and from what she could tell, Jerome was supposed to experience a slow cooling trend over the next week.

Yes, autumn really was almost here.

Although they'd driven through Cottonwood before now and on the highway beyond, she noticed that Bill still paid close attention to everything flowing past outside the Suburban's windows. And when they passed the turnoff for Airport Mesa and began driving through the heart of Sedona and into Uptown, he was practically like a little kid with his face glued to the window.

"Gorgeous, isn't it?" she asked, and he nodded.

"The rocks here are different from the ones in the western part of town."

She supposed they were. Or at least, even if they were all red rocks, the shapes here were even more dramatic, and they also revealed a bit more of the geological strata that made up the formations, with the red sandstone giving way to paler limestone and granite on their lower elevations.

"Every part of Sedona has its own unique

character, I suppose," she said as they maneuvered around the final roundabout in Uptown and were now heading due north on Highway 89A. "There are some beautiful formations down in the Village of Oak Creek, too, but we're heading in the opposite direction today."

His brows pulled together for a moment—she had a feeling he was wondering why the village named after the creek wasn't their destination—but he didn't say anything. "You were right when you told me the other day that there's a lot to explore around here."

"Of course I was," she said with a grin. "Gotta listen to the people who grew up in the area, you know?"

He smiled as well. "I do know."

They crossed Midgley Bridge, which Bree always thought of as the true entrance to the canyon, although Oak Creek had been glittering far beneath the highway for a while now. But the water had begun to climb with them, and now it was there to their right, waters dancing in the sun as the creek made its way over rocks smoothed by millennia of flow and flood. The landscape grew lusher, with a canopy of cottonwood leaves sheltering them overhead. A few of those leaves had just begun to turn gold, but most of them were still bright green, making it seem as if they'd entered another world.

"It feels so different," Bill said.

"That's because it is," she replied. "Totally different biome. People come up here all the time to escape the heat—not that it doesn't get plenty warm in the canyon at the height of summer, but there's a lot more shade."

An understatement, to be sure, since there were spots where the road grew almost dark thanks to the high canyon walls on either side and the old, old trees that spread their wide branches in all directions. Crews came through every once in a while to cut things back, true, but she could still feel a twig scrape against Sally's roof every once in a while.

Well, to be fair, she sat a lot higher than most modern, low-slung electric vehicles.

"So, where exactly are we going?" Bill asked after they passed the Indian Gardens market, its parking lot crowded with cars, and showed no signs of slowing.

"West Fork," she said. "The trailhead is about two more miles farther into the canyon."

And she had to pray it wouldn't be too crowded. There hadn't been a lot of traffic on 89A so far, but she'd spied more cars than she'd expected as they drove past Slide Rock State Park, which meant she wasn't sure what to expect.

Part of being a local, though, was knowing where they could park if the lot at the trailhead was full. They could go a little farther and then slip down a private driveway onto a property that belonged to the same people who owned the Haunted Hamburger and a bunch of other local restaurants. That driveway was open season for any McAllister who wanted to use it, and since Bree knew the Suburban was instantly recognizable as hers, she doubted there would be any problem with her leaving it there.

However, the lot at the trailhead was only half full, so she didn't have to resort to that particular backup plan. Most likely, a lot of the hikers had come and gone already, which meant that the ten-odd people or so who'd left their cars in the parking lot were probably spread out enough on the trail that the chances of bumping into them were pretty low.

Bree couldn't even say for sure why it was so important for her and Bill to have some privacy. It wasn't as though she expected anything to happen between them out here.

Not really.

But she knew she liked peace and quiet when she hiked, and having a bunch of people chattering about the scenery or their dinner plans or whatever didn't exactly make for an optimal experience. Talking quietly with Bill was one thing, but getting stuck in the middle of other people's conversations was something else entirely.

They got out of the SUV and went around to the back, where she'd stowed the pack that held several bottles of water and a few snacks.

"Do you mind carrying that?" she asked. "I mean, I could, but I've already got my own backpack."

"Not at all," he said, then reached into the cargo area so he could pick up the backpack and slide it on. "Which way?"

She probably should have known he wouldn't have a single complaint about being the designated pack mule. Her backpack purse wasn't exactly for show, either, since she had a first aid kit, sunscreen, and various other useful odds and ends in there, but still, it was good to know he hadn't even considered that she probably could have carried both.

The GPS app on her phone was running, too, although the West Fork trail was so well-marked and traveled that it would be pretty difficult for them to lose their way. Cell reception in the canyon was crap, but the GPS worked whether or not they were in reach of a tower.

"Over here," she said as she made her way to the sign pointing toward the trailhead. "Honestly, it's pretty easy to follow."

"Good to know," he replied, then slipped on his sunglasses. "I'm not what you could call the world's most experienced hiker."

"Indoor guy?" she asked with a grin. She wasn't sure she entirely believed that—the muscles his T-shirt showed off could have been acquired in a home gym, she supposed, but his tan looked entirely natural.

"I like to walk," he said. "And garden. I just don't do a lot of hiking."

A gardener, huh? Bree hadn't really imagined that hobby for him, but she had to admit it was a useful and interesting one. She'd always helped her mother in the garden at home, and actually missed being there to deadhead the roses and pull weeds now that she was living at the apartment. Sure, she had some houseplants to tend and a planter with flowers on the balcony, but it wasn't exactly the same thing.

"You have a big yard?" she asked as they began to make their way along the trail. Here at the starting point, it was only a path that cut through sycamores and cottonwoods and pines, but soon enough, they began to wind their way along the bank of Oak Creek, and the red rock canyon walls grew closer, nearly overhanging the water in some places.

"Big enough," he said. "Anyway, there's something peaceful about working with plants. It's good to watch them grow and flourish."

Not for the first time, Brianna reflected that Bill Garrett was quite an unusual guy. No flaunting of his wealth, no pretense, just someone who'd been lucky enough to inherit a bunch of money but wasn't about to let it change him into something he wasn't.

"My mother would love to hear that," she remarked. "She's always puttering around in the garden."

And then Bree wondered if that had been entirely the wrong thing to say. After all, Bill hadn't met her parents, and there was no reason for him to. You didn't introduce a guy you were seeing to your parents until things were pretty serious, and she knew the situation with him was anything but that.

Or…maybe it was serious, in some strange way, but not in the way most people would probably think.

But then he startled her by saying, "Your parents seem very nice."

She came to a stop then and stared up at him in surprise. "You *met* them?"

"I did," he said, looking singularly unperturbed. "That is, I didn't know they were your parents at first. We bumped into each other while we were watching you play at the folk festival."

All right, that explanation made a little more sense. The crowd had been big, but it wasn't so big that you might not run into someone you knew… or someone that a person you knew was acquainted with. And her parents would have done their best to be near the stage, just as Bill probably had.

She hadn't seen them standing near each other, but that didn't mean much. The crowd had been one big blur to her, probably her mind's way of trying to prevent her from paying attention to any single person's reaction to her performance.

Still….

"Why didn't you tell me you met them?" she asked, and now he looked a little confused.

"I suppose I didn't think it was all that important," he replied. "We spoke a little, but mostly, we were just listening to you play and sing. And afterward, I headed off to Vino Zona because I thought you might like a drink as a way to decompress. Was that wrong?"

No, it wasn't. He'd known exactly what she needed, and she had a feeling that if he'd brought up how he'd seen her parents in the crowd, she would have tensed up again, wondering if she should ask him what they'd thought or whether she should dismiss the encounter.

Really, this was a silly thing to get worked up over. He'd told her now, when the stakes were a lot lower, so she should probably just let it go.

"It's fine," she said. "Maybe even a little funny that you were standing near them out of all the people in that crowd."

"I suppose that's one way of looking at it." He slid the backpack off his shoulder, unzipped it, and then pulled out a bottle of water. "Do you want some?"

They'd only gone about a half mile, but she was still a little thirsty. "Sure."

He handed it over to her, and she drank about a quarter of the bottle before giving it back.

"You can open a fresh one," she told him, since he was now looking a little hesitant.

"That would be wasteful, wouldn't it?"

And he lifted the bottle to his lips and drank a bit more than she had.

Well, at least now you know he isn't worried about swapping spit with you, ran through her mind.

She brushed away the thought as best she could. Sharing a bottle was one thing.

Sharing a kiss?

That was something else altogether.

No point in shaking her head at herself, not when Bill had already returned the half-drunk bottle to the backpack and replaced it on his shoulders.

They set out again, with her keeping to the same leisurely pace. She didn't have any real intention of doing the entire fourteen-mile hike, not when they'd have to wade in the creek at some point to keep going, so there was no reason to push themselves. This was all about getting out in nature and enjoying the sights, and sticking with the easy but still scenic part of the route, which was just a little over three miles.

He seemed content to be quiet and pay attention to the nature all around them, and she was grateful for that. Of course she liked talking to him—he was easier to talk to than any other man she'd ever known—but when she was out on a hike like this, she wanted to pay attention to her surroundings. They could save the conversation for drinks afterward, or dinner, or whatever they decided to do.

If anything at all. He hadn't said anything about that on the drive here, so maybe he was expecting to just head back to Jerome after they were done with their hike and call it a day.

She sure hoped not, though.

Up ahead was one of her favorite spots, a sort of natural shelf that jutted into the creek and was a perfect place to stop and maybe dangle their feet in the water. Although the air was cooler here, the steady uphill climb had warmed her enough that she thought it might be good to peel off her socks and hiking boots and give her a chance to cool down.

When she mentioned the idea to Bill, he seemed just fine with it, so after they reached the spot in question, she stopped and took off her purse backpack, then bent down to unlace her hiking boots and remove them, and finally her socks. He followed suit, and soon they were both sitting on the ledge, their feet dangling in the water. It was quite cold—it always was, even at the height of summer, since the creek was fed by snow melt from the San Francisco Peaks in Flagstaff—but it was also refreshing, even though she knew she couldn't sit here like this forever.

"It feels so far away from the rest of the world here," he said.

"Well, we're almost a mile off the highway now, so it's hard to hear much of anything."

Only the soft whisper of the breeze in the leaves, and the murmur of the creek, and the happy songs of the birds in the trees. Far overhead, a dark shape in the sky might have been a hawk or even an eagle, but it was too high for Bree to be able to tell for sure.

"I like that about this part of the world," Bill commented. He'd also lifted his head to the sky, as though he'd spotted the hawk as well. "There are plenty of people, but it's not difficult to find a place where you can be alone with your thoughts."

She shifted a little on the rock, just enough so she could see him better instead of looking directly at the creek. His expression was thoughtful, but because he still wore his sunglasses, she had a harder time guessing exactly what he might be thinking.

"Yes, I suppose it's harder to be alone in L.A."

He didn't answer at once. Bree thought she saw his jaw tighten, but she wasn't quite sure what to make of that response.

When he spoke, his words were unexpected.

"It's always difficult when you don't want to listen to what those thoughts are trying to tell you."

She wasn't sure how to reply to such a remark. As far as she could tell, he was being completely honest with her, so saying something lighthearted didn't feel right.

"Maybe they were telling you that you needed to get away."

Now his mouth curved just a little, although she still couldn't call the expression he wore a smile.

"And I did get away," he said. "I got away to Jerome…and I found you."

His voice was quiet, but she couldn't mistake the intensity of his tone.

At a loss, she sat there, toes still dipping into the cold water, a cardinal somewhere off in the distance singing out its distinctive *chip chip chip,* followed by a small trill.

She wanted to tell Bill how glad she was that they'd found each other, but even though she had no problem spilling the contents of her thoughts into her songs, her tongue felt somehow tied when it came to saying those sorts of things out loud.

Then he shifted his position just enough so he could reach into the front pocket of his jeans and pull out a small box. "I got you something," he said.

Everything about her seemed to freeze. Then the rational side of her brain took over, and she realized that wasn't a ring box he was holding, but one that was much flatter, the kind of thing you might use for a pendant or maybe a pair of earrings.

Her heart began beating again. "You didn't have to do that."

"I know," he said calmly. "But I wanted to."

And he handed the box to her.

It wasn't very heavy. Her fingers closed around it, even as her brain registered that this kind of brown recycled paper box was the kind they used at McAllister Mercantile.

Plus probably a million other stores, her brain added, but she had a feeling her first instinct had been correct, if for no other reason than Bill didn't seem to want to go very far afield unless she was playing chauffeur.

Sitting there and holding it for too long

would have been impossibly awkward. So she swallowed and opened the little box.

Lying inside was a silver pendant set with a greenish-blue, heavily veined stone surrounded by a framework of dark blue topaz and small rose-cut diamonds. Bree recognized the piece at once, mostly because she'd been coveting the thing ever since she first saw it in the display case at McAllister Mercantile. It was Angela's work, and fairly priced for what it was, but she hadn't been able to justify the cost when she already had plenty of jewelry.

"It's—it's beautiful," she said, and something about Bill's posture seemed to relax a little.

"You like it? When I saw it earlier today, something about it reminded me of you."

Shades of blue and green, just like they'd discussed a few days earlier. The London blue topaz had the faintest greenish undertone, making it an interesting but also perfect companion to the center variscite. Angela did a lot of that, pairing stones that at first you might not have imagined together but then couldn't see any other way.

"I love it," Bree said. "And I'd put it on right now, but it's probably safer in the box."

"It didn't come with a chain anyway," Bill responded, now practical. "You wouldn't have had anything to hang it on."

Well, that was true. She probably had a cord

stashed somewhere in her backpack because she always carried stuff like that around just in case, but better to wait until she could put it on a real chain, or maybe one of the thin leather cords with silver clasps she tended to prefer for hanging her pendants.

She carefully closed the box and then secured it in one of the inner pockets of her purse, zipping it tight so there was no chance of her present going anywhere. Then she turned back to him.

"Thank you, Bill. That was...super thoughtful."

While she was messing with her backpack, he must have taken off his sunglasses, because now his eyes met hers, intensely green, reflecting the hues of the leaves overhead.

"I'm always thinking of you," he said simply.

Did he lean in first, or was she the one who moved closer to him? She couldn't say for sure. All she knew was that in the next moment, their lips were touching. His arms went around her, stronger than she'd expected despite the muscles his T-shirt revealed.

Time seemed to stop, or at the very least, the world went on around them while Bree thought she and Bill must have been suspended somewhere outside it, in a perfect moment when nothing mattered except the sensation of his mouth against hers, a certain sweetness to his taste that might have been from the water they'd drunk a while earlier.

Or maybe that was just him.

The kiss went on and on, her entire body thrilling at the embrace, all honey and gold, but at last, he let go. His gaze met hers, worried.

"Should I have done that? I thought—"

She needed to let him know that yes, it was exactly what he should have done, so she pulled him close again and kissed him, kissed him hard, hoping that he could sense the passion in her touch, the need…the belief that this was the perfect thing for both of them.

It seemed she got through, because when they pulled apart again, that delicious mouth of his had lifted at the corners.

"I see you're all right with this."

"More than all right," she said frankly. "If I'm going to be perfectly honest about it, I've been thinking about kissing you for the past couple of days. But I wasn't sure if that was what you wanted, not when…."

The words trailed off. She had the feeling that if she uttered them out loud, then she'd make that part of their situation far too real.

Not when you'll have to go back to L.A. at some point.

His hand found hers, and he squeezed it gently.

"We don't have to talk about that right now," he said. "I'll be here through the end of the week, and then—"

"And then what?" she broke in. Maybe that was rude of her, but she needed to have some idea of where she stood.

"And then we'll decide what to do next." He paused there, his eyes locking on her face as if he hoped the mere intensity of his gaze would be enough to show her that he didn't plan on going anywhere.

It wasn't a promise to stay here forever. Then again, it also wasn't a statement that he planned to get on the next plane headed for L.A.

Bree wasn't going to push things.

Not when she knew she'd found the only man in the world for her.

She also gave his fingers a squeeze, then let go and pushed herself to her feet. During their kiss, she'd pulled them from the water, so they were damp but not dripping wet and probably ready for her to put her socks and hiking boots back on.

"Okay," she said clearly. "Now, let's go finish our hike."

14

H<small>E'D DONE IT, EVEN THOUGH ALL OF HIS</small> instincts had been screaming at him not to succumb, not to lean over and press his mouth against Brianna McAllister's sweet, full lips.

Was it this human body he wore? Had its own needs somehow managed to overtake his common sense, making him do something that under normal circumstances, he would never have even considered?

Belshegar couldn't begin to say. The only thing he knew for certain was that there was no coming back from what had just happened.

If he truly were Bill Garrett, the man he was pretending to be, then he supposed he could have called an airport shuttle to take him to Phoenix and get him safely away. Unfortunately, he didn't have that option, cowardly as such an escape might have been.

He was bound to stay in Jerome until the artifacts were found.

But even though he knew he had made a colossal mistake…even though he knew there was no possible future for him and Brianna… all he could think about was how much he wanted to kiss her again.

And they had kissed one more time before they rose and put on their hiking boots and socks, and followed the path of Oak Creek until the passage became somewhat treacherous, and Bree told him this was where they should turn around and head home.

Neither of them had spoken very much, and he could tell she was lost in her own thoughts, doing her best to process what had happened. For all he knew, she was berating herself just as much as he; while she wasn't an extradimensional being pretending to be mortal, she was still a witch with a father who was a little more than that, and no doubt she thought that getting involved with a civilian who lived so far away wasn't a very wise thing to do.

And yet, here they both were.

It was nearing five when they reached the parking lot, which was now empty. They'd passed one couple on the trail and heard voices in another spot, but otherwise, they seemed to have had the creek and its accompanying path all to themselves.

Probably a good thing. Belshegar wasn't sure if he could have managed to maintain his composure if they'd been surrounded by humans wanting to chat about the trail and the scenery, or whatever inane subject such interlopers might have thought of.

When that thought passed through his mind, however, he knew he wasn't being entirely fair. Under other circumstances, he might have found such conversations enlightening, since he learned a little bit more about humans every time he had a chance to talk with them.

Today, however, he only wanted to climb into Brianna's ancient, lumbering hulk of a vehicle and get out of here.

It wasn't until after they'd pulled out of the parking lot and were driving back down the highway that she spoke again.

"If you—if you think that was a mistake, I understand. We can just be casual. I know starting up a long-distance thing is kind of a lot."

His mind wanted to tell him it had been a mistake. His heart, on the other hand, knew better.

"It wasn't a mistake," he replied at once, then reached over to touch her hand briefly where it rested on the steering wheel. "I've felt drawn to you since the first time we met. But…."

"But your life is in Los Angeles," she finished for him. "I get it."

Well, she thought she did. The truth was just a bit more complicated.

"It isn't much of a life," he said frankly, and she sent him a sideways look, obviously surprised by the comment.

To be fair, he was a little startled himself. True, he'd been talking about his existence on his own plane, and not this mythical life in L.A. that he'd concocted for himself, and yet the bones of the remark had been true enough. Perhaps once he'd been content to tend his gardens and just be, but ever since Elena had summoned him that first time so many years ago, he'd found himself increasingly fascinated by all the intricacies of human existence, by its utter messiness and passion and vibrancy. Every time he returned to his own plane, he tried to tell himself that this was better, that the peace and calm and gentle monotony were far preferable to being caught up in so many complications.

Those inner arguments had rung more and more hollow as the years progressed.

But what in the world was he supposed to do? Surely he couldn't be contemplating staying here and pretending to be Bill Garrett for the rest of his days.

Even if such a thing was physically possible, Belshegar had a feeling the voice might have a few words to say on the subject, none of them what he wanted to hear.

"I...stay at home most of the time," he continued, since he could tell Brianna had been waiting for him to elaborate.

"Why?"

Another lie, although this one was at least somewhat close to the truth.

"Because it seemed simpler that way."

She went silent then, graceful brows pulling together slightly as she maneuvered her oversized vehicle with grace and skill along the winding road. "You don't strike me as an antisocial person. Maybe not a party animal, but...."

Belshegar hadn't heard the phrase before, but he could guess at its meaning well enough...especially since he'd met a few specimens, most notably Elena's cousin Tony Castillo, who fit that description well enough based on their behavior at her wedding reception.

"That's because I'm here," he said. "Jerome feels...different."

Now Brianna chuckled, a laugh that sounded natural enough. "Well, that's true. Jerome does have a certain magic."

A lot of magic, considering how many witch-folk lived there. However, her comment wasn't anything that would have raised eyebrows among the civilian population, not when they used that word in plenty of situations that had nothing to do with real magic.

"It does," he agreed, then surprised himself by adding, "And so do you."

Her lips—those beautiful, kissable lips—pursed for a moment. "I don't know about that. But…thank you."

They left it there as they continued to drive through the canyon. Strangely, though, Belshegar thought they'd both come to an agreement…even if neither of them wanted to discuss the topic further.

The next morning, the guilt hadn't abated much—especially since he and Brianna had kissed goodnight when he saw her to her door after an extended dinner at a place in Page Springs called Up the Creek—but he knew he had to do what he could to find the artifacts. Doing so was the only way to atone for the way he'd all but ignored his mission and instead had focused on spending as much time as possible with the woman he loved.

It was the first time the word "love" had

passed through his mind. As much as he wanted to ignore it, or tell himself he was making this out to be much more than it was, he knew better. He loved Brianna McAllister.

And he had no idea what to do about it.

Today, luckily, he'd been granted something of a reprieve, just because she'd told him she would be busy for most of the day, first watching the gallery because the owner had business down in Phoenix, and then teaching several music lessons late in the afternoon. He didn't want to think of being away from Brianna as a blessing or anything close to it, but he knew if she was safely occupied elsewhere and he wasn't distracted by her presence, then he'd have a much better chance of locating the artifacts.

He had his usual breakfast of toast and fruit, accompanied by green tea, and then settled down to strategize. A few online searches had told him it wouldn't be as easy as simply typing in Angela McAllister's name and discovering her current address. A helpful comment in an online forum told him one could usually look up the owner of a property by typing in an address or parcel number, but he didn't have that, obviously. No, he'd have to use the power of deduction.

It seemed clear enough to him that her home must be located somewhere on Paradise Lane. The street wasn't all that large, and probably comprised twenty houses at most. He already knew it wasn't the big yellow house with the green trim, since that one belonged to Levi and Hayley McAllister.

And although he hadn't particularly noticed a pink house—probably because it was too small to be a viable home for the clan's *prima* and her consort—he also knew to ignore that one when he saw it, since it belonged to Brianna's older brother, Shane.

So that narrowed things down to roughly eighteen houses or so. Most likely, he could eliminate even more based purely on size, since there were only about five or six that appeared to be around the same square footage as Levi's home.

Also, Brianna's father had already seen him sketching on the street and appeared to have given him his blessing to continue with such activities— and, perhaps, had told his neighbors not to be alarmed by a stranger standing around in their neighborhood and drawing this house or that—so Belshegar had no reason to believe anyone who lived there would have much of a problem if he made a repeat appearance today.

That was why he picked up his sketchbook, slid two pencils into the spiral binding, and headed out of the hotel a little before eleven. He thought by that hour everyone should be up and about and off to work or school, so there would be less chance of him disturbing the residents.

Or being seen by them.

Sure enough, Paradise Lane appeared utterly deserted when he arrived. He paused in front of the yellow house that was Brianna's childhood home and surveyed the rest of the houses on the street. The white one with the green shutters appeared to be the largest, but there was also a home several doors down that nearly rivaled it in size, and boasted a fancy turret with stained-glass windows as well.

Either of them seemed to be likely candidates to be the *prima's* house, and Belshegar frowned, not sure which one he should try first.

Perhaps the one with the turret, if for no other reason than it seemed slightly more architecturally interesting than the other, and if he had to start somewhere, he might as well begin with the one that would be more of a challenge to draw.

He had only taken a few steps in that direction, however, when the door to the big white house opened and Levi McAllister emerged.

Belshegar froze. Every instinct was telling him to flee, even though he knew doing so would make him look much more guilty than standing his ground and acting as if he had every right to be there.

Besides, Levi had caught sight of him and lifted his hand in a wave, and Belshegar could do little else but wave back.

It's fine, he told himself. *Levi McAllister knows why you like to come up here and sketch. In fact, he practically gave you permission. You have nothing to worry about.*

He wished he could tell that to the human heart beating within his breast, for it had sped up more than he would have liked.

By that point, Levi was only a few feet away, so Belshegar managed to smile at the other man as he approached.

"Back to sketching?" the man who wasn't quite a man asked, and Belshegar nodded.

"It's cooler today, so I thought it would be good to spend more time outdoors."

At least that wasn't a lie. The temperatures had remained much more comfortable, and he could practically sense the arrival of autumn now—not so surprising, considering that October was only a few days off.

"Yes, it sounds as if we're going to have a run of good weather," Levi agreed.

However, he didn't follow up that comment with a casual "goodbye" or "have a nice day," but instead remained standing there, his eyes narrowing ever so slightly, as if in speculation.

A thrill of unease went through Belshegar, even as he told himself there was no reason to be so on edge. He didn't know the other man well at all, so he couldn't pretend to be an expert in his shifts in expression or how he reacted to certain comments.

But then he smiled…although the expression wasn't much more than a lift of his lips. It certainly didn't reach his eyes.

"I think," he said slowly, "that you and I have much to discuss. Why don't you come inside, and we can have a little talk?"

It was framed as a friendly request, but Belshegar knew it wasn't. Once again, he sensed the power rippling out from the other man, an energy that was very different from what he could feel when he was around ordinary witches and warlocks.

Levi McAllister was anything but ordinary.

Perhaps he could try to make excuses, or try to pretend that he didn't understand the need for a private conversation, but he had a feeling he wouldn't get very far with that sort of maneuvering.

No, he'd been fairly caught.

"Very well," he said.

Hayley McAllister didn't appear to be at home, and Belshegar could only be grateful for that. And while Levi appeared to be cordial enough as he invited his guest to take a seat on the living room

246 | CHRISTINE POPE

sofa and asked if he wanted any water or lemonade or iced tea, it was clear enough that he wasn't going to allow his visitor to leave until he had the answers he wanted.

Water sounded like a good idea, considering how dry his human throat felt right then, so Belshegar requested a glass. Levi went into the kitchen to fetch it, and for one desperate moment, Belshegar considered leaping up from the couch and making a run for the door. If he'd been in his own body, he could have simply disappeared outright, but again, he feared that using his powers in such a way might do something to alter or even ruin the disguise the voice had given him, since doing so required much more magic than simply summoning a new shirt or a pair of hiking boots.

So he remained where he was, and a moment later, Levi reappeared with a glass of water in each hand. Something about his expression was almost satisfied, as if he'd set up his brief errand in the kitchen as a sort of test.

It seemed Belshegar had passed.

Levi set down one of the glasses in front of him and then took a seat in one of the chairs that faced the sofa. "So…what are you, exactly? You don't feel quite like Loc."

When had the two unearthly beings met? They lived with different clans in different states, so Belshegar didn't see why there had been any reason for their paths to have crossed.

But although he didn't know the whole story, he did know the past few years had been rather tumultuous for the New Mexico and Arizona witch clans, and perhaps they had worked together at some point.

"I am not like him," Belshegar said calmly. "He is a demon lord, someone who held sway over many others. I am Belshegar. I am…myself."

Levi smiled, and again, it seemed as if he was pleased that his guest hadn't tried to lie about who he was or pretend he didn't know what the other man was talking about. "And who is…yourself?"

"Some have referred to me as a demon, but that is not what I am. I suppose it is easy shorthand for humans who have no concept of how many planes of existence there truly are, and how many other beings inhabit them."

"Well, that's true enough," Levi replied. "At the same time, it's not exactly usual that someone like you would have any business on this plane. So I must ask…what precisely are you doing in Jerome?"

Although he stopped there, Belshegar got the distinct impression that Levi would have liked to follow up the one question with yet another.

And what are you doing with my daughter?

He swallowed. It had already been hard

enough to conceal who he was and dance around the truth, simply because lying was not part of his nature, and he had to work at it.

And hate himself the whole time.

Rather than reply right away, he reached for the glass of water Levi had provided and took a swallow. It helped his dry throat somewhat, but Belshegar thought he would only be truly comfortable once he was away from this place... and the piercing stare of Levi McAllister's cool blue eyes.

Levi's next question was an unexpected one. "Are you being coerced?"

Belshegar sat up a little straighter. Could he answer honestly?

Perhaps. As long as he didn't say who was doing the coercing, at any rate.

Because if he could somehow make Levi understand the truth of his situation, then perhaps the other man would be able to come up with a way to get him out from under the voice's thumb.

"I—"

"So you are," Levi cut in. His tone was mild, but a flicker of anger still showed in his eyes. "That is...unfortunate. May I ask what you are being forced to do?"

Belshegar shifted on the sofa. It was comfortable enough, he supposed, and yet he wished with all his might that he could get out of there.

For some reason, his gaze moved upward.

Could the voice hear what they were saying?

Levi must have noticed, because he said quietly, "This house is warded…and protected by my powers as well. Nothing that happens here can be detected by anyone else, no matter how powerful the being attempting such an intrusion might be."

Those words were something of a relief, and yet Belshegar couldn't help wondering how true they actually were. Although he didn't doubt that Levi was certainly powerful enough to repel any magical intrusions from a mortal user of magic, did that apply to someone as powerful as the voice, a being who had a seat on the Council?

"I fear that those whose bidding I must do are not precisely human."

For some reason, Levi didn't look too perturbed by his guest's statement. He also reached over to pick up his glass of water, although he didn't drink right away, instead saying, "Just because they aren't human doesn't mean they're innately more powerful. I've lived among mortals for nearly thirty years, and yet they still continue to surprise me."

"I want to believe you," Belshegar replied.

Levi didn't blink. "You should."

A brief silence fell. Both men drank some water—probably because they couldn't think of what else to do—and it became clear to Belshegar that Levi was waiting for him to respond, and seemed content to remain quiet until his guest found the courage to speak.

What could he say, though?

The truth, of course.

Those words echoed in his mind, and he realized they were correct. It seemed that Levi was trying to offer some form of help, and Belshegar would be foolish to refuse it.

"Several artifacts are being held in Jerome by your *prima*," he said. "The voice told me they were here, but it was unable to provide an exact location—I assume because of whatever warding spells might have been placed upon them."

"You assume correctly."

Levi still appeared relaxed enough, but Belshegar had noticed the way he'd sat up a little straighter when the artifacts were mentioned.

So…not quite as casual as he appeared.

But at least now it seemed clear that the wards Angela and Connor—and most likely Levi as well—had placed to conceal the treasures the voice desired were so effective that not even the voice had been able to pierce that powerful magic to discover their location.

"Who is this voice?" Levi asked.

"A member of the Council, I assume."

The other man's head tilted to one side. "And what is this Council? Do they function like the clan elders here in Jerome?"

Belshegar couldn't say for certain, since he knew nothing about the McAllister elders. Brianna certainly wouldn't have mentioned them, not when she was doing her best to conceal her witch nature from everyone around her who wasn't also a witch.

"Possibly," he replied, then sent a curious glance at the other man. "The Council sits above many planes of existence, and has many powerful beings who have roles in ensuring its rules are followed. You are not originally from Earth, so how is it you have never heard of them?"

To his surprise, Levi smiled. "My case is an unusual one. I had consciousness of a sort, but no form, no true reality. It was then that Zoe Sandoval's magic ensnared me and brought me to this plane. I was nearly shapeless when I arrived, and a horror she fled from. It was only after several days that I became the man you see before you now." A pause, and he still appeared somewhat amused as he looked down at himself. "Well, a much younger version, I suppose. But because I had no true existence before I came here, there is very little for me to remember."

Odd, and yet Belshegar knew there were other

consciousnesses like Levi's out there, beings who one day might take shape and form, but who for now were little more than energy with just a bit of self-awareness.

No wonder he had never heard of the Council.

"However," Levi continued, his voice turning brisk, "something about this doesn't feel quite right. I'll admit I don't know anything of this Council of yours, and yet it seems to me that a body so worried about the behavior of those who also exist on other planes shouldn't be concerned with corporeal objects like the artifacts currently in Connor and Angela's keeping."

Belshegar had to admit the other man had a point. However, he knew better than to analyze the Council's motivations, not when they operated on such a higher plane than his.

"I cannot say," he replied. A weak response, but the only one he felt he could possibly give. "I never had any dealings with them before now, so I have no real frame of reference."

For a moment, Levi was silent. "This is something I will need to discuss with Angela and Connor—and the other two elders. It's possible they'll see something I can't."

Alarm went through him. The other man's tone had been casual enough, but Belshegar wondered if Levi knew what he was truly saying. To simply reveal his existence, just like that?

"I will explain the situation to them," Levi said, a note of understanding now in his tone. "You don't need to worry that they'll make you leave. I'll vouch for you."

Belshegar wanted to believe that.

But....

"Even though—" he began, and Levi smiled again.

"Yes, even though you're seeing my daughter."

While he'd never been on a rollercoaster, Belshegar thought the ebb and flow of his emotions during this conversation must be something like that—worry, then relief…then worry all over again.

He found his voice. "Brianna told you?"

"No," Levi replied at once. "She doesn't discuss her private life with us very much…well, not until things get serious, which hasn't happened very often. But her mother told me she's sounded happier when she's talked to her on the phone these past few days…and I saw the way you were looking at her when she was performing at the folk festival on Saturday. It seemed clear to me that something was going on between you two, even if I couldn't say for sure exactly what it was."

So many thoughts were passing through

Belshegar's mind, he wasn't quite sure where to start. Somehow he found his voice, though, and said, "You're not going to forbid me to see her, when you know what I am?"

Now Levi chuckled—but not in a scornful way. No, it seemed more that he was laughing at himself.

"Considering who I am and where I came from, that would make me quite the hypocrite, wouldn't it?"

It was an angle Belshegar hadn't considered, but he supposed he could see why Levi might think that. "So…I have your permission to continue to see her?"

"She's a grown woman who can make her own choices," Levi replied. "She certainly doesn't need my permission—or her mother's—when it comes to her private life. However…."

The words trailed off, as if Levi wasn't quite sure what he should say next.

"However?" Belshegar prompted.

Those blue eyes were suddenly sharp as lasers.

"If you hurt her…if you're only amusing yourself while you're here…then I'll make sure you have justice, whether on this plane or the next."

15

THANK THE GODDESS FOR BUSYWORK. CHELLE had left a bunch of invoices for Brianna to orga-nize—a task she guessed wasn't strictly necessary, considering the gallery's books were all digital—but she didn't mind.

Not when making sure each invoice went in the right file folder helped somewhat to keep her mind off Bill Garrett.

All right, she was totally fooling herself. No matter what she did, she couldn't seem to stop herself from thinking about how his mouth had felt pressed against hers…how she still got flutters all through her body at the mere memory of that kiss, or the ones that had followed.

Always the gentleman, he hadn't asked to come inside when he walked her to her apartment door. He'd kissed her again, of course, but then said he'd be in touch about dinner, that he wasn't sure when he'd be able to call, but he'd make contact well before six.

From some men, that might have sounded like a total brush-off, although she had a feeling a lot of them wouldn't have tried to ghost her until after they got her in bed. Joke was on them, though—she might have been fooled like that when she was young and stupid and in her first year of college, but now that she was the ripe old age of almost twenty-four, no way was she doing anything with a guy until at least the fourth or fifth date, just to be safe.

Although she supposed that if you counted up all her various dinners and outings with Bill and wanted to be technical about it, then they'd already reached that milestone.

However, it seemed clear he wasn't going to push things. And because she somehow knew with the same certainty as the sun rising in the morning that he'd call her right when he promised, she wasn't going to let herself worry about that part of the equation.

No, she should really be worrying about what was going to happen on Monday, the day he'd said he was going back to Los Angeles. True, he'd switched his travel dates before, so there was no reason in the world why he couldn't switch them again, but she assumed at some point the rubber would meet the road and he'd have to go home, if only to handle any business he couldn't take care of online or over the phone.

She didn't think she could bear that.

Maybe she could go with him? L.A. was in Santiago clan territory, but they'd been neutrally friendly with the McAllisters ever since the Escobars had been ousted, so maybe it wasn't outside the bounds of possibility that she might be able to tag along for a visit.

Assuming, of course, that Bill even wanted her there.

She had to believe he did. Maybe she'd dated a couple of scumbags over the years, but none of their kisses had felt anything like Bill's, and she wanted to believe he cared about her just as much as she cared about him. If he was faking the connection between them, then someone needed to give that man an Oscar.

A few customers came and went. Not many, because it was a Tuesday and even when the weather was as lovely as it was today, you just didn't get as many visitors to Jerome as you did on a weekend or holiday.

But then the bells on the shop door jingled, and Bree was surprised to see her mother walk in.

"Hi, Mom," she said, and began to stuff the unsorted invoices back into their original manila envelope. There was no way she would have been able to sort them all in one day, anyway.

Her mother looked beautiful and breezy as always, her long blonde hair pulled back into a ponytail and tied with a scarf in happy shades of green and yellow and blue. "Hi, Bree," she said. "I was just down at a meeting at Helen's, so I thought I'd drop by and see how you were doing."

How her mom managed to stay in the same room with Helen Doyle for longer than ten minutes and not want to pull her hair out, Brianna had no idea. But Hayley McAllister was passionate about preserving Jerome's history—maybe even more passionate than some of those who'd been born there—and Bree supposed her mother simply bit her tongue when necessary and reminded herself that she was working for the greater good.

"Didn't you just have a meeting last week?" she asked. After all, that was the whole reason why Helen had insisted on having her new painting hung right away—so it would be in place when the historical preservation society showed up for tea that afternoon.

"We did," Hayley replied, looking unperturbed. "But that was just our usual monthly meeting. This time we were getting together to discuss the rummage sale."

Right. Time had been slipping by so quickly

that Bree had almost forgotten that the society's famous rummage sale would be happening in less than two weeks. Jerome's residents unearthed an astonishing collection of treasures from the attics and basements of their vintage homes, and people came from all over the region to shop for that one special antique they needed to complete their collections.

"That's a lot of Helen in a short amount of time," Bree said with a grin.

Her mother only shrugged. "It's fine. And this year's sale is going to be even bigger and better, so we're all willing to put up with a little pain to make it happen." She paused there, head tilted to one side as she regarded her daughter. "But that's not really why I stopped by."

"It isn't?" Brianna responded. She kept her tone light…but she also had a feeling she already knew the reason for her mother's visit.

"You know we'd never tell you not to date a civilian—" Hayley began, but Bree didn't let her get any further than that.

"I do know," she cut in. "Because I've already done it several times."

"Yes," her mother said. "I can't help thinking this situation is different, though. I've heard this Bill Garrett isn't even from Arizona?"

She made the comment on a slightly upward

inflection, but Bree had no doubt that her mother already knew a whole lot about Bill.

Small town living, she thought, and held back a sigh. It was hardly worth wondering who'd been blabbing, although she did it anyway. Tally, down at Bocce? Lila, who worked part-time at the Grand Hotel?

Word always got around, no matter how careful you were.

"He seems very nice," Hayley continued.

"But?" Bree ventured. Since Bill had already told her that he'd bumped into her parents at the folk festival, she couldn't be surprised to hear from her mother that they'd met. "I mean, I assume there must be a 'but.'"

"Just that long-distance relationships can be difficult," her mother said.

"How would you know?"

All right, that question sounded more than a little hostile. Still, Brianna thought it was fair enough. Her mother had met her father right here in Jerome, and they'd never been separated since —not for more than a few hours at a time, anyway. The only things Hayley McAllister could have possibly known about being in a long-distance relationship would have been whatever she gleaned from books and movies and maybe online magazine articles or blogs.

It seemed her mother must have been

thinking about the same thing, because she didn't look angry at her daughter's confrontational tone, only worried. "I don't have any personal experience with it, true," she said. "But still, it complicates things. And that's not even taking into account the whole witch/civilian thing."

"Maybe I'm just amusing myself," Bree suggested, but her mother only gave her a smile that was somehow sad and knowing at the same time.

"You know you don't do that," Hayley said. "Most of us don't. It's just not in our natures. We want to be with the person who's our other half, and we don't waste time on anyone who isn't a real possibility of being 'the one.'"

Since her mother was only speaking the truth, Brianna knew there weren't many arguments she could present that would make a lot of sense. Sure, here and there you'd find the odd witch or warlock who seemed okay with casual dating and hook-ups and wasn't looking to settle down, but they were few and far between.

And she'd never been like that. She hadn't been as set on being with civilians as her brother, but she'd gone out with a couple when it seemed as if the pool of Wilcoxes or safely distant McAllister cousins was starting to feel a little shallow. Although she knew she would have bristled at being called romantic, she knew she was, deep down.

She wanted to believe she would have the kind of happily ever after that her parents had enjoyed…the same thing that most of the witches and warlocks of her acquaintance shared.

Was it possible to have that with Bill, despite his being a civilian and from somewhere far away? During their last talk, he'd almost made it sound as if he was all right with picking up stakes and leaving L.A. behind. Not in so many words, true, but she couldn't blame him for being the slightest bit cagey, considering how new their relationship was.

At least she thought it was all right to think of their connection in those terms now that they'd shared several kisses.

"I suppose I'm just seeing where it all goes," she said, which was about all she could tell her mother at this point. "Maybe we'll enjoy each other's company for a bit and then go our separate ways. The only thing I know for sure is that he's a good guy."

Hayley tilted her head, and one end of the scarf tied around her ponytail slipped over one shoulder. "You tried looking into his mind?"

"No," Bree said a little more severely than she needed to. The sharpness in her tone probably arose from the realization that she actually had considered doing that very thing and then had decided against it. It just hadn't felt right.

Also, there was the very real possibility that she wouldn't have been able to manage it at all. She might have possessed a baker's dozen of talents, but getting any one of them to cooperate at a given time was problematic at best.

"I just know he's a good person," she went on. "He's shown it to me in dozens of little ways. We might not have known each other for very long, but we've spent a lot of time together. If he was playing me, I have to believe I would feel it."

For a long moment, her mother didn't say anything. Then she raised her shoulders ever so slightly, not in a shrug but in a sort of acknowledgment that Bree most likely knew better than she what was going on with Bill Garrett.

"Are you seeing him again soon?" Hayley asked, apparently deciding that she needed to go with the flow on this one for now…and also realizing that she'd provide a shoulder to cry on if necessary.

Bree doubted that was going to happen. Even if she and Bill came to nothing in the end, she just wasn't the sort to indulge in histrionics when a relationship fell apart.

Then again, if any person had the ability to crush her soul when he walked away, she had a feeling Bill Garrett was that man.

She didn't want to think about that, however.

"Tonight, I think," Bree said. "He was going to call me after I was done with my students late this afternoon."

"Then I suppose we shouldn't expect you for dinner this evening," Hayley said.

Bree wouldn't let herself feel too guilty about that, not when she'd been there just this past week. Although her parents would have liked to have both their kids at the house for Tuesday dinner as often as possible, they all knew that wasn't feasible a lot of the time.

"So, what's Dad up to today?" she asked, thinking it was high time they changed the subject.

"A little of this, a little of that," her mother replied. "He mentioned he was going to meet with Angela and Connor and the other elders today, but he didn't say why."

That bit of information wasn't too unusual. The elders and the *prima* and her consort got together to talk at least once or twice a week when Connor and Angela were in Jerome, and Bree had noticed that those meetings had only increased in frequency after the Collector came on the scene and they had to make doubly sure that the artifacts in their possession were well warded. She had a feeling no one was too thrilled about the extra security measures, especially after the McAllisters had thought the episode with the Escobars was now safely behind them and they could breathe a little easier.

Apparently not.

But since she was just a peon in the greater scheme of things, no one had found the need to discuss such matters with her in depth. It wasn't as if she had a great talent for creating warding spells or could pop off a quick fireball in case Angela and Connor's house was physically threatened. The only thing she could do—the same as the rest of the McAllisters—was to keep her guard up and make sure she reported anything out of the ordinary.

There hadn't been much out of the ordinary in Jerome lately, that was for sure.

Well, except Bill, she supposed, but he was an ordinary sort of extraordinary. He was just a guy, after all. Yes, one who made her heart do a funny little dance and who was the most amazing person she'd ever met, but still, he was a civilian, and the world was full of those.

"I guess let me know if the meeting was about anything important," Brianna said, and her mother nodded.

"I will." She went over to her daughter and gave her a quick hug. "You two have fun tonight."

"Absolutely."

A smile, and then Hayley let herself out the

door. The whole time, they hadn't been interrupted by any customers…it was a very slow day…but almost as soon as she left, an older couple came in and began inspecting the paintings that hung in the main part of the gallery. They had the air of those who didn't want to be disturbed while they browsed, and Bree was just fine with that.

She hated pushy salespeople.

Holding back a sigh, she reached under the counter and brought out the box of invoices to be filed.

16

Belshegar might have been surprised by the swiftness with which the meeting was organized, but if there was anything he'd learned during his friendship with Elena and his brief time among the Castillos, it was that witches could act with surprising speed when sufficiently motivated.

Levi had told him to go back to the hotel while he contacted the other elders and Connor Wilcox and Angela McAllister, but Belshegar had been there for less than an hour when his phone beeped to reveal a brief message.

Come to my house at eleven.

He hadn't recognized the phone number but knew the text must have come from Levi. Besides Brianna, her father was the only person in the world who had his contact information.

Anxiety had rippled along all of Belshegar's human nerve endings, but he told himself it was better to sit down with the McAllister elders and see if there was anything they could do to help him. At least they would know the truth…even though he still had no idea how to explain to Brianna why he had come here and why he had been forced to conceal who…what…he really was.

It seemed that Levi must have arranged for his fellow elders to be there before his guest arrived, since they were already seated in the living room when Belshegar was ushered in. Two women, one quite elderly and frail, with her wispy white hair piled up in a messy bun on top of her head and faded blue eyes. In contrast, the other woman was at least a decade younger, if not more, and although her hair was almost entirely silver except for a few strands of its original red around her face, it had been cut in a sleek style that just hit her jaw, and her clothing appeared to be quite stylish.

"Allegra, Tricia," Levi said, inclining his head first toward the older of the two women, and then at the younger one with the bobbed hair, "this is Belshegar, although he is going by the name Bill Garrett while he's here with us."

Belshegar couldn't help being startled by Levi's introduction, simply because he knew he'd never given the man the human name he'd been using. Word must have gotten around somehow, although he hoped the people in the town hadn't learned anything about him beyond that false name.

Both women regarded him with intent eyes, although he didn't detect any real surprise in their expressions. Well, he supposed that Levi would have already explained the situation, and since they had been working for decades with someone whose origins were also not of this world, Belshegar supposed he wasn't quite as much of a novelty as he might have originally thought.

"So, Belshegar," said the woman with the bob —Tricia, he reminded himself, "you were sent here to spy on us?"

"Not precisely," he replied smoothly, although something inside him bristled at the question. "More that I was sent to recover the artifacts that are currently in your *prima's* keeping."

As he spoke, he couldn't help wondering where Angela and Connor were. Surely they should have been included in this conversation?

Levi must have noticed a shift in his expression, because he said, "Connor and Angela are on their way over here now. They were in Prescott because Connor was delivering several of his paintings to a gallery there, but they should be back shortly."

That made some sense, especially when Belshegar recalled how the woman at the artist's co-op had mentioned that Connor also displayed his work in a gallery in that town. A ridiculous sort of name, too. Van Gogh's Ear?

He supposed that didn't matter so much. What mattered was that the *prima* and her consort were even now on their way back to Jerome.

"Why didn't the person who sent you just get the artifacts themselves?" Allegra, the older of the two women, asked.

Belshegar found himself shrugging. Odd how it became easier and easier to use human mannerisms the longer he was among mortals...the longer he inhabited this human body.

"I cannot say," he replied. "But the Council is made up of beings from a plane as far above mine as my own world is above yours, and I suppose it is possible that the voice's non-corporeal form would not allow it to interact with physical artifacts in such a way."

"Which begs the question as to why this 'voice' of yours would even be interested in physical objects at all," Tricia observed, her tone dry.

He had to admit that he hadn't considered that aspect of the situation. "I do not think the voice planned to use them," he said, speaking slowly as he picked his way through the conundrum. "It is more that he believes they have no place on this plane. They are far too powerful."

"Even though they were created by human hands?" Levi said, speaking for the first time after making the introductions.

Belshegar stared at him for a moment. Because he'd known very little about the artifacts other than the mere fact of their existence, he'd had no idea that mortals had made the things in the first place.

"You know this for certain?" he asked, and all three elders exchanged what he thought were worried glances.

"There's very little we know 'for certain,'" Levi said, and now his tone was quite dry. "One of the artifacts was brought to us from the past, and the witch and warlock who found it told us that the McAllister elders of that time had said it was made by witch-folk centuries earlier, users of magic who poured some of their life force into their talismans to give them their power."

Belshegar had never heard of such a thing—everything he knew of witch-kind was that their powers were born within them and awakened after they had been on this earth for a decade or so, and that those gifts certainly did not come from external amulets and talismans and so on.

However, he also knew enough to realize how little he actually did know.

"And the other artifact?"

"That one's origins are far murkier," Tricia said. "It was found very recently, and we know very little about where it came from, since the man carrying it is no longer alive to explain its history."

"Another reason why we have them both locked up and as warded as we can make them," Levi put in. "We know a little about how both of them work, but it just seemed safer to keep them away from everyone."

Yes, that made sense. It was unfortunate there wasn't more information to be had, but Belshegar was relieved to see that the McAllisters were proceeding with an abundance of caution.

The doorbell sounded then, and Levi immediately turned away from the rest of the little group, saying, "That must be Connor and Angela."

He headed toward the foyer, while Allegra glanced over at Belshegar with bright eyes. "How are you enjoying your time in Jerome? It must be very different from what you're used to."

"It is," he replied, relieved that the three of them weren't going to sit there in awkward silence during Levi's absence. "But I like it here very much. The land in this region is quite beautiful."

And it was, whether the view consisted of the purple bulk of the Black Mountain range high above Jerome, or the glowing, energy-charged red rocks of Sedona, or the gently rolling hills with their acres upon acres of sun-golden grass.

She seemed satisfied with that response, settling against the back of her chair even as Levi returned, Connor and Angela a few feet behind him. Since Belshegar had already met them, he knew something of what to expect. However, they seemed far more tense than they'd been at the folk festival—for good reason, he supposed.

Both of them immediately looked over in his direction as soon as they entered the living room. "So, you came here to take the artifacts?" Angela said abruptly, not bothering with any sort of formal introductions.

"To retrieve them," Belshegar replied. A fine point of distinction, he supposed, and yet he wanted everyone listening to understand that he would never have come after them if he hadn't been directed to do so by the voice.

"For this person on the Council, according to what Levi told us," Connor said, and Belshegar nodded.

"Yes. The members of the Council seem to believe those items are far too powerful to be placed in human hands."

"Even though humans made them," Angela said. Her lip didn't quite curl, but he could tell from the angry sparkle in her emerald-hued eyes that she didn't have much use for that particular argument.

"You *believe* they were created by human hands," Belshegar said mildly. "But do you know that as a verified fact, or do you accept that explanation for their origins because you don't have any others?"

A silence fell then, as Angela slanted a look up at her husband, and his shoulders lifted ever so slightly. Both Tricia and Allegra also seemed unsure as to how they should react to such a question.

Levi spoke then, saying, "I've only handled each of the artifacts briefly, but I couldn't sense anything particularly otherworldly about them. And although I'd be the first to admit I don't know as much as I should about this sort of thing, I want to believe that I'd be able to detect something if they weren't of this earth. After all, I was able to note your...unusual energy...easily enough."

He made a good point, Belshegar realized. If Levi really had held the artifacts in his hands, then he should have sensed their strangeness just as easily as he was able to detect Belshegar's.

But if they had been made by humans, the Council shouldn't have had any interest in the things. They were mortal business, something to be ignored, as it couldn't possibly affect anyone on the higher planes.

There seemed to be only one true way to know for certain, though.

"Let me feel them," he said. "I am from one of the higher planes—although not as high as the one the Council occupies—and it should be easy enough for me to tell for certain whether they are as much a part of this earth as the chair I'm sitting on or the rug under my feet."

The three elders looked over at Angela and Connor, both of whom were frowning mightily. It was easy enough to tell that neither of them was too happy with his suggestion.

And yet it might answer this particular question once and for all.

Belshegar spread his hands wide, hoping they could see from his expression and demeanor that he was not trying to play a trick on them.

"You will all be there with me," he said simply. "I am not going to abscond with the artifacts. Even if I wanted to, your combined powers would be more than enough to stop me."

Angela glanced at Levi, whom she clearly viewed as the expert on all things otherworldly, even if he had, as he'd explained, come to this plane as not much more than an unformed spirit and had no real knowledge of other worlds save that they existed.

"He's telling the truth," Levi said, his tone quiet but firm. "While he possesses powers that might seem miraculous to some, he is no demon lord like Loc. We would be able to contain him easily enough."

"I think we should let him see the artifacts," Connor said then. "Because I'm starting to have a suspicion, but there's no point in bringing it up if it turns out that they really were made someplace other than this world."

Questions crowded Angela's eyes, and yet it seemed she was willing to listen to her husband's suggestion, since she nodded after a slight hesitation. "All right. If Levi thinks we can handle him, then I suppose it should be okay."

By some unspoken signal, Tricia and Allegra stood, and Belshegar got up from his chair as well. In that moment, he didn't think he could have even begun to describe the thoughts running through his mind. It seemed almost impossible that they were going to allow him to see the artifacts, to even touch them—but he also knew their assessment of the situation was accurate enough. He was powerful, but in combination, they could defeat him without even blinking an eye.

Not that he would ever go back on his word. He didn't want to think about how the voice would react if it learned that he had held the artifacts in his hands and hadn't made even a single attempt to take them, but he supposed he would deal with that eventuality when the time came.

For now, though, it was enough to follow Connor and Angela out of Levi's home and down the street to the big white Victorian he'd thought could be the *prima's*. However, Belshegar couldn't be too triumphant about that correct guess, not when he'd also speculated that several other houses on Paradise Lane were equally plausible candidates.

In contrast to the almost fussy architecture outside, the interior of the home was simple and yet grand at the same time, with polished dark wood floors and Navajo rugs and plain furniture that had the solidity of something crafted by hand rather than created in a factory. Connor's paintings hung on all the walls, giving the space the sense that it had many more windows than the ones incorporated into the structure.

"Just a moment," he said, then left them all in the living room so he could go upstairs, presumably to fetch the artifacts.

"You can sit down, Belshegar," Angela told him, but he shook his head.

"I think I would like to remain standing while I do this."

Her shoulders lifted, but she didn't insist. Perhaps following his lead, all the others stayed on their feet as well, even Allegra Moss, although he noticed that she had one hand on the arm of the big leather sofa, as if to steady herself.

Connor returned quickly enough, however, now carrying a small steel box measuring a little less than a foot on all sides. He set it down on the coffee table, which appeared to be carved from a single hunk of juniper, and looked up at his wife. Something in his expression was almost amused.

"Good thing we convinced Devynn that we should key our thumbprints to these locks."

Belshegar had no idea who Devynn was—perhaps the person who discovered the first amulet in the past—but he supposed he could find out from Brianna at some point.

If he ever gained the courage to tell her the truth about himself.

Angela grinned. "Yes, this makes it easier."

And she bent and pressed her thumb against a small square of glass on one side of the metal box.

At once, a light next to it flashed green, and Belshegar heard a faint *click*. Angela lifted the lid and drew out two small items, both of them wrapped in black silk.

"This is the one that Devynn and her fiancé Seth found back in 1884," the *prima* said as she pulled away the silk that had shrouded the object.

Lying on her palm was a lozenge-shaped amulet that appeared to be made of gold, although Belshegar guessed it was more likely bronze. Embedded in the center was a large garnet cabochon that gleamed dully in the sunlight streaming through the windows on either side of the living room's stone fireplace.

That light revealed some sort of runes or symbols that had been engraved in the surface, but he didn't recognize any of them.

What mattered more was how the thing would feel in his hand.

"May I?" he asked, and although Angela tensed for a second or two, at length she nodded and placed it gently in his palm.

It felt warm to the touch, even though he wouldn't have thought the *prima* had held it long enough to transfer any of her body heat to the metal. Belshegar wrapped the fingers of both hands around the object and closed his eyes.

The thing was very powerful. Its energy seemed to radiate up both arms and then somehow spread throughout his body, even though he seemed to understand at an instinctive level that the magic it conveyed was nothing he required, since his own powers were more than sufficient and needed no enhancement.

Beyond that, though, he thought he saw a shadowy figure pouring molten bronze into a mold to create the basic shape, and then painstakingly setting the smooth garnet in its bezel. After that, clever fingers etched the symbols he'd seen into the now-cool surface.

And through all of this, the artisan's magic had shimmered around him or her—whoever it was, they'd worn a hooded cloak that concealed their face, so Belshegar couldn't quite make out their sex—pouring through their fingertips and into the amulet they'd created.

He opened his eyes to see everyone watching him expectantly. This spacious room with the clear sunlight streaming through the windows and the magnificent landscapes on the wall was so different from the fire-lit chamber he'd seen in his vision that he found himself blinking, doing his best to bring himself back to the here and now.

"It was definitely made by human hands," he said. "I saw it being created, and I felt the magic flowing into it. But I couldn't see exactly who it was that made the amulet."

Triumph flickered in Connor Wilcox's smoky green eyes. "That's all right," he replied. "The important thing is that you were able to tell it didn't come from anywhere except here on this plane."

Yes, that piece of pertinent information had been clear enough.

"Try this one," Angela said as she unwrapped the second object in her hand. "This is the one I'm really curious about, since it was found on a dead man and we have absolutely no idea where he got it."

A dead man? Belshegar's eyebrows lifted, even as he understood this was not the time for questions.

This new talisman looked quite different from the first amulet. It appeared to be rock crystal carved into a perfect sphere, with a housing of thin bronze protecting one side of the piece. Here, too, were symbols engraved in the metal, although they were much fainter, as if they'd been worn down by the passage of time.

He took it in his hands and at once felt its purpose, although its power couldn't affect him, otherworldly being that he was. This amulet had been created to block magic, just as the first one had been designed to amplify it.

The rock crystal was cool and smooth in his hands. Once again, he closed his eyes and tried to absorb the energies of the object so he might know something of its origins.

This time, he could tell it was a woman who'd created the thing, because he could see her kneeling in a dark forest, her copper-colored hair falling forward to hide her face. She appeared to be utterly alone in the woods, and although her waist-length locks concealed her features just as well as any cloak, he could practically feel the despair radiating out from her.

Belshegar couldn't begin to say how he knew, but he somehow understood that this unknown witch had created the talisman out of desperation, and not out of any desire to triumph over others or perhaps gain control of them. It pained him to see her desolation, even though he knew she must have been dead for centuries.

All he could do now was hope that the amulet she'd created had given her some relief during the time she was alive.

"This was also made on this world," he said as he opened his eyes. "By a witch with red hair in a dark forest. I know nothing more than that."

"Maybe she was a long-ago McAllister," Angela said in musing tones. "Our ancestors were originally from Scotland, and we still have red hair that pops up every once in a while, like Tricia here, or my cousin Bellamy."

Tricia's hair was now mostly silver, but some of its original coppery tones could still be seen in the strands surrounding her face. Belshegar supposed it was possible that what he'd seen was a McAllister witch kneeling in a dark Scottish forest.

"But again, the amulet was made by a regular witch," Connor said. "A powerful one, obviously, but we aren't talking about extradimensional beings here. And that just proves my suspicions."

"Which are?" Levi inquired. His expression showed only mild curiosity, but for some reason,

Belshegar got the impression that both men had been thinking roughly the same thing.

"That this 'voice' that instructed our friend to come here and steal these things isn't a member of the Council at all." Connor paused there and sent a sideways glance at Belshegar, one that again seemed oddly triumphant.

"Then who was it?" Allegra asked in her quavery voice.

"The Collector, of course."

Belshegar could only stare at Connor Wilcox with puzzled eyes.

Who in the world was the Collector?

Clearly, everyone else there understood the reference, because although they seemed a little startled by this revelation, no one asked any questions as to who Connor was talking about.

Belshegar had no problem with that, however.

"What's a Collector?"

"Who," Angela corrected him gently. "To be honest, we don't know a whole lot about the guy. The only thing we do know is that he's on some kind of a tear to grab as many magical objects like these as he possibly can. He came out of nowhere last month to try to steal the first amulet, the one with the garnet."

"Well, to be more accurate, it was one of his lackeys who tried to steal it," Connor said, his tone now much grimmer. "He broke into the house and laid hands on the safe, but it seems the thief wasn't powerful enough to get past the biometric lock or to take the safe beyond all the wards we put on the house. Still, it was kind of a shock to know he was able to get inside at all."

Belshegar could see how that would have startled the *prima* and her consort. Although they'd lowered the wards to allow him entry, he could still sense them humming in the background, ready to be deployed once again. It was hard to believe that a single warlock would have been able to breach them on his own.

"We think he used that," Angela said, inclining her head toward the rock crystal amulet Belshegar still held in one hand. "One of our witches found it on him after he fell to his death, and it makes sense that it might have been enough to help him weaken the wards to get inside the house."

Such an explanation made some sense. Still, so many questions crowded his mind, Belshegar wasn't sure which one he should ask first.

"Is this Collector human?" he asked, and Angela glanced over at Levi, whose shoulders lifted slightly.

"We don't know," Levi said. "We know he

exists, and we know he is on the hunt for magical artifacts, for whatever reason, but other than that —and that he seems to have some witch-folk working for him—we can't really say."

"If he's human, I can't see how he could have possibly known about the Council," Belshegar replied. "It exists, many, many planes above this one, and mortals would have had no reason to interact with anyone on it."

To his surprise, Tricia was the one who responded to that comment. "If this person has been collecting magical objects for a while, isn't there a chance that he might have picked up something along the way that would give him access to that knowledge?"

Belshegar hadn't considered that angle to the problem, but her suggestion made some sense. Both of the artifacts in the McAllisters' keeping appeared to have a direct effect on magical powers, and yet that certainly didn't mean others couldn't exist that had an entirely different purpose. Clearly, human magic had its own way of reaching out to other dimensions, or the witch who'd summoned Levi here all those years ago would never have been able to accomplish such a feat.

And Elena would never have been able to sense Belshegar in his world, or the other "demons" she had visit her when he was unable to be there, for whatever reason. What if some long-ago witch or warlock had found a way to harness such a power and then placed it in an amulet or other talisman of some sort so it might be used by anyone who possessed it?

It was possible, although Belshegar didn't much like knowing that an artifact with such powers was now apparently held by someone who appeared to be ruthless in his pursuit of anything that might benefit him.

Angela's mouth had compressed, and he had the impression that her thoughts had run along the same lines and she wasn't overly happy with them, either.

"Have you had any contact with your 'voice' since you came here?" she asked, and he shook his head.

"None," he replied. "I'll admit it has seemed rather odd to me, just because I have now been in Jerome for a week and thought for certain I would be called upon to provide some sort of progress report. But there has been nothing."

Both the elders and Connor and Angela seemed nonplussed by this statement, which seemed to indicate they had no real idea why the voice—the Collector—hadn't demanded to know why it was taking so long to retrieve his treasures.

But then Levi spoke. "Possibly he hasn't demanded an accounting because he would rather you take your time than risk the chance of rattling you to the point where you might make a mistake." He paused there, and then offered Belshegar an incongruous smile. "That is, I'm assuming you've never done anything like this before."

"No," he replied at once. "I live a very quiet life."

Angela crossed her arms. "And yet the Collector still had enough dirt on you to coerce you into doing this in the first place."

"'Dirt'?" Belshegar repeated, not sure what she was trying to say.

Once again, Levi smiled. "Something to hold over your head." He directed his next words to Angela, adding, "He came here and put on a human form and went to a friend's wedding."

"That's it?" she demanded, clearly surprised that such a small thing would have been enough to force compliance.

"Perhaps that was the final straw," Belshegar said. "I had also spent many years visiting her and offering her what comfort I could. In the grand scheme of things, I suppose it is not the sort of thing that beings from my plane should do. But Elena was my friend, and I had told her I would be at her wedding. I do not go back on my promises. Also," he continued, thinking he should clarify what Levi had just said, "I did not assume this human form on my own. I do not have the power to do such a thing. Loc took care of it for me, since my friend Elena is a member of the Castillo clan."

To anyone else, this would have all sounded hopelessly opaque. But it seemed Angela and Connor understood the mechanics of the situation well enough that they found no need to ask any further questions.

It was Allegra who spoke up then, her tone obviously puzzled. "If Loc provided the human form you wore to your friend's wedding, who gave you the one you wear now?"

"The voice," Belshegar replied at once. "Or rather, the Collector, if he's truly the one behind all of this."

No one listening seemed to like the sound of that very much. Angela's full mouth thinned, and she said, "He's really that powerful?"

"I doubt he is on his own," Levi told her. "But it seems likely he's 'collected' a magical artifact that allowed him to give Belshegar this human body."

If he'd given it, then he could also take it away if he liked.

A chill moved through Belshegar's form, even as he did his best to tell himself that the Collector wouldn't do such a thing if he thought his reluctant servant had even the slightest chance of obtaining the artifacts he wanted.

But if he should decide that Belshegar was no longer of any use to him….

A swallow, and he forced himself to say, "It is a reality I must face, I suppose. Although I do hope it will not come to that."

After he made that remark, Conner and Angela shared a look Belshegar couldn't quite interpret.

Did they know something of his relationship with Brianna?

Perhaps. After all, she was a member of their clan, and even though the clan elders didn't appear to be too involved in the day-to-day doings of the family, he also guessed they were still aware of many more things than one might think.

If they did know, then of course, they would also realize that for him to suddenly assume his true form would cause a very large problem for his and Brianna's burgeoning romance. No one here had any idea what he actually looked like, but if they knew Loc, then they also would understand that otherworldly beings such as they never looked like ordinary humans.

Or even not-so-ordinary ones.

"What must I do?" he asked, glad that his voice sounded so steady. Some might have thought it odd for a being such as he to ask for advice from a group of humans—Levi excepted, of course—but he had never encountered a situation like this before, and he thought he could use all the help he could get.

"Keep on with what you're doing," Angela said immediately. "Make it look as if you're poking around. Now that we know why you're here, we won't have to worry about what you're up to, but if the Collector is watching, that should assure him you're doing everything you can."

It didn't sound like a terribly strong plan, and yet Belshegar knew the *prima* was only trying to clear the way for him as best she could. And he had to believe they would spread the word, and while not providing all of the story, would at least let the other people in the clan know there was nothing to fear from him and not to worry if they saw him wandering near their homes.

"Even when I'm not," he said softly.

The corners of her mouth lifted slightly. "Well, the way I see it, the Collector wasn't exactly honest with you, so I don't see why you should be honest with him."

A very human way of looking at the situation.

Belshegar thought he liked it.

17

SOME PART OF HER HAD BEEN WORRIED THAT maybe Bill wouldn't contact her after all, especially when most of the afternoon ticked by and she hadn't heard a single thing from him.

But then her phone pinged just a minute or so after she got home from her final music lesson for the day.

> I haven't been to the Haunted
> Hamburger yet. Would you mind
> going there for dinner?

Most of the time, Brianna avoided the restaurant—not because she didn't like the food, but because it tended to be even more overrun with tourists than the other places to eat in Jerome. On a Tuesday evening, though, they had a chance of actually finding a place to sit down.

> Sounds like fun. What time?

6:30?

> Meet you there.

That was all, but it was enough to push away the unease that had been nagging her all after-noon. She couldn't even say why she'd been feeling so off. It could have been simple worry that Bill really was going to ghost her after all, and yet she still thought something else was going on, even if she couldn't yet put her finger on it. Her students had all done well, and the one couple who'd come into the gallery had ended up walking out with almost three grand in purchases.

Pretty good for a Tuesday.

But….

She told her brain to shut up and then headed into the bathroom to refresh her lip gloss and brush her hair. No point in changing out of the jeans and striped top she'd been wearing that day, not when the Haunted Hamburger didn't exactly have a dress code. All the same, she didn't want to look like an utter mess.

It was already past five-thirty, so she didn't have a huge amount of time to kill before she needed to walk up the hill to meet Bill at the restaurant. Just as she was about to sit down and pick up the neglected book she'd been reading, however, her phone pinged again.

Was he canceling after all?

The message on her home screen put that paranoid thought immediately to bed.

> We bought a house!

Bellamy, of course. She and Marc had been house hunting for the past month, ever since she'd had that massive lottery win. Angela and Connor hadn't been too thrilled with her about it, mostly because being a MegaMillions winner didn't exactly fit their idea of lying low and not attracting attention.

But Bellamy had kept her big win anonymous, so it was only the other members of the clan who knew about her windfall.

Because she'd won so much, Bellamy and Marc could have bought pretty much anything they wanted, up to and including some of those gorgeous ranch properties in Sedona that usually were the vacation homes of the rich and famous, since no one else could afford them.

Well, except for the part that nobody of witch-kind was allowed to live there, thanks to the way vortex energy affected their magic.

> Where?

> In Page Springs. It's the old
> Rainbow Canyon winery.

Brianna couldn't help blinking at that piece of information. Yes, Bellamy had a degree in enology, but she'd said on more than one occasion that she wasn't interested in making wine necessarily and would rather educate people about it. That was why she'd been so good at working in the tasting rooms.

I thought you didn't want a winery.

> I thought I didn't, either, but the
> property is gorgeous, and we'll
> hire someone to manage the
> vines. And I got to thinking and
> realized it would be kind of fun to
> have our own private label. Not
> to sell, but to share with family
> and friends.

A teeny tiny boutique winery. Yes, that sounded more like Bellamy's speed.

When do you get to move in?

> A couple of weeks. It's an all-
> cash purchase so it'll go fast, but
> the current owners need time to
> get their stuff cleared out. After
> that, though, it's all ours.

> Sounds great. You'll have to have a housewarming party when the place is ready.

> Absolutely! Keep you posted!

> Congrats! 🍾

> Thanks!

That was the end of the convo, and Brianna put down her phone, annoyed with herself at the flare of jealousy that went through her. Here Bellamy was going to have her own winery, and she was living in an apartment above a gallery.

Shut up, Ms. Sour Grapes, she told herself, and that helped a little. No one could deny that Bellamy had been very lucky—a lot luckier than the previous owner of the winning lottery ticket, who'd met a bad end after he tried to murder both her and Marc Trujillo—but she still deserved every speck of happiness that came her way.

Besides, it would be lots of fun to go to any parties Bellamy and Marc might want to throw. Brianna had gone out to Rainbow Canyon once when she was back in high school, since a friend's parents had rented the spot for Mindy's sweet sixteen. A small creek ran through a corner of the property, which was shaded with dozens of old oak trees, and the house was a big Craftsman-style structure with a wide porch that wrapped around the building. The tasting room was a second, smaller structure set behind the main house and had a large patio covered by a pergola.

All in all, it was a gorgeous place, and although she guessed that Bellamy would probably have to put some money into updating the house, it wasn't as though it wouldn't be livable right away if they wanted to move in now and then deal with the renovations later.

Or maybe they were going to fix it up first and continue renting various high-end vacation homes until it was ready. Either way, Brianna knew her friend wouldn't have to worry about what any of it cost.

A very brief sigh, and then she picked up her purse and slung it over her shoulder. If she sat here brooding for much longer, she'd be late for dinner with Bill. While she was sure he would excuse her tardiness without asking any questions, she didn't want to be that person.

The gallery had been closed for almost an hour, so she didn't have to worry that anyone would be nearby to see her touch her index finger to the lock on her apartment door after she let herself out. Down the stairs, then up the street and up the steps that would lead her to the level where the Haunted Hamburger was located.

As soon as she walked in, she saw Bill sitting

at a table near one of the windows that overlooked the deck. When the weather was warm enough, she preferred to sit outside, but there had been a definite bite in the air today as the sun went down, enough that she'd slid on a jean jacket before she left the apartment.

He must have gotten here a little early, because as far as she could tell, she was right on time. As soon as he caught sight of her, he smiled and stood up so he wouldn't be seated when she got to the table.

Always the gentleman, that was for sure.

Despite the smile, though, Brianna thought she saw a certain tension in his handsome features, a tautness to his jaw that normally wasn't there.

Had something happened today?

Was he steeling himself to tell her that he'd decided this wasn't going to work out after all, and he was leaving tomorrow?

With all the trouble she kept borrowing, she was going to pay a serious amount of interest if she kept this up.

"Hi," she said. "I hope I'm not late."

"No," he responded immediately. "I was a little early. I wanted to make sure we got a good table."

He pulled out the chair opposite his, and she went ahead and sat down while he returned to his original seat.

Even though it was a Tuesday night, enough people were eating at the Haunted Hamburger that Brianna thought it was probably a good thing Bill had gotten here before her—especially since she noticed that a big family group, eight people in all, had just stopped at the hostess station. Getting stuck behind them in the queue probably wouldn't have been too much fun.

"How were your lessons?" he asked as she unfolded the napkin from her place setting and put it on her lap.

"Fine," she replied. "Everyone seems to be making good progress. And the gallery wasn't too busy, so I was able to get some paperwork taken care of."

Busywork, more to the point, but Bill didn't need to hear about that.

"How was your day?" she asked next.

There it was again—a tensing of his jaw so slight that she doubted she would have noticed if she hadn't been looking for it.

"Fine," he replied without hesitation. "I did some more sketches and walked out to the old Gold King mine."

"That tourist trap?" she asked with a grin, and he only smiled in return.

"I suppose it is sort of touristy. But it was still interesting to see the old mine equipment and all the old vehicles parked everywhere. It gave me more of an idea of what Jerome must have been like back in its glory days."

Brianna supposed she could see that, even though the Gold King technically hadn't been part of Jerome but instead had been its own small settlement. However, since it was only a quarter-mile or so outside Jerome's main street, she understood why a lot of people would think they were all part of the same place.

"Did you do some sketching out there, too?"

He nodded. "Some, but not as much as I would have liked. I suppose I got too caught up in looking at everything around me."

There was definitely a lot to look at, especially if you counted the chickens that ran free on the property, not to mention the pen full of goats and the special enclosure for a very large black and white pig named Abner.

"Sounds like you had a full day."

"I did."

Their waiter came by—a guy Brianna had known in high school, Harris Twohey. She'd always had the impression that he'd had a crush on her back then, but since their paths hadn't crossed much after they'd graduated, she'd never been able to confirm that suspicion.

In fact, she'd heard through the grapevine that he'd moved to Phoenix a year or so ago, but apparently that hadn't lasted.

Anyway, judging by the way his dark blond brows together as he took in her companion, Bree guessed that her initial impressions had been correct…and that Harris's crush hadn't lessened too much over the years.

But at least he sounded polite enough as he asked, "Something to drink?"

"A glass of merlot," she said. No wine by the bottle here, which was probably just as well. She'd have the one glass with her burger and call it a day. At least that way, there'd probably be less chance of her getting too amorous before the end of the evening.

Oh, who was she kidding? Like she would need to be a little tipsy to convince herself to kiss Bill Garrett again.

As rattled as she might have been that day, she knew she still wanted to take his hands and pull him toward her so their lips could touch and she could experience the thrill of that contact all over again.

With the table where they sat squarely in the way, though, she doubted that was going to happen.

He also ordered a glass of wine, and Harris told them he'd get their drinks while they looked over the menu.

Not that Brianna really needed to. She didn't eat here as often as she did at some other places, but that didn't mean she still didn't know what was on offer.

A barbecue burger this time, probably, just because it had been a while since she'd had one and it sounded good to her. She'd only had salad for lunch, so she figured indulging herself for dinner shouldn't be too big a deal.

However, Bill picked up his menu and studied it for a moment, then set it aside.

"You know what you want?" she asked.

"I was thinking of the mushroom burger," he said. "Is it good?"

"Everything here is good," she told him. "It's just more a matter of what you're in the mood for."

His gaze lingered on her mouth for a moment, and warmth pooled in her stomach. Clearly, his thoughts were running along the same lines that hers had been only a moment earlier.

Harris came back with their wine, though, effectively interrupting that moment of connection. To her relief, however, he didn't seem to notice the sexual tension she'd thought must have been just as visible as the clouds of pot smoke that tended to hang in the air outside the Spirit Room whenever one of the locals' favorite bands was playing.

And then they placed their orders, and Harris

headed off to the kitchen to take care of things. As soon as he was gone, Bill lifted his wine glass.

"To burgers, haunted or otherwise," he said, and she couldn't help grinning.

"Sounds good."

They clinked glasses and drank. Even though the Haunted Hamburger only served house wine, it was still pretty decent. The merlot sliding down to her stomach helped relax her a little, and she leaned against the back of her chair.

"Do you sense any of the ghosts?" she asked, only half joking.

Bill glanced around them. People were eating and talking and laughing, and Bree had to admit the restaurant didn't look very haunted…even though she knew better.

"They're here," he said quietly. "But I get the sense that they're not very active when the restaurant is busy."

A valid impression, since she'd heard pretty much the same thing from the people she knew who'd worked here over the years. You could get a sense of a presence, but doors didn't slam and pans didn't get knocked to the floor by unseen hands until the place was closed and all the customers had gone home.

And there was also her cousin Dayna's horror story about getting locked in the meat freezer one night while she was at the restaurant cleaning up after her shift. Luckily, someone had come back because they'd left their phone in their locker and had heard her beating on the freezer door, so Dayna hadn't been trapped in there for more than ten minutes at the most.

Still, she'd quit the next day and had never set foot in the place since then, even though that had happened more than five years ago now.

"I suppose they don't want to feel like they're putting on a show or something," she said, then sipped some more of her wine.

"That could be it," Bill agreed. "Or possibly the vibrations of all these people help to keep them away. I don't really know that much about ghosts."

Neither did she. That was Angela's thing, since she'd been talking to ghosts since she was ten years old, long before she became *prima*. Probably if asked, she would have said every ghost was different, just as all people were different, so you couldn't expect them to all act the same.

In this particular case, though, Bree could only be glad that the Haunted Hamburger's resident ghosts were quiescent at the moment. She had enough on her plate already.

"What about the Gold King?" she asked, and Bill's head tilted to one side, as though he wasn't quite sure what she was asking. She smiled, then figured she'd better elaborate. "I mean, if you sensed any ghosts there."

His expression turned thoughtful. "No, I didn't. Not that I was trying to, either, but that place didn't feel haunted, unless you're talking about haunted by the memories that were made there or the memories of what it used to be."

"Makes sense," she said. "I've never heard of any real hauntings at the Gold King, unlike at least half the buildings here in Jerome. Maybe the encampment there felt too temporary to any of the people who might have died in that spot, and they didn't see any need to stick around."

Bill nodded, but Harris came back with their food then, effectively cutting off any answer he might have made. And after Harris told them he'd check back in a while to see how they were doing, there didn't seem to be much point in pursuing that particular topic.

No, they were quiet for a few minutes as they bit into their cheeseburgers and stopped every now and then to eat a French fry or drink some wine, and Bree thought she was okay with that. She was hungrier than she'd expected, and the vague notion she'd had pass through her head of saving half her burger for later evaporated almost right away.

And even when she and Bill spoke again, it was about commonplace things, like her gig at

Tantrum wines on Thursday evening and the way she'd been stewing over whether to hold a recital so her students could show off their talents. She didn't have that many pupils—only five at the moment—but Callie's mother and Luke's father had asked about a recital as well, and she thought maybe it would be a good idea if she could find someplace to hold the event. Since it wouldn't be a very big crowd, the living room of her childhood home would probably work...if she could get her parents to agree to let a group of civilians into the house for an evening or maybe a Sunday afternoon.

Bill seemed interested, and agreed that a house seemed like a more likely place rather than trying to book a real performance hall. And once again, he deftly snagged the check before she could even reach for it, a knowing little smile playing around his mouth as he did so.

Well, the Haunted Hamburger had been his idea, so she supposed she should go ahead and let him pay.

Afterward, she slipped on her jean jacket and they headed outside. He didn't seem to need anything other than the T-shirt he was wearing to protect himself from the cool evening air, but she'd known lots of guys like that, men who would only lower themselves to put on outerwear if temperatures dipped into the forties or lower.

"I'll walk you home," he said, and his tone was firm enough that Bree guessed there was no point in arguing.

Especially since he'd already been to her place and knew exactly what kind of climb it entailed.

They went a little way past the restaurant so they could get to the steep staircase that led down to Main Street. Even though she'd lived here all her life and knew there was nothing to fear from those steps…or the little alley that awaited them at the bottom…she always felt her heart speed up a bit as she made the descent.

It was just creepy, no matter how you looked at it.

Especially now, with the sun gone down and no one anywhere around them. Some orange-hued light from the sparsely spaced sodium vapor street lamps down on Main Street made its way here, but not enough to truly illuminate anything. No, it was mostly to keep you from tripping over your own feet.

Oddly, the air felt colder the lower they went, which didn't make a lot of sense. Her mind playing tricks, she supposed, although she didn't know why she should feel so hinky when she had Bill there with her. Any would-be mugger would probably take one glance at the width of his shoulders and the muscles of his biceps as they strained against the sleeves of his T-shirt and decide to look for easier prey.

When they reached the bottom of the steps, Bill stopped abruptly, head up in the air like a dog detecting a strange scent.

"Something's wrong," he said.

Brianna hadn't yet lifted her hand from the stair railing, and her fingers curled around it, the metal cold against her skin. "What do you mean, 'wrong'?"

"Just…wrong."

Before she could respond, the air in the alley at the base of the steps appeared to shimmer, almost like heat waves rising from the pavement on a hot summer day.

Except it wasn't hot. In fact, the air seemed to be getting colder by the second.

The shadows darkened, becoming blacker than black, almost as if they weren't shadows at all, but gaping tears in the fabric of reality.

A figure emerged from one of those shadows —as tall as Bill, so she guessed it must be male even though she couldn't see the person's face, thanks to the hooded cloak it wore. Something about it seemed not quite real, though, the edges of the black fabric seeming to bleed into nothingness, as if it wasn't quite anchored to this plane.

"The Council sends its greetings," the figure said. Its voice sounded human enough, but it still echoed off the alley walls with a strange sort of distortion, like it was being put through some sort of filter.

And it raised one hand. Resting in the stranger's palm was a dark orb that glowed with odd colors that moved across its spherical surface, almost like animated oil slicks. Even from where she stood, Bree could feel the wrongness of the thing.

Immediately, Bill positioned himself so that his body blocked her from the device. "A dimensional anchor! Stand back, Brianna!"

A dimensional what? Some kind of magical device, she supposed, but how in the world would Bill Garrett even know about such a thing?

Her lips parted so she could ask the question, but before she could form a single syllable, a beam of oily, purple-black light shot out of the orb, aimed directly at Bill.

Except... *was* that Bill?

His form flickered, became something monstrous and huge, eight feet tall or more, with heavy black hair hanging down his back and coppery skin. Then he was Bill again, his face tight with strain.

Her mind tried to grasp what it had just seen, but she knew she had bigger problems to worry about right then. The energy that had shot out of the orb had wrapped itself around his wrists and ankles, binding him in place.

"You can explain yourself to my master," the robed figure said, and the energy chains seemed to tighten and then pull him inexorably forward.

Once again, Bill's form shifted, becoming that huge demonic creature. Its muscles strained as it tried to free itself from its bonds, but all its struggles didn't appear to make any difference.

Not "it," Brianna told herself. *Bill. That thing...it's* him.

She didn't know how or why, but she knew she'd have to worry about that later.

Right now, she had much bigger problems to deal with.

Whatever was going on with Bill, she knew she had to prevent that person in the hooded robe from doing whatever he or she was trying to accomplish. They could sort the rest of this out later.

"Stop it!" she cried out, and rushed toward Bill.

But...she passed right through him—or whoever he was...and realized his attacker had almost succeeded in tearing him from this plane of existence.

Her heartbeat was now a panicky drumbeat, all her nerve endings surging with adrenaline. She still didn't know what the hell was going on, but she knew one thing.

If she didn't act fast, Bill would be ripped from this planet and sent the Goddess knew where.

The world felt as if it was collapsing around her. All she could see was the man she loved, his familiar face and form shifting back and forth between the person she knew and that improbably huge figure, all gleaming copper skin and night-black hair and eyes, a being whose head towered above her by at least two feet, maybe more.

Time slowed. There was Bill caught in his attacker's energy field, but she realized there was so much more to the moment than that—the slow, steady pulse of the earth beneath her feet, the far more delicate energies of the stars wheeling overhead, the ancient wisdom of the night wind that played with the ends of her loose hair.

All these combined were so much more than the unstable, distorted power of the orb whose energy chains were trying their best to drag Bill away from this world.

Well, that wasn't going to happen.

Her magic, which had always felt scattered and sparse to her, spread out over too many indi-vidual talents, surged within her. Somehow knowing without knowing, she understood that her own powers and the energy of the earth beneath her feet—yes, and the energy of those terrible purple-black beams that were trying to pull Bill somewhere else, somewhere *other*—were all just a group of disparate frequencies.

Not exactly music, not quite, but she still guessed she would be able to control those frequencies, just as her fingers knew which chords to play while she strummed on her guitar or which harmonies to choose when she was working out the notes of a new song.

She lifted her hands, and the energies she'd sensed just a moment before now wrapped around them, making her feel as if she was playing an utterly new instrument, one without a corporeal form but which still could create its own unique harmonies.

Harmonies that would utterly destroy the evil magic pulsing from the oil-slick orb their attacker held.

At the same time, she found herself humming, and the sound that emerged from her throat somehow combined with the notes emanating from her fingertips, creating a song with its own power.

"What are you doing?" their attacker gasped, but she paid him no mind.

No, she needed to keep on with what she was doing…even if her conscious mind couldn't quite comprehend how she was able to manage such a thing.

Blue-white light now drifted from her fingertips and moved toward Bill. When it touched the dark energy chains that held him in place, those bonds shuddered and then disappeared.

And as each chain was destroyed, he became more and more solid, as though whatever had been trying to drag him away from this dimension was losing more and more power.

The light emanating from her fingers grew even more solid, rippling across the dark little alley like the dancing currents in Oak Creek. One of those waves struck their attacker, who took several steps backward, his breath coming in heaving gasps.

"How are you doing this?" he demanded, voice cracking.

Brianna didn't know. This was all coming from some subconscious force within her, something she couldn't have even begun to understand.

The only thing she knew was that it seemed to be working.

With a sharp sound that made her think of ice breaking during a spring thaw, the orb in their assailant's hand began to crack, dark energy seeping out like purple pus.

Sensing its weakness, she brought her hands together in a single abrupt clap, and at once the orb shattered into a thousand pieces. Bill sank to his knees, fully himself again.

"The Council will hear of this!" their attacker spat, and then dissolved into darkness.

Brianna gasped, even as the energy she'd summoned seemed to flow out and away from her, like waves receding from a shore right before a tsunami swept in. Her knees buckled, and she found herself falling.

But there was Bill, catching her in his strong arms before she collapsed to the pavement. He steadied her, holding her up, until he seemed to realize she could stand on her own. Then he let go and took a step backward.

During all of this, he'd looked exactly the way he had when she first met him. Those brief glimpses she'd caught during his struggle with their assailant told her that he was far more than what he pretended to be, however.

They could discuss that later. For now....

"What...what just happened?" she stammered as she stared down at her hands in confusion. They looked the same as they ever had, lightly tanned and with the nails cut short so they wouldn't get in the way of her guitar or piano playing.

But she'd seen the blue light that had flowed out from them...had seen how that laser-clear light had somehow broken the dark chains that bound Bill in place.

Just what the *hell* was going on?

"That's your true gift," Belshegar told her, his voice hushed, almost awestruck. "You're a harmonic—you can balance energies across dimensions."

She'd never heard of such a thing, although she understood there were plenty of magical talents out there that she had no real experience with, just because they hadn't occurred in any of the Arizona witch clans. But she'd seen with her own eyes what her magic—her supposedly wimpy, unfocused magic—had just done.

It had cut through those magical chains as if they didn't exist, had shattered the magical orb their attacker had held as if it had been as fragile as spun glass.

Not exactly the actions of someone with magic that everyone around her had thought was far weaker than average.

As best she could, she gathered her thoughts, straining to analyze and absorb everything that had just happened. Bill stood nearby, expression concerned and wary at the same time, as if he was just waiting for her to ask why his appearance had kept slipping.

Oh, she would ask…just not right now.

"Is that why my magic always felt…scattered?" she asked, trying to sort her racing thoughts into something halfway coherent. "Because it wasn't one kind of magic, but sort of everything all at once?"

Bill nodded, now looking relieved. Clearly, he understood she wasn't going to press him about the way his appearance had kept shifting during the encounter.

Well, not yet, anyway.

"You don't create energy or destroy it," he told her. "You harmonize it. And that, Brianna, is a gift much rarer and more powerful than you can imagine."

She looked down at her hands again. They appeared completely normal, but she knew better.

"We should get you inside," he went on, his gaze roving across the dark alley where they stood. "I don't sense any other hostile intentions nearby, but I still think it's better if we don't stay out here."

A point she heartily agreed with. The unnatural cold had disappeared along with their assailant, and as far as she could tell, everything had gone back to normal. Still, she knew she would much rather be inside her apartment.

Could these strange gifts that had just surfaced help her ward the place? Brianna didn't

316 | CHRISTINE POPE

know for sure, but she figured it couldn't hurt to try.

They began walking down Main Street to her apartment. The only real signs of life on the street were the sounds of voices and music drifting out from the Spirit Room and Paul and Jerry's Saloon just a block away, but she still found herself heartened by them. They told her she and Bill weren't the only living beings in town, even though she couldn't detect any sign that anyone had even noticed the altercation that had taken place just a few minutes earlier.

Thank the Goddess that she always left a light on inside the apartment. Right then, she didn't think she could have handled walking into an entirely dark space. Her imagination would have conjured all sorts of attackers, even though she knew the place was empty.

All the same, she flicked on more lights as soon as she was inside, doing her best to send all the shadows fleeing. Bill came in and waited as she shut the door, his expression diffident, as though he knew the inquisition was about to start at any moment.

Once she was sure the door was safely locked behind them—for whatever reason, she feared the person in the hooded robe who'd attacked them far more than she did the person...creature...

whatever…who faced her now—she turned toward him and set her hands on her hips.

"Okay, are you going to tell me just what the *hell* is going on?"

18

BELSHEGAR HAD ALWAYS KNOWN THIS moment would come. Perhaps he hadn't thought it would arrive in such a spectacular fashion— clearly, the Collector had wearied of his stalling and had sent one of his minions to rectify the situation—but still, it would have been impossible to forever hide the truth of his nature from Brianna McAllister even without such an attack to precipitate the revelation.

Brianna, who had just proven herself to be far more than she appeared. True, she had never spoken of her magical gifts with him, simply because she had believed him to be a civilian, but still, he'd never sensed that she carried such a deep well of talent within herself.

And, if her utter astonishment at what she had

just done was any indication, she'd never realized it, either.

"Perhaps you should sit down," he said.

For a moment, she remained resolutely in the same spot where she'd been standing, her jaw set at a stubborn angle. But then she seemed to realize she would only be hurting herself if she didn't allow herself to be seated, because she took a few steps backward and collapsed onto the overstuffed sofa behind her.

"Okay, I'm sitting," she said, and shot him a defiant stare. "Now will you explain yourself?"

As much as he would have liked to sit down next to her, he doubted she would welcome such proximity at that moment.

Perhaps never.

Belshegar did his best to banish the unwelcome thought, especially since he knew the attacker and his motivations were of far greater importance than their relationship…if he would even have one with Brianna after all this. The attack by the Collector's minion had been far more painful than he could have ever imagined, and each second those magical chains had been wrapped around his wrists and ankles, he'd felt more and more of his life force being drained from him, even as he had gotten closer and closer to being removed from this plane entirely.

It was not an experience he wished to repeat anytime soon.

Although he'd only paused to gather his thoughts, it seemed Brianna believed even that scant second or two was too long to go without some sort of explanation, for she said, "What's this Council? Why would they have come after you?"

Those were, he thought, easier questions to answer than any that might have pertained to his actual identity.

"The Council," he said, "is made up of a group of extradimensional beings who resonate on a far higher plane than yours—or mine, to be honest. However, I believe our assailant was purposely misrepresenting himself and that he was not sent by the Council at all. No, I believe he must have been working for the Collector."

At once, Brianna's big blue eyes flared even wider, and her fingers splayed against the pale linen couch cushions as she made herself sit up a little straighter. "How do you know about the Collector?" she demanded.

"Because your father told me about him," Belshegar said simply.

Her fingers dug into the sofa. "My father knows who you really are?"

It was something of a relief that she'd said

"who" and not "what." Still, this was going to be uncomfortable no matter what he said or did.

"Yes," he replied. "Your father is not originally from this dimension, of course, and neither am I. That is why he was able to sense that I was not the simple human I was pretending to be."

Brianna went silent for a moment. Then her brows pulled together, and she gave him a very direct stare.

"Those artifacts that Angela and Connor are babysitting," she said slowly. "Are those why you're here?"

Again it seemed as if she wished to focus on the externals of the situation and not on anything that had passed between them over these last few days. Belshegar could not fault her for that, not when some cowardly part of him wished to avoid that topic for as long as possible.

"Yes," he replied. "I was summoned by a being whom I thought was a member of the Council. He told me I needed to find those artifacts and return them to him, that they were far too powerful to be kept in the hands of mortals."

"But it was really the Collector who was asking you to steal them."

A bald way of phrasing it, but accurate. "Yes," he said heavily.

Now Bree crossed her arms, making it look almost as if she was hugging herself, doing her best to maintain her composure while she attempted to process what he had told her. "Why would you believe him? Why would you go along with what he wanted?"

Both very good questions. A single chair faced the couch—the only other piece of furniture the room could really hold without feeling overcrowded—and he went ahead and sat down on it, thinking it felt strange to stand there and loom over her while they spoke. True, this human body was much smaller than his true form…he'd experienced moments of almost vertigo while he switched between them during the attack, struggling to acclimate to how much bigger and taller he was when he lost his mortal disguise…but still, he thought it might be more comfortable for them to be mostly at eye level with one another.

"The Council—the real one," he added, just to clarify, "in general does not interfere in the lives of those they watch over. At the same time, it is their business to ensure that all runs smoothly. I still have no idea how the Collector could have learned all this, but somehow he knew that I had been on this plane before, and used this same body once during that time."

One tawny brow lifted at an ironic angle. "What, to pick up chicks?"

Belshegar wasn't quite sure what "chick"

meant in that particular context, but he guessed it was some sort of reference to female humans.

"No," he said, wounded that she would believe him capable of such shallow interactions. "I had been here in my true form when I was summoned by a girl named Elena Salazar. That is her magical gift—calling in beings from other planes."

To his surprise, Brianna looked almost sympathetic. "That's kind of a rough talent."

"It did pose her quite a few difficulties," he allowed, thinking there was no need to elaborate too much. "But she overcame those difficulties and married the man she loved about a year ago. I had promised her I would dance with her at her wedding, and of course I needed a human guise to do such a thing."

Bree went silent again, her brain clearly working away at everything he'd just told her. "And you didn't think it was suspicious that someone on the Council would give you grief over something so trivial, something that happened so long ago?"

"I did," he said heavily. "But you must understand that the higher up you go on these planes of existence, the less meaning time has. I merely told myself that the voice—the person who tasked me with retrieving the artifacts—did not have a clear grasp of exactly when Elena's wedding had taken place, or of the times when I visited her before then."

"You couldn't have refused?"

"I could have," Belshegar replied, then paused to consider the best words to give her to explain how he truly had little room to maneuver when the voice—the Collector—had summoned him. "But the Council has broad power. If they'd determined that my transgressions were too egregious to be forgiven, they could have simply made sure I no longer existed."

Brianna's eyes widened again, and now she seemed pale under the light tan that still lingered even as summer faded. "They would have *killed* you?"

"That is a crude way to put it. They would have ensured my energies would have been dispersed and that I, myself—Belshegar—would cease to exist."

"That's your name?" she asked. "Belshegar?"

He nodded.

"That's kind of a mouthful," she continued, and now she appeared almost amused. "No wonder you were going by 'Bill.'"

"Yes, I needed to blend in as much as possible."

She uncrossed her arms and set her hands on her thighs, something about the movement signaling that she wasn't quite sure what to do with them. Right then, she looked oddly vulnerable, like a child who'd just been told the truth about Santa Claus and didn't know what to do next.

Her next question was the one Belshegar had been dreading the most.

"And this…this thing between us? Was that more protective camouflage?"

How he wished he could get up from his chair and go over to the couch so he could take her in his arms. However, her posture remained stiff, as though she was holding herself still with every ounce of control she possessed, and he doubted she would appreciate such an overture.

"No," he said at once. He was new to this body, to making it do what he wished, but he hoped Brianna would be able to hear the sincerity in his voice and see it in his face. "I didn't even know of your existence when I came here to Jerome. My sole thought was to retrieve the artifacts and deliver them to the voice so I could go back to my quiet existence. And then I met you… and I began to realize there was so much more to myself than I had previously understood."

Those words felt hopelessly inadequate to explain the sea change that had taken place within him over the past week, but again, he could only hope that she would understand what he was trying to say.

"You never...?" she began, then paused delicately, every beautiful plane and angle of her face showing she didn't quite know how to phrase the question.

"Never," he said firmly. "The body you saw me shift into—that is my true form. It would not have been feasible for such a thing to occur, even if I had wished it. If we are being honest with one another, the thought had never even entered my mind. I interacted with humans at Elena's wedding reception, but I did not experience an attraction to any of them."

Brianna was quiet, those sunlit-sky eyes of hers fixed on him for a long moment. "Then... why me? I'm nobody."

He wanted to tell her she was far from "nobody," but he guessed those were not the words she needed to hear. "Why does anyone feel an attraction to one person and not another? That is one of the mysteries of the universe that I doubt even the greatest minds have been able to solve."

For just a second, her lips quirked. It wasn't much of a shift in expression, but it was still enough to give him some hope.

Surely if she hated him and wanted nothing to do with him, he wouldn't have been able to arouse even the beginnings of a smile.

"Do you think it has something to do with my father?" she asked next, and Belshegar blinked at her, not sure what she meant by the question. He must have looked utterly blank, because she added, "Because of who he is. I mean, my brother and I look completely human—of course we do, because my father's body is just as mortal as anyone else's—but even with that, there's something very different about his essence. His soul, I suppose."

Belshegar hadn't thought of the situation in those terms, and yet he thought she might have something of a point there. After all, he had met quite a few beautiful Castillo witches at Elena and Alessandro's reception, but none of them had stirred this spark inside him. Could it be that he'd recognized the other in Brianna and his soul had realized there might be a chance at some kind of connection?

"I don't know," he said frankly. "There is so much about all of this I can't begin to explain. There is only one thing I know, Brianna McAllister, and that is that I love you. Out of nowhere, against all odds…but there it is."

Her jaw tightened, but he noticed how she didn't look away. No, she sat there with those forthright blue eyes fixed on his face as she appeared to consider what he'd just said.

Then something about her expression seemed to relax, and once again, the faintest hint of a smile touched the corners of her mouth. "Well, I suppose that's a good thing," she said. "Because I fell in love with you a few days ago and had no idea what to do about it."

She'd said those words, perhaps the most important in any language, whether on this plane or the uncounted others that occupied all of existence.

But….

"Even…." He made himself take in a breath, then another. The question needed to be asked, even though he hated to bring it up. "Even knowing that I am not human?"

"Well, some part of me isn't, either," Brianna replied frankly. She pushed herself up from the couch, and he found himself rising from his chair at the same time. For the first time, she smiled outright. "Although I have to admit that it would be easier if you were able to maintain this form." Her expression turned curious as she added, "Can you?"

"I'm not sure," he replied. "The voice bestowed this form upon me, but he was only borrowing what the demon lord Loc had done for me so I might attend Elena's wedding. I suppose we could always go to Loc for assistance if the voice decides to return me to my original form as a sort of punishment."

"That's good," she said.

The coffee table still separated them, but

Belshegar didn't see its presence as too much of an impediment. He simply walked around it so he could stand next to her, although he made no other movement.

This must be her decision.

A slight tremor went through her slender body, but then she reached out and laced her fingers through his, pulling him closer. Another step, and she was lifting her beautiful face toward him so he might lean down and kiss her, taste the sweetness of the wine she'd had with dinner.

Or perhaps that was simply herself and nothing more.

Need surged through him, even though he knew this was not yet the time. Brianna was the one who needed to make that decision, and he knew he would wait for as long as necessary. She had suffered multiple shocks tonight—the attack by the Collector's minion, the emergence of her true powers, the realization that the man she'd come to care for wasn't even human at all—and he guessed she would need some time to get used to the situation.

Those same thoughts appeared to have passed through her mind as well, because although the kiss lasted far longer than any of the others they'd shared, after a few moments, she gently pulled her fingers from his even as she broke off the embrace and took a step backward.

"This is…a lot," she said. "But even putting aside what's going on between us, we really need to talk to my father—and the other elders and Connor and Angela—to let them know what happened tonight. I doubt they'll be too thrilled to learn the Collector went on another rampage."

Or one of his minions, more likely. Based on what he'd been able to glean from the things Levi and the other elders had said, it didn't sound as if that master of magical artifacts had much of a desire to get his hands dirty and tended to send others to do his bidding.

For all Belshegar knew, the "voice" wasn't the Collector, either, but yet another of his lackeys.

Were any of them human?

Impossible to say. If he had been collecting magical items for years, then the properties of those talismans and amulets and what-have-you would probably be enough to make it seem as if those who held them were far more than mere mortals.

"Yes, that would be a good idea," Belshegar replied. "They need to know that there's been an attack here in Jerome. Perhaps they even sensed a tremor in the wards protecting this place." He paused there, then made himself go on, even though he knew Brianna would probably not be too happy to hear his next words. "And they also need to know how your powers presented themselves tonight."

As expected, she appeared less than thrilled by that comment. Her mouth pursed, and she glanced down at the patterned rug beneath their feet before she looked up once again, her expression now resigned.

"I suppose there's no real way to get around it," she said. "Much as I might like to. I just don't want people making a fuss because my powers decided to take a left turn at Albuquerque."

He had absolutely no idea what she meant by that remark. Yes, he knew that Albuquerque was a city in New Mexico, but he failed to see how it could have any bearing on the current situation.

Well, he could leave that aside for now.

"Your father doesn't seem like the sort of person to make a fuss," he replied gently. "And I don't get that feeling from Angela and Connor, either."

Nor Tricia McAllister, who appeared to be a no-nonsense sort of person. Belshegar was less sure of Allegra Moss, but he had to believe the presence of the others would prevent her from making any uncomfortable outbursts.

Brianna's shoulders lifted. "You're probably right. I just hate this kind of thing."

She reached up to rub the back of her neck, then released a breath and went over to her purse, which she'd dropped on the dining room table as they came in. After she got out her phone, she touched a finger to the screen and brought it up to her ear. A pause, and she said, "Hi, Dad? Bill and I have something we need to talk to you about—well, you and the other elders and Connor and Angela."

Another pause, and Belshegar guessed that was Levi responding to his daughter's unusual request.

"Sure," she replied. "We'll be there in five."

Then she pulled the phone away from her ear and returned it to her purse. A bit of scrabbling around, and she got out a set of keys.

"We're driving," she said. "No way am I walking back up that hill in the dark."

And that, Belshegar thought, was an excellent idea.

19

HER SHOULDERS HITCHED THE SECOND THEY left the apartment and descended the stairs, expecting some kind of supernatural attack, even though Bill—Belshegar—was right behind her and she knew he would do whatever he could to ward off another assault.

Not that he'd done such a great job earlier this evening.

Which she knew wasn't an entirely fair thing to think. There was no way in the world either of them could have anticipated that they'd be attacked by one of the Collector's minions on the way home from dinner.

Was that entirely true, though? Although Belshegar hadn't provided a lot of details, she had to believe the warlock—or whatever the Collector turned out to be—who was trying to scoop up all those magical trinkets probably hadn't been too thrilled that the person he'd blackmailed into doing his dirty work was instead playing footsie with a local witch. It didn't seem too out of bounds to think he might lose his patience in such a scenario.

Well, that was neither here nor there. She couldn't start doubting Belshegar now, not when he'd come clean and even told her that he loved her.

Just a few hours ago, she would have been thrilled to hear him say such a thing. And all right, she was still sort of thrilled…and had told him she loved him too, since that was the simple truth…but she'd also realized that her worries about hooking up with a civilian from out of town now seemed downright quaint when you compared them to the reality of the situation.

Deep breaths, she told herself as she guided Sally up the hill toward Paradise Lane. Belshegar sat quietly in the passenger seat, as though he knew she was worried about traveling even that short distance.

And she was. Sure, she could have driven this route blindfolded, but she still white-knuckled it all the way to her parents' house and didn't begin to relax even the slightest bit until she'd pulled into the driveway.

All the lights were on, both inside the house

and glowing from either side of the garage and the front door, as if her father had known she would want the place as brightly illuminated as possible. The various fixtures weren't utterly obnoxious, since they'd been designed to abide by "dark sky" rules and not shed all sorts of unwanted glare upward to interfere with the patterns of the night sky, but still, it was more than enough to guide her and Belshegar safely to the front door.

She'd barely lifted her hand to knock when her father opened the door. "We're all waiting in the living room," he said, and ushered her and Belshegar inside. "What happened?"

"A lot," she replied briefly. Yes, she was going to have to tell everyone what had gone down only a half hour earlier, but damn it, she wasn't going to do it more than once.

Her father seemed to understand, even though she could tell he'd already guessed that her relationship with Belshegar had undergone a seismic change. Otherwise, she would never have brought him to a meeting that included not just the clan elders but the *prima* and her consort was well.

When Brianna entered the living room—which, as in most older houses, was separate from the foyer—she saw that everyone had already assembled there, including her mother. Maybe Hayley wasn't strictly an elder, but Bree had a feeling she'd put her foot down when she realized that whatever was going on, it had affected her daughter directly.

One of the couches was unoccupied, and she guessed they'd left it that way so she and Belshegar could take a seat there without having to share with anyone else. She headed over to the empty sofa and sat down, and a few seconds later, he settled himself beside her.

"I felt something earlier," Levi said quietly. "I didn't know exactly what it was, but it felt...wrong."

Bree knew she probably shouldn't have been surprised that her father was the one who'd sensed the attack. While the others were strong witches, they weren't beings whose essence had originated in an entirely different dimension. He would have felt those shockwaves, even if he might not have known anything about where they'd originated.

"One of the Collector's lackeys attacked us when we were walking back from the Haunted Hamburger," she said bluntly, and Connor and Angela exchanged a worried glance, even as her mother let out a gasp and Tricia and Allegra both turned quiet and tense.

But Angela wasn't so shocked that she still wasn't the first to respond. "How do you know this person was working with the Collector?"

"We don't," Belshegar replied. "Or at least, we don't have any concrete proof. But he claimed he was from the Council, and since we've already all decided that it's much more likely there is no Council involvement in the situation at all and that the Collector was only using them as a convenient cover story, it seems much more plausible that the Collector was displaying his displeasure."

"Toward you for not getting him the prizes he wanted," Levi said, and Belshegar nodded.

"Are you both all right?" Hayley asked, and Brianna sent her mother a smile she hoped was reassuring.

"We're fine. We were able to fight him off."

Next to her, Belshegar shifted, and Bree guessed he wasn't too happy about the deliberate obfuscation in her reply.

"More to the point, Brianna fought him off," he said, and everyone else in the room stared at her as if she'd just grown two heads.

"Bree?" Allegra said, her tone doubtful. "She has some useful gifts, I suppose, but none of them could ever be described as defensive in nature."

"That's the thing," Belshegar responded. He gave Bree a very small sideways glance, as if asking permission to go on, and she shrugged. The truth was going to come out at some point, and maybe it would be better if he was the one to describe what had happened.

After all, the encounter had moved pretty quickly, and a lot of it now felt like a total blur.

Also, he was the one who knew about other dimensions and the ways to move between them and tap into their energies. She'd done something, she knew, but trying to describe it to other people sounded hopelessly difficult right then.

"She fought him off," Belshegar went on. "All those small gifts of hers—they were only manifestations of her true power, which is being able to get the frequencies of different realities to resonate together. Something about the encounter woke up that gift, made it so she was able to fight back effectively and dispel the intruder. It was…rather astonishing."

Bree supposed that was one word for it. Afterward, she'd been tired and more than a little freaked out, but she'd still felt like herself. She had no idea where that gift had come from…or whether she'd ever be able to use it again.

If it only awakened during times of duress, then maybe she could pretend that it didn't exist.

Everyone assembled in the living room was still staring at her as if they'd never seen her before. Or rather, Connor and Angela and Tricia and Allegra were. Both her parents seemed a little stunned, but her mother sent her an encouraging smile, and Levi also appeared very thoughtful.

"I've often wondered…." he began, then shook his head. "That is, some part of me always believed there was much more to your talents than met the eye, although I couldn't think what it might be. But this incident seems to prove we simply weren't looking in the right place."

"I wouldn't beat yourself up too much, Dad," Brianna replied. "None of us could have possibly guessed that my talents would have manifested themselves like this."

"No," Belshegar put in. "It was only because of the nature of the attack that they finally surfaced. If that hadn't happened, I believe they would have remained dormant."

Would that have been better? In a way, she thought so, simply because she could have continued to think of herself as completely ordinary, just a regular witch with an undistinguished grab bag of talents.

Now, though...now she had a power she'd never even heard of, and neither had anyone else in the room, if their original reaction to Belshegar's revelations had been genuine.

"Well, those talents are here now," Connor said briskly. "I think the next order of business is to try to decide the best course of action to keep the Collector from dropping in anytime he feels like it and causing havoc in our town."

Everyone nodded, and Brianna was inclined to agree. Bad enough that the guy thought he had a claim to every magical artifact in existence, but the troubling fact that he also seemed to be just fine with creating a little mayhem in the pursuit of those objects made this a situation which needed to be dealt with quickly.

"It's unfortunate that we know nothing about this person," Belshegar replied. "Other than his obsession with any magical objects he can lay his hands on. It's difficult to defend against someone when we don't know where his home base is, or what methods he might use next to obtain the treasures he desires."

That was for sure. The boogeyman who had terrified Brianna when she was around five or six had nothing on this guy. At least the boogeyman was always either hiding under her bed or lurking inside the closet. The Collector, on the other hand, could come from anywhere.

Or at least, his minions could.

Angela had been silent during this exchange as she listened to the others speak. Now, though, she tilted her head to one side as she glanced over at her husband. "Maybe we shouldn't be worried about defense. Maybe we should be going on the offense."

Connor's dark, level brows lifted. "How are we supposed to go on the offense against someone when we don't even know where to find him?"

"Also," Levi cut in, "we have to keep in mind that we have no real idea as to how many magical artifacts he currently possesses. They could give him all sorts of advantages."

The *prima* didn't look too deterred, though. There was a martial spirit in her brilliant green eyes, and Brianna had the feeling she was royally pissed off about the way the Collector had sent someone to attack a member of the McAllister clan right on their home turf.

"We've got plenty of advantages of our own," she said. "We have you, Levi, and we have Hayley to bolster the powers of anyone who would be of help in this fight. And now we have Brianna, too. If the Collector or his lackeys try to use any sort of dimensional magic against us, she should be able to neutralize it."

Bree thought that was a pretty big "should." After all, she'd only used those powers once, and it had all been pure reaction. There hadn't been anything calculated or thoughtful about the way she'd jumped in to save Belshegar.

No, she'd only done what needed to be done because she couldn't bear to consider the alternative.

"I don't know," she said, not bothering to hide the doubt in her tone. "We're working with a lot of big 'if's here. We don't know if my powers will manifest the same way during a second attack, and we have absolutely no idea what kind of magical objects the Collector might be working with. It sounds like a recipe for disaster to me."

Angela's lips pursed, and she looked over at her husband. It seemed pretty clear she wasn't happy about being contradicted like this…even as she probably realized they were working with far too many unknowns for any of them to be certain about how this all might shake out.

But then Connor said, "I know this isn't a sure thing. On the other hand, do we want to spend the rest of our lives—or even the next few months or years—always looking over our shoulders, never sure when the Collector or his servants might show up? Because I don't think that would be very much fun…do you?"

No, probably not. On the other hand, Bree thought an extra level of vigilance might be better than a magical confrontation that could get someone hurt or worse, or maybe cause enough havoc in their small town that the civilians would be sure to notice something very wrong was happening in Jerome. So far, they'd managed to keep their magical conflicts hidden from the general public, but if the Collector had the enchanted equivalent of an atom bomb or something, that might be a little more difficult.

"What are you proposing?" Belshegar asked. His tone was so neutral that Bree got the feeling he wasn't entirely happy about any of this, either, but he must have still wanted to hear what the *primus* had to say.

"A trap," Connor replied at once. "It's pretty clear that what the Collector wants most of all is to grab those two artifacts we have in the safe. So we make it so he thinks they'd be easy to obtain— maybe we let the wards slack a little, something that would give him an opening. And when he swoops in to get them, we capture him."

"And then what?" Tricia said, her voice openly skeptical. "We're just going to keep this guy prisoner indefinitely?"

"And that doesn't even take into account that it could be another servant of his who shows up to take the artifacts rather than the man himself," Bree added before Connor could respond, glad that not everyone seemed to be on board with the *primus's* plan. While it would be great to get rid of the threat the Collector presented, there did seem to be the very real possibility that they wouldn't even be dealing with their real target when they sprang their trap.

Once he found out they'd been lying in wait for him, he probably wouldn't be too thrilled with the McAllister clan.

Connor's jade-hued eyes narrowed, and she could tell he was thinking over her words, even if he wasn't very happy to be contradicted like that. Most of the time, he was just as chill as his wife, but every once in a while, some of the Wilcox stubbornness would pop up to make things difficult.

"Maybe it's not about trapping the Collector," Allegra said in her wispy voice, and everyone turned to look at her.

"What do you mean?" Angela asked. Her tone was noticeably gentler now, and Bree could tell the *prima* was doing her best to show the oldest elder the proper deference.

Allegra sat up a little straighter. Most of the time, Brianna found her almost a figure of fun, with her wispy, flyaway buns and layers of long skirts and tops, all of which served to make her look a little like an ambulatory pile of clothes from a thrift store. Now, though, there was almost something stern about the way she lifted her chin, reminding Bree that this woman had been a McAllister elder for more than fifty years, had been alive to work with Angela's Great-Aunt Ruby during the dark days when the clan had still been involved in a cold war with the Wilcoxes.

Her age and wisdom shouldn't be discounted, not when she'd seen and experienced so much.

"Tricia and Brianna are right," she said. "Holding a being as powerful as the Collector indefinitely isn't a practical solution to our problem. It would be much better to make sure we're so well protected that he gives up and goes to collect his magical items elsewhere."

"Well, yes, that would be the best outcome," Angela agreed. She crossed her legs and wrapped her fingers around her knee, all the while fixing Allegra with a direct stare. "But I thought we were already doing that."

"No," Tricia cut in, nodding slightly, as if she'd suddenly understood what Allegra had been getting at. "We've been setting the wards and doing what we can on that front, but it clearly hasn't been enough, not when the Collector's servant was able to break into your house, even if he wasn't able to remove the safe with the amulets. That was probably enough to embolden him and make him realize he could be successful if he kept at it. But now we have Brianna."

Everyone's gaze fixed on Bree then, and she found herself shifting uncomfortably as she sat on the couch next to Belshegar.

Funny how she was already just fine with thinking of him by his real name.

"Her gift," Angela said softly. "The way she seems to be able to weave harmonies across dimensions. If she could use that power as we create the wards, their strength will be bound not just to this world, but to many others. I doubt even the Collector or his minions would be able to get past something like that."

Everyone nodded, although Bree couldn't help thinking they were placing a lot of trust in something they didn't even know would work. She'd only used these strange new powers of hers once. How could they all be so sure that they'd activate at the proper time?

But Belshegar seemed to be on board with the idea, because he said, "This is true. The Collector wields powers we don't entirely understand—mainly because none of us knows exactly which magical items he has in his arsenal—but for now, it does seem as if he's mostly operating on this plane. By drawing in energies from other dimensions, we should be able to create a barrier that he can't penetrate."

"He hasn't been working entirely on this plane," Brianna argued as a thought occurred to her. "I mean, unless the place where you spoke with him was somewhere in this world, too."

Belshegar's brows drew together, and she could tell he was pondering what she had just said. But then his expression cleared and he replied, "I can't say for sure. It was a place of mist where there didn't seem to be any discernible landmarks or anything that might have identified exactly where we were. Of course I assumed we were on the plane where the Council gathers, but it's entirely possible that we were instead someplace in this world, with the Collector doing everything he could to make me think otherwise."

Bree thought she could see why that might be possible. Belshegar clearly had his own gifts, but he wasn't some omnipotent being, couldn't completely control his environment. Because of that, she supposed the Collector might have been able to trick him into believing they had met in an impossibly alien dimension when in fact they might have been standing on a sound stage in L.A. or something.

"How would we even do something like this?" she asked, and her father sent her a reassuring smile.

"Connor and Angela and we elders will take care of the mechanics," he told her. "All you'll have to do is add your power at the right time, and the wards we'll create will be completely different from what we've been using so far. Like Angela said, those protective spells will have energy that extends far beyond this plane, and the Collector will have a much more difficult time getting past them."

He'd said "difficult," but not impossible. Since none of them knew what sorts of relics the Collector already had in his possession, it would also be very hard to know for sure whether he had an artifact that could rip through their newly constructed wards like fingernails through parachute silk.

And yet, despite all these worries, Brianna knew this plan was the one that would serve them best. Capturing the Collector might solve their immediate problem, but they were witches and warlocks, not jailers. Holding him indefinitely would only stir up a whole host of other issues.

Much better to create an environment so hostile that he would take his treasure-hunting activities elsewhere.

"All right," she said, then lifted her chin.

"Just tell me what I need to do."

20

BELSHEGAR WAS SOMEWHAT RELIEVED TO HEAR that the McAllister elders—and their *prima* and her consort—intended to lay most of the groundwork for the protection ritual themselves, with no need to involve Brianna.

"We'll call you in when we need you," Angela assured Bree, who looked almost disappointed by her comment, as if she'd thought she would be involved in all the planning.

"Your power is still new," Levi told his daughter. "The best thing you can do is try to be as rested as possible."

This comment didn't appear to sit very well with her, since she crossed her arms and gave her father a very direct look. "How am I supposed to rest when I have no idea when this jerk is going to pop up out of nowhere and attack us again?"

To Belshegar's surprise, Levi chuckled before laying a reassuring hand on his daughter's shoulder. "I have a feeling he isn't going to try anything again for a while. Probably, he wasn't expecting that kind of defense."

No, most likely not. Belshegar was still somewhat shocked by the way Brianna had gathered all those disparate energies and used them to break the hold the minion's orb had on him.

And then to destroy the thing utterly, rather than merely render it useless?

He had to admit he still had much to learn about the way magic operated on this plane, but he had to believe such a feat was not something most witches or warlocks could easily manage.

However, he could also tell Brianna was frightened, and no one could blame her for that.

A thought crept into his mind, one he knew he would not speak aloud until he was alone with her. If she was afraid, he thought he knew how he could help…even though he realized she had been the one to save him during that encounter, rather than vice versa.

"Maybe not," Brianna allowed. Her gaze moved toward Belshegar, almost pleading, and he realized then how tired she looked.

Beautiful, yes…but also at the utter limit of what she could handle in one evening.

It seemed her mother had thought much the

same thing, because Hayley spoke up then, saying, "It's getting late, and Bree looks like she's about to fall over. I say we end things here. The rest of you have a lot you probably need to do, but there's no need to keep her when I can tell she needs her rest."

Brianna looked as if she wanted to roll her eyes, but managed to restrain herself. "Mom, it's not even ten o'clock yet."

"And?" her mother returned. "The time doesn't matter. Your exhaustion does. And you need to be in bed."

For just a second, Bree's full mouth went tight. Then she seemed to realize there wasn't any point in arguing, not when she must be feeling the same weariness the rest of them could so obviously see.

"Okay, you're right," she said. "I'll pack it in, then." Her gaze moved to Belshegar. "But I'll take you back to your hotel first."

Under normal circumstances, he would have protested and told her there was no reason for her to do such a thing, not when the Grand Hotel was less than a five-minute walk from the house where they all sat.

However, since her offer fit in neatly with what he'd already been planning, he only inclined his head. "That would be kind of you."

She rose from her chair and he got up as well,

and so did everyone else. Levi and Hayley walked Belshegar and their daughter out to the big Suburban where it waited at the curb, and they remained on the sidewalk until Brianna had started the engine and begun the laborious process of turning the bulky vehicle around on the narrow street.

"We'll go to the hotel," he said once they were pointing in the right direction. "But only so I can get some of my things. There is no way in this world or any other that I'm going to allow you to sleep alone tonight."

The glow from the dashboard caught the ironic lift of her eyebrow. "Inviting yourself over? Don't you think it's a little soon for that?"

As most humans judged such things… perhaps. However, a tryst was the last thing on his mind.

Or at least, several other matters certainly came before any thought of becoming intimate with Brianna McAllister.

"You misread me," he said, and hoped he didn't sound too stiff. "I was not suggesting anything other than sleeping on your sofa and offering whatever protection I can."

Some women might have pointed out that he hadn't done a very good job of protecting her so far…quite the opposite, in fact. But Brianna wasn't some women.

No, she was her own unique, beautiful self.

"Sorry," she said, and let out a breath as she began to ease the Suburban into the hotel's cramped parking lot. "I shouldn't have jumped to conclusions like that. Today…it's just been a lot more than I was expecting."

"I understand," he replied. "Now, though, you'll come inside with me while I gather my things, and then we will go down the hill to your apartment."

Her lips parted, and he wondered if she was going to tell him that she would be quite safe here in the parking lot, since there seemed to be always someone who was coming and going from the hotel, and there was a far lower chance of the Collector and his minions trying to attack when they most likely would have an audience.

However, she closed her mouth without saying a word, which told him she'd realized she shouldn't take any unnecessary risks, as unlikely as the prospect of another assault might be.

The two of them climbed out of the vehicle, and she locked it before following him up the steps into the hotel lobby. Luckily, one of the elevators was free—of both human and ghostly travelers—so they got inside and rode up to the third floor. The whole time, he couldn't help wondering if the Collector or one of his servants might choose this moment to attack them in the cramped space...and what in the world they would do if such a thing should happen.

However, all remained peaceful, and they progressed to his room without incident. Once there, he packed as quickly as he could, deciding to take several changes of clothing with him since he wasn't sure how long his tenure as guardian might last.

Forever would be fine with him, but he guessed Brianna might have a few words to say on that subject.

Soon enough, though, they were descending the stairs from the lobby and back in her lumbering vehicle, and only a few minutes after that, she'd pulled into the parking space at the rear of the building that housed both the gallery and her apartment. Not for the first time, he marveled at how she was able to fit the oversized SUV in such a narrow place, although he supposed she'd had plenty of practice.

As they got out, he looked all around them, using his sight and every other sense he possessed to determine whether a hostile being lurked nearby, but he saw nothing, no hint that anyone had been watching and waiting for their arrival. A motion-activated light had been installed on the rear of the building, and it turned on as soon as they approached, which made him feel slightly better. Surely no one who was used to attacking under cover of darkness would risk an assault under the glare of such harsh illumination.

He went up the stairs first, just to be safe, but the landing outside her apartment was similarly empty, nothing there except a painted metal flowerbox with some late-season blooms happily growing inside.

"I think we're okay," she said with a smile as she laid her hand on the door handle.

At once, the door swung inward. This time, he let her go first, but he was close behind.

Just in case.

But her apartment appeared to be empty, one small lamp on the bookcase opposite the door providing some faint illumination before she touched a switch and a much larger floor lamp flared to light, banishing the rest of the shadows.

He hadn't quite been holding his breath, and yet he couldn't help being relieved that everything seemed to be in order here.

"I'm not sure where to put your stuff," she said, now sounding faintly worried. "There's only one closet, and it's stuffed to the gills."

Although he hadn't stopped to think about it, he realized that he'd been in Jerome for more than a week and hadn't seen her wear the same outfit twice. Perhaps a pair of jeans or some sandals had made a repeat appearance, but overall, her wardrobe appeared to possess quite a bewildering variety.

No wonder the closet was already full.

"It's not a problem," he replied. "My things can remain in the suitcase until I need them."

"Won't they get wrinkled?"

"Probably," he said. "But I can take care of that."

For a long moment, her gaze met his. It seemed to say, *Yes, I suppose you can.*

"I know this must be awkward," he said, thinking he might as well get everything out in the open as best he could. "It seems that we came to some sort of an agreement earlier, and yet—"

She went over to him and pressed a finger against his lips. Just that mere touch was enough to set the human blood within his veins on fire, but he guessed that was not why she had done such a thing.

No, she needed a chance to speak.

"It's okay, Belshegar," she said. "We don't have to figure all this out right now. Honestly, we should probably make sure there really will be a tomorrow before we start planning ours."

Very sensible.

Despite her no-nonsense tone, she still seemed on edge, and he couldn't blame her for that.

"I feel certain tomorrow will come," he told her, "and the day after that, and the day after.

Your *prima* and her consort seem very capable, and of course your father brings talents to bear that I am sure no other witch clan possesses. And there is also you."

"Yeah, me," she said, although she didn't look terribly cheered by her inclusion in that powerful group.

Well, this was all very new to her. Up until an hour or so ago, she'd had no reason to believe she possessed anything but some very simple magical powers.

"Yes, you," he said firmly. "You dealt the Collector quite a blow, between vanquishing his servant and destroying one of his precious artifacts."

"And letting him know there's a new witch on the block," she added, a certain light in her clear blue eyes signaling that she was beginning to realize she wasn't powerless here.

"Exactly," Belshegar said. "I'm sure he didn't expect that sort of resistance. With any luck, he is now second-guessing himself—which means we might have more time to prepare than you think."

"I sure hope so." She paused there, her gaze surveying the living room with its cheerful yellow-painted walls and the golden-hued landscape… another of Connor's paintings, Belshegar guessed…hanging above the bookcase with its beveled glass doors, a piece that must have been at least a hundred years old, most likely more. It didn't look like the sort of setting where an evil collector of magical items would stage an attack.

Apparently, Brianna thought the same thing, because she surprised him by yawning then, arms stretching out from her sides as she inhaled.

"Guess I'm more tired than I thought," she said. "My mother was right."

"It seems mothers often are," he replied, although those words were based more on what he'd heard from other people than because of anything he'd observed personally. Elena Salazar's civilian mother had been long gone by the time he arrived on the scene, but it seemed that Elena's husband was very close to his mother.

And certainly it appeared that Hayley was quite protective of her daughter, even though Brianna was an adult, as humans reckoned such things.

"We should both go to sleep," he said, and Bree's head tilted to one side as she considered him.

"So…you do sleep?"

"I do," he replied. "This body is human, even if the soul it contains is not. I don't require as much sleep as you do, and I can go quite a long while without food and water if I must, but I am certainly not an automaton."

In response to those words, she went on her

tiptoes and pressed her lips against his cheek. A pleased thrill went through him, but he knew she had made the gesture simply as a sign of affection and not because she wanted to initiate anything more.

"No, you're definitely not that." She moved away an inch or two but remained close enough so she could reach over and take his hand. Her fingers were slender and yet much stronger than they looked, probably from years of playing the piano and the guitar.

An incongruous smile touched her lips.

"I'm just glad you're you, Belshegar."

21

IT HAD BEEN A LITTLE WEIRD TO HAVE Belshegar sleeping on her couch—but not so weird that she hadn't basically passed out the minute her head hit the pillow and then slept soundly for the next nine hours. She guessed he hadn't been asleep that whole time, because when she finally wandered out to the living room a little after eight, he was awake and dressed, a cup of tea steaming faintly on the coffee table while he seemed absorbed in the beautiful illustrated edition of *The Hobbit* her parents had given her for her tenth birthday.

Since she'd guessed he might have woken up before she did, she'd thrown a light robe over her tank top and yoga pants, and also paused to put on some tinted lip balm so she wouldn't look quite so much like an extra from a zombie movie.

"Did you sleep okay?" she asked, and immediately he slid the green ribbon attached to the binding over the page so he wouldn't lose his place, then closed the book and set it down on the table.

"Very well, actually," he replied. "But I was not in need of as much sleep as you were, so I woke up about an hour ago."

Bree couldn't help feeling a little guilty about that, even though she understood she'd needed her rest.

Especially since none of them knew what might be coming next.

"I'm glad you found the tea," she said with a limp smile.

"I hope you didn't mind that I went looking. Perhaps I should have waited for you to wake up."

If it had been anyone else, she might have found herself a little irritated that he'd made himself free of her kitchen—and her bookshelf.

But this was Belshegar, and that meant he wasn't anyone else. No, he was just himself, as amazing and remarkable as that was.

What could a being such as he see in someone as small and limited and mortal as herself?

"No, it's fine," she said quickly. "I wouldn't expect you to sit here and just stare at the wall while I was off snoring."

"You weren't snoring," he responded at once. "Or at least, I certainly didn't hear anything."

Bree supposed she should be somewhat relieved by that. "I know you already had tea," she said, figuring it was time to move on to a more neutral topic. "But I can't function without a cup of coffee to get me going. Do you want any?"

"No, the tea is enough for me. Thank you, though."

His deep hazel eyes warmed as he looked at her, and she understood something in that moment. This was all new and strange, and she had absolutely no idea what the future might hold for them.

But despite everything—despite how they literally came from two different worlds—he loved her and would be there for her.

How could she ask for anything more than that?

It felt just a little anticlimactic to be back at the art gallery later that day, but she'd set this up with Chelle weeks earlier. The gallery's owner always took a week-long trip in late September or early October to visit other galleries and scout artists she might like to include in the collection at West by Southwest, and it was no one's fault that her time away had managed to fall right in the middle of this mess with the Collector.

Of course, Bree didn't mention any of her witchy woes to Chelle when her landlord slash part-time boss sent a quick text to make sure she'd still be able to cover as many hours as possible. At least Chelle understood that she had her music lessons to teach and gigs to play, and didn't expect her to be at the gallery eight hours a day. And since irregular shop hours tended to be the rule rather than the exception in Jerome, no one was going to have too much of a problem with the place possibly being closed when they decided to stop by.

Belshegar was up at Connor and Angela's house, meeting with them and the elders. Brianna didn't know exactly what they planned to do, but it sounded as if they intended to perform their ritual on the promontory where the clan had held its regular ceremonies honoring the four quarters of the year ever since the McAllisters first arrived in Jerome a hundred and fifty years earlier. Because it had been the site of so many rituals over the decades, they seemed to think the spot would have its own energy, something extra they could draw on to make their shielding spell as powerful as possible.

She supposed that made some sense, even though she wouldn't pretend to understand all the mechanisms involved in creating protective magic on such a large scale. Her father had assured her again that she'd know what to do when the time came, but she wasn't nearly as certain as he.

But while she had a feeling that being involved in the actual nitty-gritty of creating such an enchantment would have felt like being thrust back into calculus class—she'd passed with a B-minus and sincerely hoped she'd never have to go through anything that mentally painful again—she also didn't like the idea of being stuck here while everyone else went about much more important business.

However, bailing out on Chelle would have raised too many questions, which was why Bree found herself stuck at the gallery, watching as the hours and minutes inched past.

No busywork today, which was better in some ways and worse in others. While all that filing had been beyond tedious, it had given her something to focus on rather than watching the front door and hoping she'd get at least one or two patrons each hour to justify her being there.

Actually, there was a little more foot traffic than she'd expected—probably because it was another picture-perfect day, with puffy clouds dazzlingly white against sapphire skies and temperatures smack in that perfect zone between seventy-four and seventy-six—and she even sold a couple of pieces. Prints, true, and not originals, but they were still signed and numbered and went for around three hundred bucks each.

A little after two, a woman by herself came in. Since she smiled at Brianna, it seemed to be a signal that she wouldn't mind some help rather than exploring the place on her own.

"Are you looking for anything in particular?" she asked.

Her new customer seemed to relax slightly. She looked like she was maybe in her late thirties, and although her clothes were simple enough—a loose linen shirt in a warm brick shade over slim jeans—the wide silver cuff on her wrist looked expensive, as did the sculpted silver hoops she wore.

And both those pieces were nothing compared to the band of glittering diamonds on her left hand.

"I hope so," the woman said. "I wanted to get something for my husband for our anniversary— he's off golfing right now, so I thought I'd drive up here and see what I could find."

Buying art for other people could be tricky, and Bree hoped the woman had a good sense of her husband's taste in such things.

"Does he like modern art, or is he more traditional?"

"Traditional," the woman replied at once.

"Not Old Masters kind of stuff, but he doesn't have much use for art where he can't recognize the subject of the painting."

That helped. And since she'd already seen the woman's gaze track across the space to one of Connor's paintings on the opposite wall, a study of a big oak tree standing alone in a field, Bree thought she knew just where she wanted to direct her customer's attention.

Still, she also figured she probably shouldn't presume that the woman was willing to drop five figures on a painting for her husband, even if it was intended as an anniversary gift.

"Were you thinking of an original painting, or is a print more what you were looking for?" she inquired politely. There—that didn't sound like too much of a hard sell.

"I'd be open to an original if it was the right one." The woman moved toward the painting of the oak tree. Because the artist's name and the price were prominently displayed on the card posted on the wall next to the piece, it would have been impossible for her to miss just how much it cost. Without batting an eye, she said, "This one is lovely. Do you ship? We live down in Tucson, and I don't think this painting would fit in the trunk of our car."

Bree opened her mouth to respond that yes, they shipped anywhere in the world. But then she realized how cold it was in the gallery, how the temperature inside was beginning to feel positively arctic.

Had the mini-split that provided their climate control decided to go haywire at that exact minute?

The woman noticed it, too, and looked over at Brianna in bewilderment. "Is there something wrong with your air conditioning?"

"Feels like it," she replied. "I'll need to check on that."

As the words left her lips, though, the lights flickered, and the wooden floor under her feet shuddered ever so slightly.

What the hell? The hillsides here were unstable, but still, it wasn't as if Jerome got many earthquakes. Good thing, or even more buildings would have slid down the side of the mountain.

The temperature dropped further, and once again, the lights blinked.

"I think—I think I'm going to check out a gallery I saw in West Sedona instead," the woman said, and all but ran outside, letting in a waft of warm air before the door closed behind her.

Realization flared in Brianna's mind, sharp and frightening as a lightning strike.

It had gotten cold like this just before the Collector's minion had attacked her and Belshegar the night before.

Adrenaline surged, and she reached for her phone, thinking she would call him or her father...hell, Angela and Connor...to come and help.

But even as that thought shot through her mind, the phone went flying across the room and into the hand of a man she knew hadn't been standing there a moment earlier.

If she'd passed him on the street, she probably wouldn't have given him a second glance. He was a little taller than average, with medium brown hair and brown eyes, and he wore a white button-up shirt and khakis.

But even as the phone landed in the stranger's palm, something about his form seemed to shimmer. Not so much that she could see what lay underneath, but enough to tell her that the guise he wore wasn't his real appearance, and instead was one he'd assumed specifically for this encounter with her.

"The Collector, I presume?" she asked, surprised that she sounded so calm.

Then again, since the stores on either side of her weren't even open—they had strictly Friday through Sunday hours—who would have heard her if she screamed?

The man smiled. His teeth were even and white, which didn't tell her very much. They seemed just as calculated as the rest of the disguise he wore.

"You presume correctly," he said. His voice didn't have a trace of accent, and was friendly enough.

Not that she believed his outer aspect of good-will for a second.

"What do you want?" she demanded. "I'm not selling any magical artifacts here. Just paintings and prints and some local jewelry."

The smile he wore didn't even flicker. Or at least, while it remained in place, his appearance glitched once more. Again, not so much so she could see what he really looked like, and she wondered if he was doing that on purpose to put her even more on edge.

"Oh, I know that," he said casually, although his gaze lingered on Connor's oak tree painting before returning to her. "That's not why I'm here."

"I'm not paying you for that orb I broke," Bree remarked. "I'll admit I don't have a lot of experience with this kind of thing, but I'm pretty sure 'you broke it, you bought it' doesn't work when it's a case of self-defense."

The Collector chuckled, and she couldn't miss the amused glint in his brown eyes.

Well, the eyes he'd decided to wear for this meeting, anyway.

"No, I wasn't expecting that of you," he said.

"While I wasn't pleased that a servant of mine would be so careless with an object of such value, I can't fault you for doing what you must to protect yourself."

She crossed her arms. Her brain was working furiously, wondering if there was some way she could use her strange, multidimensional talent to reach out to Belshegar or her father, and yet she couldn't figure out how to make something like that happen.

Still, she had to try.

Belshegar! she called out with her mind, doing her best to imagine the thought flying upward and away from the gallery, rising to its destination on Paradise Lane.

A good plan, she'd thought.

Unfortunately, nothing happened.

To her relief, though, it also didn't seem as if the Collector had noticed what she was trying to do, so at least he wasn't omniscient.

"No," he went on, "I must admit I was surprised by the talent you manifested during that altercation with my servant. It isn't a gift I've ever heard of before, although I assume it must have something to do with Levi McAllister being your father."

She wanted to ask the Collector how he knew about any of that, except Belshegar had already made it sound as if their foe was someone who possessed far more information about the McAllister clan than he should.

"Maybe," she said carelessly. "We haven't had too much time to really investigate it yet."

"A mistake," he replied. "You should be doing everything you can to test your gift, experiment with it, instead of playing shopkeeper."

That same thought had passed through her mind several times today, but there was no way in the world she would admit such a thing to the man who'd caused such mayhem.

Because she only stared back at him, her expression as stony as she could make it, he seemed to realize there wasn't much point in pursuing that line of attack.

"No," he continued, "I came here because I wanted to offer you a deal."

"'A deal'?" she repeated, her tone incredulous. "Why in the world would you think I'd be willing to make a deal with someone like you?"

He didn't even blink—and his appearance held steady as well. "Because," he said softly, "I can show you how to use your extraordinary gifts. Not even your father has the same understanding of magic that I have, so you will never reach your full potential under his tutelage."

"An understanding of magic gained by stealing everything magical that isn't nailed down?" she shot back, and the Collector's mouth quirked slightly.

"I suppose you think I deserved that," he said. "But I am not here to explain to you why it is so important that these artifacts are in my keeping and no one else's. I am only here to tell you that if you want to understand how your magic truly works, then it would make the most sense to join forces with me. Also," he added, seeming to sense she was about to offer further protests, "if you do so, then I will stop trying to retrieve the amulet… and also the talisman your red-haired witch friend took from my servant. That one is definitely mine, an artifact I loaned the man so he would have a greater chance of success in his mission, and it is nothing that should have been in your clan's keeping in the first place. But I would allow it to remain here."

How magnanimous of him. At least that explained why the dreadlocked thief had had the little rock crystal amulet on him in the first place. No one had known for certain whether he'd found it while he was out doing the Collector's bidding and was bringing it back to his master, or whether it had been given to him to boost his chances of making away with the artifact Devynn and Seth had found back in 1884.

Not that it really mattered now.

What mattered was that it had been safely

locked up as well, which meant there was no way the Collector would be able to get his hands on it.

"As far as I can tell," he went on, since she hadn't quite been able to come up with words vitriolic enough to express exactly how violently she planned to refuse his offer, "this would benefit everyone involved. Your clan would no longer need to fear any incursions by me or my servants, and you would finally have the chance to develop your talents to their furthest extent."

She slowly uncrossed her arms, and he watched her carefully as she did so. Was he thinking that the shift in her posture signaled a surrender of some sort?

Well, if that was the case, then he was in for a big surprise.

"No," she said. "I'd rather keep blundering around with my magic for the rest of my life than join forces with you and betray my clan. You need to get the hell out of here before my father and the elders figure out you've breached their wards."

Not even a flicker of emotion on the Collector's face.

He would have made a damn good poker player.

"You are making a mistake," he replied.

She only lifted an eyebrow. "Some might say you've done the same thing by coming here."

Now his mouth twitched ever so slightly.

"Well, it seemed my servants couldn't be trusted to carry out my wishes, so I thought this was an errand I should handle myself."

Bree tilted her head ever so slightly. "Sorry to have wasted your time, then."

"It would seem so."

And then...he was just gone. Although she'd seen Connor and Angela teleport once or twice, this was even more disconcerting, since the Collector didn't even make the small *pop* she always associated with air rushing in to fill the vacuum left behind when the *prima* and *primus* traveled that way.

No, he simply disappeared.

Bree looked all around, but he clearly had gone elsewhere rather than just another location in the gallery. All the same, she knew she needed to let her father and the other elders know that she'd gotten a personal visit from their adversary, so she got out the key for the gallery's front door and paused for a moment to turn around the "be back at" sign that hung in the window.

Sorry, Chelle, she thought.

Clan business always came first.

22

EVERYONE HAD GATHERED IN THE LIVING room at Connor and Angela's house, with Levi explaining how they would use the two artifacts in their keeping to incorporate into their ritual and, with any luck, make it that much stronger. Belshegar thought that a good plan, since he understood how those magical items possessed an extradimensional component that he didn't think their human creators had completely comprehended. However, it was that very component which made those talismans so powerful…and which also made them uniquely suited to aid the McAllister clan now.

Someone rang the doorbell, and they all startled. However, Angela recovered herself quickly and got up from the chair where she'd been sitting so she could answer the summons. Something about her expression was almost perplexed, however, as if she knew she didn't get too many unannounced visitors and couldn't quite figure out who it might be.

A ripple of energy that Belshegar guessed no one else could sense seemed to pass through him, and he realized exactly who was waiting on the front porch.

Brianna.

Something must have happened, for otherwise, he couldn't think of a reason why she would have left the gallery unattended.

"I need to talk to everyone," she announced as Angela let her in.

"What's wrong?" the *prima* asked.

Levi and Connor had risen from their seats while Brianna made her way past the foyer and to the threshold of the living room. "It's the Collector," she said breathlessly. "He was just at the gallery."

At once, Belshegar got up as well and went to her, taking her hand in his. In that moment, he didn't care what the rest of them thought.

He only wanted to make sure she knew he was there to help her and support her in any way he possibly could.

"Are you all right?"

She nodded. Although she looked somewhat pale and strained, it didn't seem as if she'd suffered any harm during her encounter with their adversary.

"I'm fine," she said. "He tried to convince me to join forces with him—said he was the only one who could teach me to explore the full extent of my powers."

"I trust you said no," Angela commented, her wry tone belying the tension in her mouth and jaw.

"In no uncertain terms," Brianna replied. "But he also hinted that he'd shown up in person because of the way Belshegar and I defeated one of his minions."

That piece of information was not reassuring, to say the least. Belshegar knew he'd been hoping deep down that the man—if that was even what he truly was—would continue to send his servants against the McAllister clan, since they would be easier to defeat. If he'd felt comfortable appearing in the very heart of town, then that seemed to signal he was not overly concerned that they might prove to be a powerful foe.

"Testing our limits, I suppose," Angela said, and looked over at Levi. "Did you sense that he was here?"

At once, Levi shook his head. "No, I didn't feel anything strange. But I wasn't particularly looking for it, either."

Belshegar thought that a good time to offer

his own insights on their adversary's sudden appearance. "It's entirely possible that he also possesses an artifact that conceals his magic. We have no real idea of how many such items he's gathered over the years, or what their particular properties might be. Since it seems a catalogue of these various objects was never created, we are only left to speculate."

"That's for sure," Angela remarked. She'd been looking less and less happy during this exchange, and he could tell she wished they had a more concrete solution to the current situation. "Considering that none of us knew the amulets were even a thing until Devynn and Seth brought the first one back from the 1880s. Since we don't know how many of them there are or what they can do, I'm sure the Collector believes he still has the upper hand even if he's suffered a couple of defeats."

"Well, we'll make sure it ends up being more than just 'a couple,'" Connor replied. If the stern set of his jaw was any indication, he had no intention of allowing the man to get the upper hand in this conflict.

And Brianna looked frightened but also uncertain. Was she second-guessing her refusal to become their enemy's acolyte? Under no circumstances should she ever have allowed her to consider such an offer for even the barest second, but if she somehow thought by doing so she could save her clan....

"Whatever is out there, we will handle it when the time comes," Belshegar said firmly, and was glad to see that Levi and the other elders nodded in agreement.

"Yes, we've done a pretty good job so far," Angela put in. "Especially when we had no reason to believe we would even be under this kind of attack. And if this jerk thinks he can just pop in and out of here whenever he feels like it, then he's got another thing coming."

"What did he look like?" Tricia asked then. Connor and Angela both sent her glances that bordered on disapproving, and she lifted her shoulders, clearly unrepentant. "I mean, it couldn't hurt to have a description so we can let other people in the clan be on the lookout for the man."

Bree's lips curled into an ironic smile. "I could tell you what he looked like when he came into the gallery," she said. "But that's not going to help much, not when I could tell his appearance was some sort of overlay, an illusion he summoned to hide what he really looks like."

"Oh," Tricia replied, now appearing somewhat deflated. "I suppose knowing any details about his looks wouldn't be of much help, then."

"Probably not," Brianna agreed. Then she

shrugged and added, "But if it helps, he was pretty ordinary. Brown hair and brown eyes. Maybe in his early forties. Tall, but not super-tall. Normal clothes—a white shirt and khakis and boat shoes."

"In other words, he looked exactly like the sort of person you'd never pay any real attention to," Angela said sourly. "So I doubt that's going to do us any good."

Everyone went quiet for a moment. But then Levi spoke, saying, "The Collector's appearance here shows that we need to work quickly, though. I know we were talking about possibly waiting for the full moon to power our ritual, but I don't think we can afford to delay that long. We need to do it tonight."

"'Tonight'?" Allegra repeated, bird-like features aghast. "We'll barely have any time to prepare."

"I know," Levi replied. "But there is something to be said for striking when an enemy least expects it. The Collector must know the phases of the moon just as well as we do, and I have a feeling he also believes we would wait for it to be at its most favorable aspect so our enchantments would be their most powerful. That's why we should perform the ritual this evening, just as soon as it's full dark."

No one looked overly thrilled by this prospect, although Belshegar also noted that no one present raised any objections, either. While Angela was the head of the clan, and Tricia and Allegra and Connor had their own formidable powers, it seemed they all deferred to Levi on these sorts of matters, as if they understood that his magic operated at a different level and they needed to heed his advice.

And in this particular case, Belshegar thought the man was right. Delaying would only give the Collector more time to mount additional attacks against them, while striking now might provide the McAllister witches with some element of surprise.

Also, while the moon wasn't full yet, it was at least waxing and gaining strength. They would still be able to use its energies, even if not quite in the manner they'd hoped.

"So we will continue to work on the ritual," Belshegar said. "And I think I should go with Brianna to the site where we will be conducting the ceremony."

"Me?" she responded, looking startled. "How can I help with that?"

"Because you need to sense the energies of the place when it's quiet," he said. "When the time comes, it's very likely that you'll have to use your powers to keep us all anchored to this dimension. When the Collector's servant attacked last night, he was trying to drag me away from this world, although I can't say for sure whether he was simply trying to send me back to my plane where I couldn't cause any further trouble, or whether he wanted to trap me in a prison he'd created to punish me for my disobedience."

Both scenarios seemed equally likely, although Belshegar couldn't say for sure which one would have appealed more to their adversary. Most likely locking him up in some pocket dimension forever, since if he was merely banished to his home plane, he could have gone back to his quiet existence and continued as if nothing had changed at all.

He doubted the Collector would view such a fate as much of a punishment.

But Belshegar had no desire to meet either of those destinies. He loved Brianna McAllister, and being separated from her, even to an exile in his lovely, serene home, would have been utter torture.

She paled under her light, end-of-summer tan upon hearing those words, and yet she didn't protest, as if she understood the Collector was equally capable of doing both things.

Or perhaps something even worse, something that Belshegar couldn't imagine. Humans might have found his true appearance fearsome, but his was not a mind that could conjure scenarios of cruelty and torture.

The Collector, on the other hand….

"I get it," Brianna said. She paused there, brows pulling together for a moment. "But don't you think it's kind of weird that he didn't mention you once during that whole conversation I had with him?"

"Not really," Belshegar replied. "Once he realized the extent of your powers, I became superfluous to him. Also, leaving me out of your discussion might also have made you wonder why he'd overlooked my presence here, which would be some cause for dissonance and worry."

"Well, I guess he got that part right." She stopped there, and her shoulders lifted ever so slightly, almost as though she was doing her best to rid herself of any thoughts of the Collector and his machinations.

When she spoke again, her voice was firm.

"But that's the only thing that bastard is going to get right."

23

BRIANNA KNEW THEY WERE AWFULLY EXPOSED on the promontory where the McAllister clan had been performing their magical ceremonies for the past hundred-plus years. Anyone could see her and Belshegar out here and wonder just what they were up to.

Her shoulders gave a nervous hitch, and immediately, he reached out to take her hand. "You have nothing to fear."

"If you say so."

She knew how brittle her voice sounded…and she also knew it was her way of trying to cope with the tension of the situation, the reality of knowing that some eight hours from now, they would be standing out here again, doing their best to weave a web of magic that would keep the Collector away from this place forever.

"I do say so," he replied calmly. "While our enemy can see a great deal, he can't see everything. And because your father and the other elders and your *prima* and her consort are already working with the energies that will be at their greatest strength tonight, I have to believe the Collector's surveillance will be focused on them."

If that was Belshegar's way of trying to comfort her, Brianna didn't know whether it was all that effective. What was the point in feeling personally safe if her father and a whole bunch of people she cared about could be attacked at any moment?

However, she also realized that she couldn't allow herself to be so scattered. No, she needed to do what she could with whatever her companion wanted her to learn from this place. If she was a fidgety mess, how in the world would she be able to help tonight in any sort of effective way?

"All right," she said. "What am I looking for?"

"Energy," he replied promptly. "Decades of rituals performed here created their own power. You only need to sense where it's strongest and learn how to draw on it. Your own strength is already vast, but in a situation like the one we'll face tonight, you'll need all the help you can get."

Well, at least he wasn't trying to sugarcoat things. Before they'd come down here, they'd stopped at her apartment so she could change into sturdier shoes and pull out the floppy canvas hat she often wore when she went hiking, so she had to hope if any onlookers spotted her and Belshegar walking around on the flat part of the hill that overlooked the Verde Valley, they'd think they were only out getting some fresh air and nothing more.

"All right," she said, knowing that she didn't sound particularly hopeful. Even though she realized he was only trying to help, she also couldn't help thinking that she didn't know what the hell she was doing. Maybe her power only woke up during moments of extreme stress, which meant this sunny stroll through the dry grass wasn't going to do her a damn bit of good.

Way to fail before you even get started, she scolded herself. *Belshegar thinks you can do this, so that means you can, right?*

As long as his confidence in her wasn't utterly misplaced.

She moved a few paces away from him, headed toward the spot where the McAllisters always gathered at the four quarters of the year—Samhain and Yule, Ostara and Mabon. As she went, she thought she could feel something stirring, sort of like a kind of warmth seeping up through the soles of her hiking boots and moving all through her body.

Was this the power Belshegar had been talking about?

It had to be, since she'd never experienced anything like this before, even though she'd attended plenty of rituals in this location. Not all of them—she'd missed a few when she was off at college, and there had been others where she hadn't felt as if she could contribute a whole lot to the ceremony—but she'd probably been to more than most in the McAllister clan, thanks to her father being an elder and wielding his own special kind of magic.

"I feel it," she said.

"And I see it," Belshegar replied. "Look down."

She'd been gazing ahead, doing her best to let her senses flow freely rather than staring down at the earth, but when she glanced at her feet and legs, she saw a warm yellow glow surrounding her, shimmering like gold dust.

That was a little too conspicuous. No, there wasn't anyone else in their immediate vicinity, but if somebody was using the coin-operated binoculars up on the overlook, they might have been able to see a woman walking around on the promontory and glowing like she was radioactive or something.

As soon as that thought went through her head, the glow disappeared. Oddly, though, she could still sense the warm pulse of the energy behind it.

"Is it gone?" Belshegar asked from behind her, and she shook her head.

"No. I just got worried about someone seeing me looking like that, and the glow sort of went away. The energy is still there, though."

"Good. That means it wants to work with you, wants to help."

That sounded like a whole lot of anthropomorphizing to her, but she'd be the first to admit that she really didn't know too much about how any of this worked. Also, the energy that had settled here had come from generations of McAllister forebears, so it had a very human source. Maybe it was more responsive to people than she'd thought.

If that was the case, then she had to believe that energy, layered in this spot after decade upon decade of ritual work, would do everything it could to protect the people who lived and breathed now.

"It does want to help," she said softly.

She'd been so wrapped up in feeling the tingling hum of the energy beneath her feet that she hadn't realized Belshegar had approached and now stood only a foot or so away from where she stood.

"That's good," he said, his voice also an undertone, almost as if he didn't want to disturb the energy flowing around them. "And it's good that you can tap into it so easily."

Another unexpected aspect to a talent she hadn't even realized she had until a day ago?

But energy was energy, she supposed, whether it had traveled across unimaginable universes or had simply built up over the years, like layers of paint on an old door.

Thinking of it that way made the situation a little easier to accept. This was just another part of her, like the color of her hair or the sound of her voice. It wasn't anything to get freaked out about.

Although she couldn't help thinking there might be plenty to freak out about later, once the Collector realized what they were up to.

But doubting herself would only make matters worse. Belshegar believed in her, and that meant she needed to believe in herself as well, even though she'd never been very good at that kind of thing.

She twined her fingers with his and did her best to smile.

"Well, now that we've got this figured out, let's get some lunch."

Her father had told her she shouldn't cancel her classes that afternoon, so Brianna had dutifully driven down to Cottonwood to give Callie her guitar lesson, and afterward, had gone to Luke Dawson's house ten minutes or so away to work on his piano. It was inching past five-thirty by the time she started to head back up the hill.

Still too many hours to go until they performed the ritual, though. While she understood intellectually that waiting until dark was the only real way to do this, she hated the idea of trying to fill up the empty space in between.

In the end, though, it wasn't too bad. She and Belshegar had already talked about going to Grapes for dinner, so she met him there and they had pizza and wine, and talked about everything except the upcoming confrontation.

If it turned out to be a confrontation at all. Maybe the Collector would realize what they were up to but would decide not to fight back. They were only one small clan, when you got right down to it, and there had to be plenty more artifacts scattered around the globe, just ripe for the picking. Why get into a big battle here when he could turn his attentions elsewhere?

That all sounded very practical in her mind. Whether any of it was the truth was entirely up for debate.

After dinner, she and Belshegar went back to

her apartment and killed some more time by watching a couple of TV shows. She wasn't very interested in either of them, but even though one part of her brain thought it might have been a better idea to take him into her bedroom and divert themselves that way, she knew deep down that she wasn't ready for that. When they did become intimate, she wanted it to be because the moment was right, and not because she was trying to distract herself from the very real possibility that maybe none of them would survive this encounter with the Collector.

No, she was imagining worst-case scenarios because she didn't know what to expect. However powerful he might be, he was still only one man. There was no way in the world he could beat Belshegar and her father and Angela and Connor and the two elders.

But if he brought enough servants with him….

Around and around her thoughts chased themselves, but eventually it was not quite nine o'clock and time to go. Belshegar had been quiet for most of the evening, as if he understood that any pep talks wouldn't find a very receptive audience.

He held her hand as they walked down to the promontory, though, and she couldn't help being comforted by the strength and warmth of his

fingers. With the sun down, the mild temperatures of the day were long gone, and she'd had to
put on a jacket before they left the apartment.
Unlike her, he didn't seem to need any extra
protection from the cold air, and that small difference reminded her again that he wasn't human, no
matter what he looked like.

It didn't matter, though. After all, half of her
wasn't exactly human, either, so what was the big
deal?

Better to think about that, and to let her mind
tease out the possibilities of a future with someone
not of this world, than to allow her thoughts to
run into dark alleys that might only lessen their
chances of successfully banishing the Collector
once and for all.

The others were already gathered on the
promontory, all of them wearing jackets or wraps
against the chill of the evening. Still, they looked
like an ordinary enough bunch—and Brianna
even spied a large telescope set off to one side, a
device she knew belonged to Connor and Angela
and usually had a place of honor in one of the
eastward-looking bedrooms on the second floor of
their home. Most likely, they'd brought it along as
protective cover just in case anyone spied them
out here in the dark and wondered just what the
heck they were doing.

No moon yet; she'd checked the almanac

online earlier today and knew it wouldn't be peeking over the Mogollon Rim to the east until around midnight. In a way, she supposed it was better to do this under cover of darkness, and yet she couldn't help thinking it would have been nice to have some friendly moonlight to guide them.

Her father came over and gave her a quick hug. "Are you ready?"

"Ready as I'll ever be," she said, even as she wondered where her mother was. Safe at home, she guessed; Hayley McAllister's powers were strong, but she wasn't an elder and didn't have any real experience with this sort of ritual, which meant it was better for her to stand back and wait...especially when it didn't seem as if her magic-amplification gift had any real effect on Brianna.

"Then it's time to form the circle," Angela said. She'd been standing a few feet away and obviously had realized that she needed to allow father and daughter to have their moment, but now they needed to get started.

No point in putting this off any longer, after all.

The *prima* moved so she was standing in the spot that denoted true north, while Connor positioned himself so he faced her from the southern pole of the circle. Levi and Tricia and Allegra filled

in around them, while Belshegar held out a hand
to Brianna.

"We must stand in the middle."

Brianna followed Belshegar to the center of
the circle, her heart pounding so loudly she was
sure everyone could hear it. The energy from
earlier that day rose to meet her at once, stronger
now in the darkness, as if it had been waiting for
this moment.

"You'll be fine," Belshegar murmured, his
fingers still wrapped around hers. "Just let the
power move through you. Don't try to control it
—instead, act as its guide."

"Easy for you to say," she returned in a similar
undertone, but there was no real bite to her
words. He was right. If she thought too much
about what she was doing, she'd probably mess it
all up. Better to relax into it, to let her body
remember what her conscious mind was still
struggling to accept.

Angela began to chant something in a voice
low enough that Brianna couldn't make out the
words, although she guessed they were simple
English, only put together in the proper order to
help focus the energies rising all around them. The
other members of the circle began to chant, too,
their voices weaving together in an intricate
pattern of sound and rhythm. Her father joined in

as well, even though she knew he wasn't normally big on this way of using magic.

The significance of the moment wasn't lost on her.

Suddenly, the earth began to glow, just as she'd seen when she and Belshegar walked along this promontory earlier today.

"It's beginning," he said. His grip on her hand tightened, although she could tell he was taking care not to press too hard. "Remember what I told you. Direct the energy upward, like a shield."

Brianna nodded, guessing it was better to remain silent just in case her words might have an unintended effect on the spell Angela and Connor and the elders were weaving. The air around them began to thicken, becoming almost soupy. She felt a strange pressure against her skin, as if reality itself was doing whatever it could to push back against the enchantment they were weaving. The words of the chant grew more insistent, and she sensed the power building beneath her feet, rising through her body, ready to be shaped and directed.

Without conscious thought, she raised her free hand toward the sky. The golden glow flowed upward, enveloping her in a cocoon of light. This time, she didn't try to hide it. Let anyone watching think what they would—she and the rest of the spell-casters had more important concerns to occupy them right now.

The space above them seemed to waver, like the world seen through a layer of plastic wrap. Brianna experienced a strange doubling of her vision, as if she was seeing multiple realities layered on top of each other. For a brief, disorienting moment, she thought she glimpsed other versions of the promontory—one covered with snow, another lush and green with vegetation that had no place in Arizona.

"The dimensions are thinning," Belshegar told her, his voice tight and yet hushed at the same time. "The ritual is working."

Whatever relief she might have felt at that news evaporated as the air right above them suddenly ripped open. There was no other way to describe it—a tear appeared in the fabric of reality, jagged and bleeding sickly greenish light around its edges. The rip widened, expanding until it was large enough for a person to step through.

And someone did.

A man emerged from the dimensional tear, his movements unhurried and elegant, as if he were simply walking through a doorway rather than crossing between worlds. He wore an immaculately tailored charcoal suit, and even in the strange lighting, Brianna could see that his features were the same as those of the man who'd confronted her in the gallery earlier that day, unassuming enough…unless you looked closely. His eyes gleamed with dark knowledge, deep and ancient and utterly devoid of compassion.

Behind him came several figures in long, hooded robes, their faces hidden in shadow. They moved with eerie synchronicity, taking up positions around their master like pieces on a chessboard.

"Belshegar," the Collector said, his voice casual, as though they'd just bumped into each other in line at Starbucks. "How nice to find you here in the company of your little witch friends." His gaze swept over the circle, assessing each person, before returning to Brianna. "And who might this be? A new pet?"

Belshegar stepped in front of her, shielding her with his body. Even though she would have liked to think she could take care of herself, she still experienced a rush of gratitude at the protective gesture. "You know exactly who she is…and she is none of your concern."

"Everything that happens in this miserable little town is my concern," the Collector replied, an edge entering his tone. He raised a hand, and Brianna noticed the large ring on the middle finger of his right hand, made of heavy gold and set with a stone that seemed to shimmer with all the colors of the rainbow, shifting and twisting in a way that made her just a little queasy.

Then he smiled, and despite the pretended warmth of his expression, a chill still ran down her spine.

"I had planned to conclude our business quickly tonight," he told Belshegar, "but seeing you here has changed my mind." He took a step forward, and the air around him rippled, as if his very presence disturbed the fabric of creation. "I'll give you one last chance, my friend. One final opportunity for redemption." He extended a hand. "Leave this place and return to your home. It seems you were not the right agent for me, but I will excuse your weakness if you give up this foolish mission to fight for these people."

Belshegar tensed beside her, every muscle in his human body now seeming as if it had been made of honed steel rather than simple flesh. His hand in hers had grown almost unbearably hot, and she could sense the way his power had begun to build, preparing for a confrontation she wasn't sure any of them could survive.

"I have made my choice," Belshegar said, and his voice was a low rumble, very different from the pleasant baritone Bree had grown used to. For just a second, his body began to shift, to grow huge and hulking, before it slipped back into the human shape he'd been wearing for the past week.

The Collector's pleasant expression froze, then slowly transformed into something much darker. Right then, he didn't look as much like an accountant on vacation as a mob boss planning his next hit. "So you have." He sighed, a sound of genuine regret. "Then I'm afraid we must do this the hard way."

He raised both hands toward the sky, and the ring he wore flared to life, coruscating with dark shimmers of multicolored light that looked like oil slicks on a sunless ocean. The night seemed to shatter around them as the power of dozens of worlds converged on one point.

And Brianna realized, as a wave of vertigo nearly made her stumble, that she was the convergence point.

24

THE ENERGY FLARING OUT FROM THE Collector's ring was stronger than anything Belshegar had ever encountered before. He was already having a difficult time holding on to his human form, but now he could practically feel the way this borrowed flesh wanted to release its hold on his spirit, the bond between the two disparate bodies becoming weaker and weaker.

Brianna had already seen his true self, and he doubted that Levi would be too surprised by it. How the rest of their group would react to seeing him unshielded by his human disguise, Belshegar wasn't sure, but he hoped they would understand that he was not the one they needed to worry about.

And yet, he wasn't ready to surrender. Perhaps it would be easier to stop fighting and allow his spirit to be blown across the universe to the place he called home, but he knew he would never do that. Somewhere within the depths of his heart, he understood that he had already given his allegiance to these people, this place.

Especially the woman who stood next to him in the center of the circle, her golden hair whipping around her in an invisible gale. She was the fulcrum of all worlds converging at once, the tipping point that would determine whether they fell to the Collector's onslaught or whether they managed to stay free.

All around them, the elders and the clan's *prima* and her consort continued their chanting. Belshegar realized it wasn't the words themselves that were important, but the connection between the five of them, the way they shared power among everyone in their circle, drawing it from the very ground beneath their feet. The golden glow that surrounded all of them might have wavered from time to time, but it still remained strong and bright despite the dark, shimmering energy the Collector had sent forth from the artifact he wore on his hand.

During the initial assault, the four servants the Collector brought with him had stood motionless, clearly told to stand by until they were needed. None of the group even appeared to be paying attention to the battle of magical wills taking place before them, and Belshegar found himself wondering if they were human at all, like the thief who had first attempted to steal the amulet Angela and Connor had been keeping safe, or whether they were some kind of strange automata their adversary had conjured, knowing that human assistants might not have been reliable enough during such a confrontation.

But then Allegra Moss seemed to stumble, her knees giving way under the weight of the magical burden she was being forced to bear. At once, Levi hurried over to her, lending her his arm so she might stagger upright once again. Next to him, Brianna sucked in a worried breath and began to move as though she intended to offer what assistance she could, but Belshegar tightened his grip on her hand, holding her back.

"You must stay inside the circle," he murmured. "All depends upon it."

Desperate blue eyes stared up at him, but she nodded without speaking. The lines of her lovely throat and jaw were so tight, he could see the tendons standing out against her smooth skin.

And yet she didn't waver, and instead stood a little straighter and tilted her head up toward the sky, as if the force of her stare might be sufficient to hold back the dimensional energies pressing down on them.

Maybe it would. Belshegar guessed that none

of them—most of all Brianna herself—fully understood the extent of her powers.

But one of the Collector's servants, obviously sensing her moment of weakness, chose that moment to dart forward as if to physically assault the elderly woman, to break the connection between the McAllister witches and allow his master the opening he needed. In the next moment, however, bright energy flashed from Angela and Connor's conjoined hands, green and brilliant as their eyes.

It drove the minion back. For a second, the hood he was wearing slipped, and Belshegar caught sight of a man not much older than Brianna, expression startled and frightened, before he pulled up his hood with shaking fingers.

So, they were human after all. Perhaps the Collector had realized that mortal witches and warlocks had their own peculiar strengths, something that an artifact could never possess.

A spasm of irritation passed over their enemy's face, although he sounded pleasant enough as he spoke again.

"You are more powerful than I thought."

"We're not a bunch of amateurs," Brianna said. Her voice was still tight with strain, but it seemed clear enough that she had no intention of backing down.

"No, it would seem not," the Collector

replied. His appearance shimmered for just a second, and Belshegar thought he caught a glimpse of long, pale hair before the face and form of the ordinary, brown-haired man he'd been wearing reasserted itself. "But you still have no real comprehension of why I need to be the keeper of these artifacts, and not those who have no idea how to properly take care of them."

He lifted his hands, and the dark energy pulsing around him seemed to intensify, pouring out of his ring like a geyser gushing black oil. Brianna's breath caught, and Belshegar tightened his grip on her fingers.

"Stay with me," he said.

Her gaze met his, and an incongruous smile touched her beautiful mouth.

"Always."

The chanting of the circle grew louder. Out of the corner of his eye, Belshegar saw how Levi continued to support Allegra, while the other members of the McAllister clan had rearranged themselves to fill in the gap his shift in position had created.

Clearly, these people were no strangers to facing down dark magic, even though he doubted they'd ever confronted an enemy like this before.

Still, they seemed to intrinsically understand that they couldn't falter, that they needed to make their stand here.

After all, even if they could have no clear idea as to how many artifacts the Collector had already gathered to him, they still must know that if he was allowed to continue on this current path, at some point he would be so powerful that no one —not even, perhaps, many witch clans working together—would be enough to defeat him.

Dark lightning crackled overhead, and although Belshegar couldn't see the physical evidence of such a shift, he sensed how the pressure on this fulcrum point intensified, how all the energies of thousands of dimensions were descending on this lonely hilltop.

Brianna's breath caught, and a terrible shudder went through her slender body.

"It's too much," she gasped.

Yes, it was. She should never have been forced to bear such a burden, no matter what power she carried within her.

And yet...she was the only one who could drive back the intensity of countless collapsing realities.

"I know, beloved," he murmured. "But I'm here with you. We all are."

Her lips pressed together. Under the crackle of those brutal energies, her beauty still shone forth, no matter how pale and frightened she looked.

Then she seemed to straighten, and she drew in a breath. Her blue eyes blazed bright as laser beams, and she stared at the Collector with the cold calm of a queen about to pronounce a sentence on a wayward subject.

Voice clear, she replied, "And I know we're going to stay together...no matter what happens."

25

NOT JUST THIS UNIVERSE, BUT UNCOUNTED others seemed as if they were holding their breath.

Waiting.

Waiting for her to save them.

Just a moment before, she'd felt like one of those witches sentenced to death in Salem, slowly crushed beneath the weight of the stones that stole their oxygen, their life.

Something had shifted, though. Brianna couldn't say why—maybe it had been the stubborn golden glow that continued to rise from the earth, telling her that this place, this crazy little town that was the only thing she'd ever known, wasn't about to give up without a fight.

Or maybe it was the way Angela and Connor and her father and Tricia and Allegra hadn't stopped chanting for a single moment, not when

414 | CHRISTINE POPE

the fragile Allegra had fallen to her knees and Levi had gone to help her back to her feet, not even when one of the Collector's servants and tried to take advantage of that moment of weakness.

Or maybe…just maybe…it had been the glow of love in Belshegar's eyes, his fierce belief that she wouldn't fail them, even when he had to understand that she didn't know what the hell she was doing.

The evil magic the Collector had summoned surged overhead, blotting out the stars, bringing with it a hellish fire like black lightning. For all its dark strength, though, it wasn't enough to hide the energies she sensed surging around them. As she looked around with vision that now seemed oddly enhanced, it seemed as though rivers of pure energy in all the colors of the rainbow— searing violet, and serene green, and sunny yellow —bore down upon the hilltop.

Those beams of energy crisscrossed the promontory, connecting to the witches and warlocks in the circle around her, to Belshegar and Brianna, to the Collector and his minions, telling her that even though they might be at odds right now, they still had their own place in creation. Her magic surged, reminding her that even the most dissonant chords could make their own harmony.

Without consciously knowing exactly how she

was doing it, Bree reached out and grasped the Collector's magic, pulling at it like she might pluck the strings of a harp. With each note, it began to shift and change, its sharp edges smoothing, becoming one with all the other energies at play, whether they came from the ground beneath her feet or her fellow McAllisters...or Belshegar.

And he seemed to understand what she was attempting, because it was as if he'd lifted his voice to join with hers, even though neither of them was singing.

No, this was all about their powers coming together, each finding the right space to complement the other, becoming stronger and purer the longer they were mingled.

The glowing energy of Jerome shifted, became in her altered vision more like a huge net that covered the promontory. Not one to capture those within, however, but instead to ensure that nothing could pass that protective barrier.

And somehow Bree also realized that the glowing net extended far beyond this space and time, spanning multiple realities at once, as if it had recognized that an attack didn't necessarily have to come from this world, not when the Collector possessed talismans that could cross dimensions and summon what he needed to him.

His eyes widened, and again she saw the way his appearance shimmered, for a second revealing a man who looked to be some ten or fifteen years older than she, with cruelly handsome features and white hair shocking against the dark garments he wore.

Was that his real face, or just another guise he'd retreated to when his first false face threatened to disappear?

She didn't know, because the disguise was back in place now, although with features twisted in fury as he seemed to understand what she was trying to do.

"It's too much," he snarled at her. "You'll never be able to keep this intersection from collapsing!"

But that, she realized, was exactly what she wanted to have happen.

As long as all the pathways to these various dimensions were open, the Collector would have a chance to retreat.

No, she needed to trap him, just like she'd use an upside-down cup to trap a particularly troublesome fly.

The glowing lines of all those dimensional energies began to shift, leaving a rift between them, a place of nothingness, a void.

"Get down!" she shouted at her father and the rest of the McAllisters. "Hold tight to the ground!"

They stared at her, eyes full of questions, but the urgency in her voice seemed to be enough to convince them that they'd better obey. All of them sank to the earth and its covering of dry, scrubby grass, although she noticed that they continued to chant as best they could…and they never let go of one another's hands.

Good.

She glanced up at Belshegar, and he nodded.

"Do what you must," he said quietly.

He'd also continued to hold on to her hand this entire time, and she knew he wouldn't let go now, not even if she commanded him to press himself flat against the ground the way the rest of them had just done.

No, he was going to stand next to her and continue to boost her powers with his own.

A scream shredded the night as one of the Collector's minions was lifted into the air as if he was being sucked into an invisible tornado. Was it the man whose face she'd glimpsed so briefly only a few minutes earlier?

Impossible to say. One by one, the remaining three met the same fate, disappearing into the void she'd created as if they had never been.

However, the Collector still stood where he'd been this whole time, although the weird, oily energies he'd summoned now swirled around him faster and faster, as if he thought their sheer velocity would be enough to save him from also being drawn into the nothingness between worlds.

"You can't do this!" he shouted at her. "You can't control what you've created. It will destroy you and everyone you love!"

The Brianna from a few minutes earlier might have believed those words. Now, though, she realized they were only a ploy, a desperate attempt to get her to reverse the magic she now controlled so their enemy might have a chance to escape.

"I don't think so," she said, and he bared his teeth, although she wasn't sure whether the grimace was in response to her stubbornness or the phantom winds that had begun to pull at his flesh.

"You are a foolish, stubborn child," he spat. "You know nothing. Do you think something like this can stop me? I, who have the power of a hundred magical tools at my disposal? I will crawl back from whatever hell you have created so I might take my revenge against you and all these foolish McAllisters. You have no idea what you're doing!"

No, she thought, *I know exactly what I'm doing.*

She wouldn't bother to say those words out loud, though. It was enough that she'd recognized her own strength, her own abilities, and was allowing herself to use them.

In that moment, though, she saw their enemy's weakness. If his own powers had been sufficient, would he really have been compelled to seek out all those artifacts to make himself invincible?

Probably not.

Speaking of weak....

The energy that had surged through her earlier was nearly depleted. Her powers had helped her shift the dimensional focuses so the void had been created, but she realized they weren't limitless. She was only a human woman, after all, not a goddess, not a being from another plane like Belshegar.

"I don't know...." she whispered, and he bent and placed the gentlest of kisses against her forehead.

"You do know," he replied, then touched her on the temple and again on her heart. "You know in the deepest of places that you can do this. You must."

Yes, she had to. She couldn't give up now, not when she was the only one who could save her clan. Even Connor and Angela...even her father...didn't have the ability to make this happen.

Just like that time you ran the Sedona marathon, she told herself. *You thought you were going to drop those last three miles, but you did it anyway.*

So do it now.

Energy surged through her. She saw the rift

between dimensions widening, reaching out like a hungry mouth to swallow the Collector whole.

Threads of darkness resembling thin, reaching fingers began to flow across him. He pulled at them, the ring on his hand pulsing wildly as he tried to summon enough energy to counter their strength.

But then the ring shattered, bits of crystal flying everywhere, and he flung up his hands to protect his face.

That seemed to be enough, because now the darkness of the void grasped him by the arms and legs and pulled him backward. For one moment, his shocked gaze met hers, imploring, begging her to stop this.

She wouldn't, though. Not when he represented a threat to everyone and everything she loved.

A final despairing shriek, and then he was gone, the darkness taking him within.

Taking him far away.

The earth rumbled beneath her feet, and Brianna let go of Belshegar's hand, falling to the earth as the world spun around her. She had to make herself lie against the ground, because she thought if she tried to lift a single finger, she would go flying off and be swallowed up just as the Collector had.

All the lines of energy that had connected the

witches and warlocks in the circle shivered once and then went flying apart, sparkling against the night sky like the world's biggest fireworks explosion.

And then they were gone, and the stars shone overhead. A cool night breeze touched her cheeks as she felt Belshegar sink into the dry grass and cradle her head in his lap.

Oddly, it felt good to be here.

She thought she'd rest for a while.

26

THE OTHERS CROWDED AROUND HIM.

"Is she…?" Levi said, and then stopped there, as though he couldn't bear to give utterance to such a terrible thought.

"She breathes," Belshegar replied. The rise and fall of her chest was very faint, but it was just enough to let him know Brianna was still alive. "I think that last push was too much for her."

"We need to get her down off this hill," Tricia said. Once again, she sounded brisk, but he guessed she was trying to be practical in an attempt to hide the very real fear that one of their own might have suffered irreparable harm while trying to protect the clan.

However, he knew the elder was right. Lying on the hard earth in this cold wind would certainly not do Brianna any good.

"I will take her to her apartment," Belshegar told the assembled witches and warlocks, and added, "In my way."

They seemed to understand he meant that he would transport her instantaneously rather than waste time carrying her down the hill and then over to her home, because they all appeared to relax slightly at those words.

"Are you sure we shouldn't have our healer look at her?" Angela inquired, delicate features still anxious. "She's only been officially on the job for a year or so, but…."

"I think what Brianna needs most is rest," Belshegar broke in, but gently, so the *prima* would understand he hadn't meant to be rude. "But if it seems she is outside herself for too long, then yes, I suppose it couldn't hurt to have the healer examine her."

To be sure, he didn't know whether even a witch healer—especially one who sounded as if she was young and only beginning to ease into her position—would be able to help Brianna. She had tapped too deeply into her powers, knowing she was the only one who stood between her clan and utter destruction. Perhaps if she had had more time to learn to work with her gifts, she wouldn't have found it necessary to tax herself so much.

But there hadn't been any time. Now all they

could do was wait and see if she could recover on her own.

"I will go, then," he said simply, and gathered her into his arms. A nod toward the watching witches and warlocks, and then he imagined himself in Brianna's apartment, with the cheerful yellow paint on the walls and the whimsical collection of local art and pottery and the table full of house plants clustered in front of the main room's picture window.

Of course, that was not his true destination, but since he'd never been in her bedroom, he had to send himself to a place he knew. From there, it was simple enough to take her into the room where she slept and to lay her down on the oversized bed there.

The walls in here were painted a soft sage green, a color he'd guessed had been chosen because of its soothing qualities. She didn't stir as he placed her on top of the quilt, which was a friendly patchwork of soft greens and blues.

Although he wouldn't presume to undress her, he did pause to unlace her hiking boots and set them on the floor next to the bed. She didn't even stir during that procedure, and he found himself frowning.

What if she'd caused herself a deeper injury than he'd first imagined?

As best he could, he pushed that unwelcome

thought out of his mind. No, she was just weary, and now all he could do was allow her to get the rest she desperately needed.

He turned on the floor lamp in the corner of the room, which cast a soft glow upward but didn't reflect directly on the bed the way the light on her nightstand might have. And since he could tell she was still breathing, he went out into the living room and then on to the kitchen so he could make himself a cup of tea.

Wasn't that what humans did when they were watching and waiting and worrying over a loved one?

He didn't have any personal experience of such things, but he'd witnessed that sort of behavior in the shows and movies he'd watched with Elena, so he assumed this particular choice of activity wasn't too unusual.

Because he'd already done this the night he'd slept on Brianna's couch, he knew where to find the box of oolong tea and how to fill the kettle on the stove. Standing there and watching the flames from the gas burner dance under the turquoise enamel of the kettle helped to ease his thoughts somewhat, but he knew he wouldn't be able to truly rest until he knew she was going to be all right.

The water inside the kettle began to make popping sounds before the whistle truly got started, so he turned off the gas and poured hot water into the cup he'd set out on the counter. Although Brianna had looked as though she wasn't going to wake up any time soon, he also didn't want to make the kind of noise that might rouse her from her sleep.

He hoped that was all she was doing, that she wasn't lost in a faint…or worse.

Perhaps he had been wrong to say that the healer didn't need to look at her right away.

But when he paused at the doorway to her room, cup of tea in one hand, he saw that Bree had opened her eyes and was staring at him, expression halfway confused, as if she wasn't sure how she'd gotten from that windy promontory to her bedroom.

"Did I pass out?" she asked, then pushed herself upward so she was resting against the pillows stacked in front of the padded headboard rather than lying flat.

"Yes, you fainted," he said as he moved farther into the room. "I thought it best to bring you here so you could rest."

She raised a hand to her temple and rubbed it. "My head hurts."

"Not so surprising, considering what you just endured." He lifted his cup of tea, adding, "Would you like this? It's oolong, and I haven't drunk any yet."

"I don't want to deprive you of your tea —" she began, and he smiled.

"I only made it because I needed something to do," he told her. "I would much prefer it if you would have some."

"Tea usually does help my headaches," she said.

He came over to the bed and handed her the mug he'd been holding. She wrapped her fingers around it, as if she needed as much of its warmth as possible.

Perhaps she would be even warmer if he took her in his arms, but he knew he shouldn't make that sort of advance, not when she needed time to recover from her faint…and the ordeal that had preceded it.

"Thank you."

She lifted the mug to her lips and took a small sip, followed by another. A faint smile touched the corners of her mouth and she said, "Yes, I think that's helping." A few more swallows, and she added, "What happened?"

"You banished the Collector to a void in creation," he replied, and now she grinned.

"I remember that part. But then it all got kind of hazy."

"You summoned all the power you could to make sure he was gone," Belshegar said. "It was too much for you, though, and you lost consciousness. I brought you back here so you could rest."

"Where's everyone else?" she asked, and her gaze moved past him to the open door and into the living room, as if she halfway expected to see the rest of the McAllister protectors assembled on the couch.

"I can't say for sure," he said. "However, I assume they probably went to Angela and Connor's home to discuss what happened."

Bree nodded and sipped some more tea. "I suppose I can see why they'd want to have a post-mortem." A long pause, and then she added, "So…he's really gone?"

A question Belshegar had known she would ask. While he didn't have a concrete answer at this point, he thought he could guess at the truth of the situation…and knew it was probably not anything she would wish to hear.

But he wouldn't lie to her. He had done enough of that already…under duress, true, but still…and yet she loved him anyway.

"Gone for now," he said, trying to sound calm and matter-of-fact. "It's difficult to say whether the rift you created is permanent. Nature abhors a vacuum, as they say, and it's possible the void will collapse eventually and the Collector will be freed. Also, even though he is trapped, that doesn't mean he has been stripped of all his powers. It's possible that he might determine some way to summon one of his artifacts to him, something that would allow him to escape."

Brianna shot him an ironic look. "If you're trying to cheer me up, Belshegar, you're not doing a very good job of it."

He allowed himself a very small smile. "Would you have preferred that I lied to you?"

At once, she shook her head. "Of course not. It's just…." The words trailed off, and she put on a rueful smile to match his.

"I understand," he said. "It would have been better if this had all been wrapped up in a neat bow, as Elena might have put it. But this past week has taught me that reality—in this world, at any rate—is much messier than that."

"You can say that again." Brianna lifted the cup of tea to her lips and drank once more. At any other time, he might have worried about her consuming so much caffeine when she should be sleeping…when he'd made the tea for himself, he'd had no need to worry about how it would affect him…but he hoped she would be so wearied from her earlier exertions that an extra dose of stimulant wouldn't be enough to prevent her from getting the rest she needed.

Then she sent him a curious glance, as if truly taking his measure for the first time.

"You still look human."

"Yes," he replied quietly.

She set the mug of tea down on a coaster that appeared to have taken up permanent residence on her nightstand, probably so she could enjoy a cup of tea or coffee in bed, as she was doing now. "Does that mean the Collector's magic is still affecting you?"

Since he'd had some time to mull the conundrum while she was resting, Belshegar hoped he might have a sufficient answer to that question. "Not precisely."

Her brows lifted, but he guessed she was willing to wait for him to provide an answer, since she didn't say anything.

"You saw how my form shifted several times during the confrontation with the Collector," he said, and she nodded.

"Yes, I was kind of wondering if you were going to change back permanently. Good thing you didn't—poor Allegra probably would have fainted for real."

Because the corners of Brianna's mouth quirked as she spoke, Belshegar thought she was most likely teasing him ever so slightly. "Yes, that would have been unfortunate," he agreed. "You know how you can wear different clothing, but you are still completely yourself underneath? This human form has become like that for me—a permanent cover I now control entirely. All my abilities, all my powers, everything that makes me Belshegar, remain exactly the same. I've simply gained the ability to wear this form whenever I choose."

Bree sat up a little straighter in bed, clear blue eyes locked on his. "So…you can stay human for as long as you want to?"

"I believe so," Belshegar replied. The eagerness in her expression made his heart swell with hope. No, he could not fault her for wanting him to remain as he was—there would have been no chance for them to be truly together if he'd reverted to the body he'd known all his long life. He would have been forced to return to his plane, to go back to quietly tending his gardens and perhaps visiting this world every once in a great while, such as to welcome any children that Elena and Alessandro might have, or to make sure the wards the McAllisters had put in place tonight showed no signs of faltering.

"That's…good to hear," Brianna said. Then, as if she'd realized her relief might appear to be a rejection of his true self, she hurriedly added, "I mean, there's nothing wrong with how you really look, of course. It's just that you might be kind of hard to explain if you hung around Jerome looking like that."

"Yes, a similar thought had crossed my mind," he replied, his tone wry. "But I don't believe it's anything we need to worry about. Also," he added, needing to reassure her that he didn't mind wearing this human body for a very long time… forever, if that was what she wanted, "I have to admit I've become rather used to this form. It is somewhat less bulky to manage."

Her mouth lifted in a smile, one so beautiful that she made his heart ache all over again. "Now you're teasing me."

"I am not," he said calmly. "I am only telling you the truth."

"And you can still do demon things if you need to?"

Now it was his turn to smile. "Yes. Although I do hope I won't be called on to use any of those abilities anytime soon."

She was silent for a moment, but he noticed that she didn't reach over for her mug of tea, as if she, too, had realized she shouldn't consume any more of the stimulant tonight.

Voice quite different, she said, "The Collector isn't gone forever, but we have some breathing space, right?"

"I believe so."

Once again, she was quiet, seeming to ponder his words. A very small nod, as if she'd accepted the truth of what he'd said and allowed herself to absorb it. Perhaps it would be years before they had to worry about their adversary, or only months.

Or perhaps Belshegar had been wrong about his assessment of the situation, and they had nothing to worry about at all.

Brianna's fingers played with the edge of the quilt that covered her. "Will you—will you sleep with me tonight? Not…not to do anything," she amended hastily, because he hadn't been able to quite prevent himself from staring at her in surprise as she made the request. "But I know I'll feel safer with you here next to me."

That was a request he could accommodate well enough. Hadn't he done the same thing for Elena many times, providing companionship so she could survive another sad and lonely night in her attic bedroom?

And true, he hadn't slept in the bed itself because his bulk would have smashed it to splinters, but he'd lain on the rug next to it while she slumbered, providing what comfort he could.

"Of course," he replied.

True, it was a little awkward to remove his shoes and his socks while Brianna watched, and then to hesitate when his fingers touched the buttons of his jeans. Perhaps he should sleep in those as well, even though they seemed rather stiff and uncomfortable for bedtime attire.

"It's okay if you take the jeans off," Brianna

said, and again she sounded almost amused. "But I hope you can sleep in your T-shirt."

"That should not be a problem," he assured her, and went ahead and unbuttoned his jeans and then climbed into the empty space in the bed next to her.

Under the covers, her fingers sought his. "Thank you, Belshegar."

"I will always be here for you," he said simply.

She leaned over and pressed a chaste kiss against his cheek. "And I'll always love you for that."

Seeming to realize they'd said what they needed to, she reached over with her other hand and turned off the bedside lamp. Darkness fell on the room, but it wasn't absolute, not with the faint illumination from the mercury glass light on the bookcase seeping in from the living room.

Beside him, Brianna settled herself down on her pillow, and Belshegar did the same, placing his head on the one provided for him, doing his best to allow his body to relax. It was odder than odd to lie here next to her and realize how much he wanted her…but also to understand he was willing to wait as long as necessary until she was ready.

He would do that because he loved her.

SOMEONE WAS IN BED WITH HER.

For just a second, Brianna's brain skidded to a halt…and then memory caught up, and she recalled how she'd asked Belshegar to lie down next to her after the battle with the Collector. Although she'd realized she would probably be just as safe if he'd slept on the couch out in the living room, it still had felt better to know he would be there beside her if she awakened from a bad dream.

Or if the worst happened and the void that had trapped their enemy failed after only a few hours.

Neither of those things had happened, though. Instead, she'd slept deeply and soundly, untroubled by any nightmares or incursions of evil men from alternate dimensions. Yes, Belshegar had warned her that the Collector might not be locked away forever, but he hadn't shown up on her doorstep last night or this morning, so she was going to take that as a win.

She shifted carefully so she could look at the clock, although she had already guessed from the quality of light streaming through the sheer curtains out in the living room that the sun must have been up for quite a while.

Sure enough, the hour was getting close to nine o'clock.

When was the last time she'd slept that late? Some of her friends were the type who seemed as though they could stay in bed all day, but she wasn't wired like that. Normally, 7 a.m. was sleeping in for her.

Well, no one could say she hadn't been through a lot the night before. Parts of the battle had already begun to grow hazy, as if her brain somehow understood it would be better for her sanity if she forgot those moments when she hadn't felt quite human, but rather a conduit for energies she couldn't begin to comprehend.

She'd survived, though…thanks in no small part to the man who slept beside her.

His eyes were closed, and his chest rose and fell with regular, deep breaths. And although he'd told her that this body needed sleep like any other regular human, she didn't know if she'd quite believed him until this moment.

Goddess, he was gorgeous.

And strong, and kind, and….

Well, pretty much every positive adjective she could think of.

In that moment, she realized she wanted him to wake up. She wanted a whole lot of things.

But did he want them as well? Of course they'd kissed more than once, and she had to believe he'd felt something of the same need and heat she'd experienced.

And yet….

He looked human, but he wasn't. It was very possible that he'd need a whole lot more time to grow into this new life, of being both Belshegar and Bill Garrett, the traveler who'd come to Jerome for a vacation and decided to make it his home.

That was all right, though. Brianna told herself she could wait as long as necessary.

Yeah, right.

Just watching him like this was enough to make desire stir in her. Sure, she'd been asleep for nearly ten hours and some of her muscles still felt sore, as if she'd done a whole lot more than simply stand out on the promontory and channel the Goddess only knew what kind of energies, but she couldn't ignore the way her body craved Belshegar's touch.

Nothing ventured, she supposed.

She shifted again, this time not being quite so careful about her movements. The bed squeaked, and immediately, his eyes opened, and he looked over at her.

However, he seemed to understand there was no emergency, that this was just a natural awakening, because he smiled and said, "Good morning. How did you sleep?"

"Like a log," she replied. "Although I'm not sure why a log should sleep any better than anything else. How about you?"

"Surprisingly well. To be honest, I hadn't expected to sleep this long. It is quite late, isn't it?"

"A little before nine," Bree told him. "But I suppose we can both be excused for sleeping in, considering everything that happened last night."

"Yes, it was something of a confrontation."

They both went quiet then. Brianna had a feeling he was mentally replaying the events of the night before, while she…well, she just wanted to reach over and pull him down on top of her.

Probably better to do this in baby steps, though.

She moved closer to him so she could reach over and take his hand. "We did good, didn't we?"

"We certainly did." His gaze caught hers, and

she thought she might get lost in those smoky hazel-green depths.

Depths that now seemed to hold a certain heat that she was pretty sure hadn't been there a moment earlier.

To her dying day, she knew she would never be able to say for sure which one of them moved first.

In the end, it probably didn't matter.

What mattered was that in the next moment, his arms were around her, pulling her close, and his mouth was on hers, warm and slightly sweet, with not a hint of morning breath.

She supposed there was something to be said for being with a guy who looked human but wasn't. Not quite, anyway.

The embrace lasted for a long moment, but then Brianna moved, sinking back against the pillows so he lay on top of her. Although he still wore his T-shirt, the jeans were long gone, and there was no denying the hardness of him against her leg, his obvious arousal.

Well, that part seemed to be pretty human, too.

He paused, though, and stared down into her face, his expression earnest and oddly sweet at the same time.

"Is this…is this what you want?"

"More than anything," she replied. "Honestly,

the only reason I didn't jump your bones last night was that I was just too damn tired."

A brush of a kiss against her cheek, and then he smiled. "But now we are both rested."

"Yes," Bree said, "we are."

And she grabbed hold of his T-shirt so she could pull it up and over his head, could take a moment to savor the perfection of his muscled body in the warm morning light filtering in from the living room.

The Collector might have been a raging dickbag, but he'd definitely conjured a gorgeous human form for Belshegar.

But she banished all thoughts of their enemy, because in that moment, all she wanted was to think of the man she loved, the surprisingly expert way he kissed her…the way his hands moved down to tug at the hem of her tank top and then pull it over her head.

His hands moved over her breasts, just the slightest bit hesitant, as though he still wasn't sure if she was ready to go any further than this.

"I want to," she told him in a whisper. "If—if you do."

"Very much so." He paused, and a hint of a wicked smile touched a corner of his mouth. "I learned something of what this is about when Elena would watch movies late at night that her grandmother had forbidden her. It was…educational, if somewhat embarrassing from time to time."

Brianna could imagine. Lord knows it had been awkward enough when she was watching a movie with her parents when she still lived at home and a sex scene popped up out of nowhere.

But there was nothing awkward or embarrassing about being here like this with Belshegar. No, it was perfect, the culmination of a desire that had its origins in that very first moment when she'd seen him standing on the sidewalk outside the Caduceus Cellars tasting room.

She ran her fingers through his thick hair and pulled him close to her again, and this time his tongue moved across her nipple. A gasp escaped her throat, and she lay back and savored the exquisite sensation for a moment...until other parts of her body let her know they wanted attention as well.

Carefully, she guided his hand to the waistband of her yoga pants, and he took hold of it—and the panties beneath—and slid them down her legs. Soon enough, they'd landed on the floor, and his warm fingers brushed against her thighs and then slid up to her mound. For just a moment, he hesitated, as if he still wasn't sure this was what she wanted.

"Yes, Belshegar," she whispered. "It's fine."

He touched her then, fingers gentle and yet

urgent at the same time, and she gasped again, closing her eyes so she could savor the pulses of pleasure moving through her, so much more intense than anything she'd experienced during foreplay before.

Not so surprising, she supposed. Those other times, she hadn't been with Belshegar.

As he continued to stroke her and suckle her breast, those waves of pleasure grew stronger, and she knew it wouldn't be very long now. She put one hand on top of his, letting him know this was exactly right, that it was perfect in every way.

Warmth flared all through her, spreading out from her core and moving through every limb. She cried out, gasping, and he held her as she rode the orgasm, breath finally slowing as she let her head fall against the pillows.

"Wow," she said, and he smiled.

"I assume that was all right?"

"So much better than all right, it's not even funny."

She lay there for a second or two longer, but she knew she couldn't rest now, not when she needed to show Belshegar everything he'd been missing.

Her hand reached down and found him, feeling how hard he was still, how ready. She wanted to feel him inside her…but first, she needed to let him know that there were plenty of ways for him to experience pleasure as well.

A line of kisses down the hard muscles of his torso, and then she ran her tongue along his shaft. Air escaped his lungs in a startled gasp, almost as if he hadn't known such a thing was possible.

Well, even HBO didn't show every little bit.

Then she pulled him into her mouth, tasting the faint saltiness of his flesh, relishing the low, almost involuntary moan he let out. Yes, this was very new to him, and she had a feeling he wasn't sure of the ways this body responded to pleasure.

He hadn't seen—or felt—anything yet.

If possible, he'd grown even harder, and she realized if she kept at this too long, he'd surely come. That would have been fine, except she didn't want to wait even a minute more to feel him inside her, and she had no idea whether he had the same refractory time as a normal human or whether he might bounce back a bit faster.

So she slowly lifted her mouth from him, then shifted so she could settle herself on his shaft, letting all his strength and his heat fill her.

His eyes met hers, shocked and at the same time needful. Yes, he'd wanted this just as badly as she did, even if he might not have been able to fully understand those desires.

Their fingers entwined, and she held on to him as they rocked together, finding their rhythm.

The way he'd touched her had been amazing, but this was even better, since now they truly had become a single being, Belshegar and Brianna, two people whose blood might have come from other worlds but who had found their home in this one.

He came first, a burst of heat within her, but she followed soon after, a cry rising from her throat that made her glad the gallery was closed today. Anyone downstairs surely must have heard them.

They were alone now, though, and they clung together as the heat and the need from their orgasms slowly subsided. After a moment, Brianna eased herself off him so she could lie down once again and feel the strength and the warmth of his oh-so-human body pressed against hers.

Silence while her heartbeat seemed to thud in her ears. Finally, he spoke.

"I had no idea."

She pushed herself up on one elbow so she could better see his face. He looked almost super-naturally calm, but she couldn't miss how his chest rose and fell, how the faintest sheen of perspiration gleamed on his forehead.

"How could you?" she asked sensibly. "You didn't even have a human body until a little over a week ago."

"Still." He went quiet again for a moment,

and then he also moved onto his side so he could gaze at her more directly. "Will I ever stop being surprised by you?"

She touched her mouth to his gently, although even that soft brush of lips against lips was enough to tell her she'd be ready to try this another time in the very near future.

For now, though, she was content just to be here like this with him.

"I sure hope not," she said.

Her phone had about ten unread texts—most of them from her parents—so after Brianna and Belshegar had showered and made some coffee, she responded to them with variations on the same theme.

I slept well. I'm fine.

And she was. Not just because her slumber had restored the energy she'd depleted the night before when she banished the Collector from this world, but because she and Belshegar had made love.

Because they loved each other, and she knew everything was going to be all right.

Now they sat on the balcony that overlooked

Main Street and offered a spectacular view of the Verde Valley and Sedona's red rocks and the darker edge of the Mogollon Rim beyond. A cool breeze stirred the air, and she thought it couldn't get much more perfect than this.

"Our battle with the Collector had an unexpected side effect," Belshegar remarked after he'd taken a bite of cinnamon raisin toast.

"Just one?" Bree responded, knowing she sounded just a bit arch.

He smiled, and the sunny day got a little brighter. "One of several, I suppose," he said. "Something about the energies we raised appears to have strengthened the permanent wards protecting Jerome, so even if the Collector somehow does manage to escape at some point, I believe he —or his servants, if any are left—will have a much harder time getting in and trying to take the artifacts you're keeping here."

That was something, she supposed. Actually, it was a whole lot. While she really didn't want to consider the possibility of their enemy being free once again, she had to admit she was somewhat comforted to know that the former mining town wouldn't present quite as tempting a target. With any luck, he'd move his treasure hunt elsewhere.

"I know my father—and the other elders and Angela and Connor—will be glad to hear that," she said. "They've had to work so hard to make sure everyone is safe."

Belshegar nodded, his gaze moving from her to the street below them. Since it was now Friday morning, there was a bit more traffic than usual as people made their way up here for a long weekend, whether they were coming from Phoenix or Flagstaff or points even farther away.

And Brianna wasn't going to let herself feel the slightest bit guilty about the way the "be back at" sign had remained firmly in place in the gallery's front window. She'd borrowed her friend Bellamy's line about a "family emergency" and had told Chelle that she wouldn't be able to work this weekend, and although Chelle hadn't sounded too thrilled—especially since she was off in Sonoma and couldn't do much about it—she hadn't put her foot down and said Bree needed to get to work or find a new place to live.

However, the idea of relocating had already floated through her mind as she and Belshegar were getting ready this morning. The apartment had suited her just fine when she was on her own, but she could already tell they'd be on top of each other if they spent too much time in the place.

Maybe it was a little too early to be thinking about cohabiting, and yet she couldn't imagine doing anything else. They loved each other, and she knew they were going to be together. Why not start thinking about the future?

He must have also been considering much the same thing, because he said quietly, "Do you think it's going to be a problem? The two of us and your clan, that is."

"Absolutely not," she said, making sure she sounded as firm as possible. "For one thing, my father's origins are just as otherworldly as yours, and the McAllisters made him an elder. If they aren't just as accepting of you, then they're a bunch of hypocrites."

"They are definitely not that," Belshegar replied, still in that quiet, musing tone. "And I will admit that knowing your clan welcomed your father so kindly has helped to put my mind at ease."

"I know they'll do the same for you," she said, and meant each and every word. Part of being a McAllister was knowing how to roll with whatever life might throw your way.

Again, they went quiet, and she knew she needed to speak the words…just to be sure.

"So…you really are staying?"

His hand found hers. "Of course I am. I can't imagine being anywhere else."

Warmth filled her then, a very different kind from the heat she'd experienced a little over an hour earlier when they'd been lost in one another's arms. "I love you," she said simply.

"And I love you."

Her fingers tightened on his. "But we're probably going to have to find someplace else to live. This apartment is way too cramped."

Again, he didn't seem at all put off by her suggestion that they live together. "You might be right. And I will admit that I would like to live someplace with more land. Back on my world, I had many gardens to tend, and it would be good to be able to do that here as well."

He'd mentioned his gardens before, so his comment didn't surprise her too much, even though at the time, she'd thought he was talking about his place in Los Angeles. "We'll figure it out," she told him. "But we'll probably need to find a house somewhere down the hill…not many of the homes here in Jerome have big yards, and the ones that do have owners who have no intention of going anywhere." A thought occurred to her, and she added, "It might be fun to find something in Page Springs, especially now that Bellamy and Marc have bought the Rainbow Canyon winery there. Then we'd have friends close by."

"'Friends,'" Belshegar repeated in musing tones. "Yes, it would be good to have friends."

Of course, all this was pie in the sky if they couldn't come up with a way to fund such a purchase. They'd have to buy, since rentals in Page Springs were few and far between. And while Bree had some money saved up, she knew it wasn't anything close to what they'd need for a decent down payment on a house. Because of the place's popularity as a tourist destination, properties in the Verde Valley tended to be expensive.

But maybe her parents could loan them some money. Or....

"You are worried about financing such a project," Belshegar said, almost as if he'd read her mind. "Homes here are quite costly, are they not?"

"They can be," she admitted.

He let go of her hand and spread open his palm. Sitting on it were several large, clear stones. Even though they hadn't received their final faceting, Bree thought she knew what they were.

"Are those...diamonds?" she asked, knowing how shocked she sounded.

"They are," Belshegar said calmly.

"Where in the world did you get diamonds?"

"I made them," he said simply. "It is easy enough to convert energy into matter, so I converted it into something that has value in this world. Would these help to buy a house?"

"Probably more than one," she said with a grin. Clearly, he hadn't been lying when he'd told her he still had access to all his demon abilities.

"I believe one is all we will need," Belshegar

said, then slipped the diamonds into her hand and closed her fingers around them.

The gems were cool and ever so slightly sharp against her skin. Brianna couldn't begin to estimate how much they were worth, but she had to guess it was well over a million dollars.

"I could have conjured the house itself," he added. "But then it occurred to me that doing so would have raised far more questions than quietly creating the means for us to buy one."

That was for sure. Most residents in the Verde Valley were used to the way the younger generation of McAllisters tended to buy houses much earlier than their nonmagical counterparts, so she doubted too many people would raise an eyebrow at her and Belshegar purchasing a property together. Besides, he'd already presented himself as someone living off a trust fund, which meant a lot of her friends and neighbors would probably think he'd financed the whole thing. Really, there wasn't anything too strange about the situation.

Well, except for the part where they'd launched into a life together after knowing one another for barely two weeks.

"But we'll probably need a Wilcox to sell these for us," she said, still smiling. "I don't think anyone in my clan would even know where to start."

"Whatever needs to be done." Belshegar's

expression turned serious then, his gaze once again holding hers. "I want to be an equal partner with you, Brianna. You are so very strong, so very talented. I want you to know that I will not be a burden."

How could he possibly believe that she would ever look at him in such a way? But both his expression and his tone were earnest, and she thought she understood.

"We'll take care of each other," she promised, and immediately, he sat up a little straighter.

"Forever?" he asked, and she nodded.

"Forever."

∾

The Witches of Mingus Mountain series continues in Christmas Past.

ALSO BY CHRISTINE POPE
(SERIES WITH ASTERISKS ARE COMPLETE)

LEGENDARY

(Urban Fantasy/Paranormal Romance)

Silver Linings

Lion's Share

Trial by Fire (February 2026)

Here Be Dragons (June 2026)

VEGAS SLAYERS

(Urban Fantasy/Paranormal Romance)

Speak of the Devil

Devil in the Details

The Devil Went Down to Laughlin (September 2025)

Devil May Care (January 2026)

Devil to Pay (May 2026)

The Devil's Due (September 2026)

THE WITCHES OF MINGUS MOUNTAIN

(Paranormal Romance)

Stolen Time

Borrowed Time

Killing Time

Wind Called

Demon Loved

Christmas Past

Season of Magic (April 2026)

Healer's Heart (July 2026)

PROJECT DEMON HUNTERS*

(Paranormal Romance)

Unquiet Souls

Unbound Spirits

Unholy Ground

Unseen Voices

Unmarked Graves

Unbroken Vows

Unholy Night

THE DJINN WARS*

(Paranormal Romance)

Chosen

Taken

Fallen

Broken

Forsaken

Forbidden

Awoken

Illuminated

Stolen

Forgotten

Driven

Unspoken

Hidden

Written

Given

Mistaken

FAMILIAR SPIRITS*

(Cozy Mystery/Paranormal Romance)

Spells and Spaniels

Cauldrons and Cats

Hexes and Hedgehogs

Charms and Chihuahuas

Runes and Ravens

LATTES AND LEVITATION*

(Cozy Mystery/Paranormal Romance)

Caffeine Before Curses

Muffins After Magic

Pastries and Prophecies

Eclairs and Ectoplasm

Sugar Skulls and Specters

Wedding Cakes and Wishes

HEDGEWITCH FOR HIRE*

(Cozy Mystery/Paranormal Romance)

Grave Mistake

Social Medium

Household Demons

Perpetual Potion

Jingle Spells

Wandering Monsters

Uninvited Ghosts

Prophet Motive

Ballroom Bits

Spell Check

Brew Confessions

Charm School

UNEXPECTED MAGIC*

(Urban Fantasy/Paranormal Romance)

Found Objects

Finders, Keepers

Lost and Found

Finding Destiny

THE WITCHES OF WHEELER PARK*

(Paranormal Romance)

Storm Born

Thunder Road

Winds of Change

Mind Games

A Wheeler Park Christmas

Blood Ties

Healing Hands

Wishful Thinking

Smoke and Mirrors

MISS PRIMM'S ACADEMY FOR WAYWARD WITCHES*

(Fantasy/Academy Romance)

Misspelled

Dispelled

Expelled

THE DEVIL YOU KNOW*

(Paranormal Romance)

Sympathy for the Devil

Charmed, I'm Sure

A Wing and a Prayer

Wish Upon a Star

THE WITCHES OF CANYON ROAD*

(Paranormal Romance)

Hidden Gifts

Darker Paths

Mysterious Ways

A Canyon Road Christmas

Demon Born

An Ill Wind

Higher Ground

Haunted Hearts

THE WITCHES OF CLEOPATRA HILL*

(Paranormal Romance)

Darkangel

Darknight

Darkmoon

Sympathetic Magic

Protector

Spellbound

A Cleopatra Hill Christmas

Impractical Magic

Strange Magic

The Arrangement

Defender

Bad Blood

Deep Magic

Darktide

Star Bright

THE WATCHERS TRILOGY*

(Paranormal Romance)

Falling Dark

Dead of Night

Rising Dawn

THE SEDONA FILES*

(Paranormal/Science Fiction Romance)

Bad Vibrations

Desert Hearts

Angel Fire

Star Crossed

Falling Angels

Enemy Mine

TALES OF THE LATTER KINGDOMS*

(Fantasy Romance)

All Fall Down

Dragon Rose

Binding Spell

Ashes of Roses

One Thousand Nights

Threads of Gold

The Wolf of Harrow Hall

Moon Dance

The Song of the Thrush

THE GAIAN CONSORTIUM SERIES*

(Science Fiction Romance)

Beast (free prequel novella)

Blood Will Tell

Breath of Life

The Gaia Gambit

The Mandala Maneuver

The Titan Trap

The Zhore Deception

The Refugee Ruse

STANDALONE TITLES

Hearts on Fire (Paranormal Romance)

Taking Dictation (Contemporary Romance)

Golden Heart (Gaslamp Fantasy Romance)

Night Music: A Modern Reimagining of The Phantom of the Opera (Contemporary Romance)

Ghost Dance: A Sequel to Gaston Leroux's The Phantom of the Opera (Historical Mystery/Romance)

Flight Before Christmas (Fantasy Romance)

* Indicates a completed series

ABOUT THE AUTHOR

USA Today bestselling author Christine Pope has been writing stories ever since she commandeered her family's Smith-Corona typewriter back in grade school. Her work includes paranormal romance, paranormal cozy mystery, fantasy romance, and science fiction/space opera romance. She makes her home in Arizona.

Christine Pope on the Web:
www.christinepope.com

facebook.com/ChristinePopeAuthor
youtube.com/@ChristinePopeAuthor